UNDEFEATED WORLD

THE EMP SURVIVOR SERIES – BOOK 5

BY CHRIS PIKE

Undefeated World
The EMP Survivor Series
by Chris Pike
Copyright © 2018. All Rights Reserved

Edited by Felicia A. Sullivan
Formatted by Kody Boye
Cover art by Hristo Kovatliev

Dedication

To my readers: Thank you. This story would not have been possible without you and your encouragement. Y'all are the best! And to my family who has put up with all my crazy ideas and work-shopping sessions, y'all are the best too.
—Chris

"Strength does not come from physical capacity. It comes from an indomitable will."
—Mahatma Ghandi

"But touch a solemn truth in collision with a dogma of a sect, though capable of the clearest proof, and you will find you have disturbed a nest, and the hornets will swarm about your eyes and hand, and fly into your face and eyes."
—John Adams

PROLOGUE

Vladivostok, Russia – Home of the Russian Pacific Fleet
Six Months Before the EMP

Standing rigidly at attention, the young soldier, whose main job was to monitor Russia's oil production, fidgeted nervously outside the door to his commander's office. The soldier cupped his damp hands to his mouth, blew cool air on them, then briskly wiped them on his pants. He had been working for twenty-four hours straight, sitting hunched over a computer monitor, checking and double checking the spreadsheet. He first thought the low oil production numbers were due to a bug or a glitch in the software, but the more he studied the numbers, the more he knew they were right.

Russia was in trouble.

His eyes were bloodshot, his skin pale.

He swallowed audibly, took a big breath to gather courage, then rapped his knuckles on the door.

"Enter," Colonel Mikhail Burkov said.

The soldier entered the dim room, lit by an old lightbulb. He saluted his commanding officer, his unblinking eyes staring straight ahead.

The furniture was bleak and dated, and about as cheery as a dull gray winter day. The commanding officer sat behind an old metal desk, something the young soldier figured was a throwback of the Cold War.

"What do you have?" Colonel Burkov asked. The chair squeaked when he leaned forward.

"Sir, I have the latest oil production numbers you requested on the Samotlor Field."

"Is it good news?"

The soldier swallowed again and wiped the sweat from his brow. "I don't interpret numbers, Sir."

"Don't lie to me, soldier!" Rising, Burkov slammed a folder down on his desk. The soldier flinched. "You eat and breathe those numbers. Tell me now. Is it good news or bad news?"

"Do you want the news only for that field, or others?"

"First tell me about the Samotlor Field."

The soldier did his best to control his shaky voice. "The field is ninety-five percent depleted. Oil production is down to the lowest it's ever been, and it continues to fall."

"What about the other top producing fields?"

"Production keeps declining as well."

"Why do you suppose that is?"

"Reserves in place were overestimated, especially for the Samotlor Field. Overproduction has depleted all fields at a faster pace than was originally estimated."

Colonel Burkov stepped over to the window and gazed at the compound. He clasped his hands behind his back. Military trucks rumbled past nondescript buildings located on a three acre plot fenced by barbed wire. Personnel walked stiffly along sidewalks. Someone laughed, which did nothing to lighten Burkov's dour mood.

"Samotlor is the biggest oil field in Russia. The money the field generates singlehandedly supplies our military and pays for our weapons." Burkov lowered his voice. "It pays to keep the Americans from attacking us."

"I am aware of that, Sir."

"Have you told anyone about this information?"

"No Sir. I only crunch numbers. My family thinks I am an accountant. Nothing more, nothing less," the soldier replied.

"Good." Burkov snatched the folder out of the soldier's hands, then sat down at his desk.

The soldier remained motionless.

"One more thing." Burkov smiled disarmingly. "I think it's time you took a vacation."

Overcome with relief, the soldier let out a breath he had been holding. His eyes flicked to Burkov. "Thank you, Sir. I shall pack immediately."

"Go someplace warm where the water is blue and the sky clear. Find a pretty girl. Have a few drinks. And be sure to keep your receipts. You will be reimbursed one hundred percent for doing a good job."

"Yes Sir. I will, Sir." The spring in the soldier's step previously missing, appeared again at the thought of a vacation.

After the soldier left, a side door leading to Burkov's office opened. A big man stepped inside.

Burkov made eye contact with the man who bore a distinctive scar running across his face. His name was Petya Ruslan. "Follow him. You know what needs to be done."

A wicked smile spread across Ruslan's cold, hard features he channeled from the literal meaning of his first name. Stone. He was as cold and hard as a slab of granite.

"I won't fail."

"I know. You never do."

Ruslan left as quietly as he had entered, leaving Burkov alone. Briefly, he pondered his next move. He unlocked a desk drawer and retrieved a plain letter sized folder. In it were oil and gas logs, seismic sections, maps, and the name of a shale oil field in the East Texas Basin: Hemphill.

The minnow of an oil and gas operating company which had discovered the new shale oil field had been easy to infiltrate. Their cyber security was laughable, and the lead geologist sang like a canary when lots of money had been waved in front of his face. His hourly pay paled in comparison to what the owners would be raking in. It was about time he had a big paycheck himself. He'd desperately needed to pay off his debts–a fact Burkov knew about from clandestine intel gathered on the man. He chose his victims carefully, just like he had handpicked the soldier who ran the numbers. He was expendable, and it didn't bother Colonel Mikhail

Burkov one iota. What Mother Russia needed was more important than the life of one lowly computer geek who knew too much.

He pulled out a map of Texas, shook it open, and placed it on his desk. His eyes gravitated to the red circle around Hemphill, Texas.

Burkov, who fancied himself an expert on American culture, had read about the rednecks of East Texas. Backwoods, uneducated hillbillies who brewed moonshine. Foul tasting stuff no doubt, unlike the vodka Burkov loved. He scoffed at the American culture. Fools they were, no pride in their homeland, crybabies who were offended by the least transgression, and slaves to their materialistic culture.

It was time now for action, the brainchild of Burkov, one he'd envisioned for years. It relied on an EMP weapon the Russians had tested on a remote area of their own country, away from the prying eyes of the world. Thousands had died, but such was the way of progress when a vital test was needed to protect the motherland.

Burkov opened a false bottom of his desk and reached for the vodka. He opened the bottle and poured himself a drink in celebration. He leaned back in his chair and thumped his boots on the desk, took a swallow of the vodka, and savored the flavor, letting it soothe his nerves. He needed some liquid bravery before he called his General, arguably one of the most ruthless men in Russia.

Burkov ran a hand over his chin. His enemies, along with those who knew too much, had disappeared one by one, and if everything went his way, he'd be climbing the ranks, and on his way to becoming a general. He'd be a hero and the one recognized as saving his beloved Russia.

Taking the last swallow of the drink, Burkov put away the bottle. He reached for the phone, punched in a few numbers and waited.

A female voice answered. *"Mikhail? Is that you?"*

"It is."

"I thought it was your number."

"Anastasia, how you are my dear?" Burkov feigned interest in the General's plain looking daughter who he considered a necessary pawn in his quest for higher office.

Giggling followed. *"I'm fine. Are you coming to see me?"*

"Hopefully tomorrow."

"Really?"

"Would you be so kind to make a dinner reservation for us at our special restaurant?"

"I'll make the call straight away." Anastasia's heart was beating fast. She hesitated when she said, *"My apartment is nearby."*

"You read my mind." Burkov's voice was smooth and reassuring, a technique he learned to satisfy the extremely needy and clingy General's daughter. What Anastasia didn't know was that after his required performance, which probably wouldn't take more than a few minutes at the max, he'd be on his way to a more worthy and desirable woman.

"Anastasia, I need to speak to General Shuvalov. Put me through to him." Burkov's tone had changed from love-smitten suitor to a by-the-book military man.

Sensing their flirting was over, Anastasia answered in a professional voice. *"One moment please."*

Burkov knew the drill: Call the General then be put on hold for an indeterminate amount of time, obviously a power play Shuvalov used to show his authority. Like a good soldier, Mikhail played along.

Finally, the line clicked on.

"Colonel Burkov," Shuvalov's voice boomed, *"it is good to hear from you. My time is short so get to the point."*

Burkov chose his words carefully. "It is time for Operation Spindletop."

There was a long silence on the other end of the line. *"Are you sure?"*

"Yes. The production numbers don't lie."

"Who else knows about this?"

"Only you and I."

"Excellent. You've taken care of all the loose ends?"

"Of course."

"Very good," Shuvalov said. *"I will call an emergency meeting to finalize the logistics for the operation. Pack your bags and be in Moscow tomorrow."*

"It will be my pleasure," Burkov said. He set the handset of the old rotary phone onto the switch hook, clicking the phone off.

He leaned back from the desk and clasped his hands around the back of his head. This moment had been a long time coming, requiring years of expert maneuvering in the political circles of the military. Having the General's daughter tied around his little finger didn't hurt either.

He had risen through the ranks through sheer cunning and he wasn't about to stop at colonel.

America would be next for him to conquer. He'd become a hero to Mother Russia. There'd be parades and babies to kiss, women would fawn over him, and the rank of general would be within his grasp.

Texas, and all the oil production, would be his first conquest. Next would be Alaska and all her spoils of the highly productive North Slope.

Americans. Burkov scoffed.

They wouldn't even know what hit them.

CHAPTER 1

Current Day
Padre Island, Texas

"Are you ready?" Nico Bell asked.

Kate Chandler was cleaning up their campsite located above the high tide line and nestled near the sandy dunes. "I think so," she answered. "I'm a little nervous, that's all."

"That's to be expected. You haven't seen your parents in over two years."

"I suppose so," Kate said. "That, and the fact you could've died last night. You scared me half to death, Nico. I thought I was going to lose you."

"If I didn't say thank you for saving my life, I'm saying it now."

Nico had escaped with his life after being stung by a Portuguese Man 'o War while swimming in the shallow beach waters of Padre Island. Highly allergic to any type of stinging insect, Nico didn't know the Man 'o War was also on the list. Fortunately, he had an Epipen with him, and with Kate's help, he survived the sting. She had implored him to go to a hospital for further treatment, but without any type of transportation other than a helicopter – which

7

Kate couldn't fly – the best she could do was to keep him warm and hydrated during the night.

"How are you feeling?" Kate asked. She reached up to brush a strand of hair out of Nico's face.

"I feel fine," Nico said. With a hint of mischievousness, he rubbed his leg with an exaggerated movement. "My leg hurts where you stabbed me with the Epipen."

"You were about to die," Kate said, somewhat aggravated. "I've never given anyone a shot before. I didn't know how hard to stick the needle in you." She moved closer to Nico and glanced at his leg. "I can tell you that you do have thick skin."

Nico laughed. "Having a thick skin comes in handy at times."

"And a thick skull," Kate added. She playfully rapped her knuckles on his head.

Nico scanned the campsite, making sure they hadn't left anything of value. After a meager breakfast, he packed the tent while Kate cleaned the campsite, leaving no trace they had been there.

"Come on," Nico said. "Time to go."

"You go on ahead. I need to do my business."

"Business?" Nico scratched his head. "Oh, yeah, right. I'll meet you at the helicopter in a few minutes. You know where it is, right?"

"I remember. Go to the sign up there," Kate pointed to the large sign spelling out beach rules, "then hang a right on the blacktop."

"Reload can come with me," Nico said.

Hearing his name, the big dog cocked his head and waited for instruction.

Kate waved him off. "He'll want to stay with me."

"Okay. See you in a bit."

Nico slung his backpack over his shoulder. "See you in a few minutes." He headed to where he had parked the helicopter on the blacktop located on the other side of the sand dunes. He hadn't checked on the helicopter since he had left it there the day before, figuring there weren't many people who knew how to fly one. He had locked the doors, not that it would stop a determined thief because the doors were easy to pick, yet he had made sure not to leave anything of value in the cockpit to tempt anyone.

Kate tracked Nico as he walked, and when he reached the break in the dunes where the blacktop was, he waved to her. She returned the wave, and once Nico was out of sight, she disappeared into the dunes, searching for a secluded place.

The wind blew over the beach and the dunes, carrying with it the peculiar smell of the salty ocean and of the sea creatures inhabiting it. The sound of tumbling waves spilling ashore then fading away washed over the beach, and Kate relished the comforting sound.

Reload trotted happily alongside Kate, his nose held high and twitching, sniffing sea grass and shells bleached white by the sun. The beach had been a new experience for him, and had stimulated his senses with new smells of the ocean and the sea creatures, and other animals that lived off the land.

The dunes had their own odors of scurrying rodents and crabs.

Reload sniffed where several seagulls had landed. A spotted ground squirrel had left its scent also. He nosed the paw prints of a coyote who had crossed the dunes during the night.

After Kate finished her business, she poured bottled water on her hands and washed them the best she could. Taking a bowl out of her backpack, she poured the remaining water for Reload. He lapped it thirstily. After stowing the bowl, she dusted the sand from her backpack. "Come on, Reload. Let's go."

The big dog wagged his tail and loped in front of her. Spying a piece of driftwood, Reload picked it up in his mouth, and playfully loped back to Kate, dropping the driftwood at her feet.

"Wanna play?"

Reload thumped his tail, and stood back eagerly waiting for Kate to toss it.

She threw the driftwood. "Go get it!"

Legs stretching out, Reload ran close to the ground, kicking up sand, and when he came to the driftwood, he skidded to a stop and took it in his mouth.

Odd scents wafted by him on a salty breeze. He lifted his snout, reading the meaning of the odors. Scents of human desperation and danger came to him, and intermingled in those scents were those of Nico.

Reload's ruff bristled. He dropped the driftwood and growled low in his throat, eyes sweeping over the beach trying to find the men associated with the scents.

Standing yards back from Reload, Kate had expected him to return the driftwood to her. She put her hands to her mouth to call him back, but before she did she was struck by his odd body posture.

UNDEFEATED WORLD

His legs were straight, ears cocked, and he was leaning forward. She had seen the posture before, where every sense of Reload's was on high alert.

Something wasn't right.

CHAPTER 2

Crouched over, Kate ran to Reload. She knelt and put her hand on his collar. "Shhh," she whispered, leading him to a concealed spot in the sand dunes. "Quiet."

Kate listened.

The wind brushed the tall sea grass growing on the dunes. Particles of loose sand blew in waves, rippling over the dunes, and a seagull squawked overhead.

Kate tapped Reload on the shoulder to get his attention. "Stay."

Crawling on her hands and knees to the top of a sand dune, she peeked through a clump of tall grass and took a quick sweep of the area. Twenty yards away, Nico had been forced face down on the blacktop and was being held at gunpoint by one man while two others searched the helicopter. Concealed by the grass, Kate thought about options.

She estimated she was about twenty yards away, and with the Glock being accurate at that distance, she might be able to get a good shot. On the other hand, if she didn't hit the guy standing over Nico on the first shot, the man might put a bullet in Nico right there. If she had a rifle it would have been an entirely different story, and she was more confident in her shooting ability with a rifle.

She unzipped her backpack and withdrew her Glock, then checked to make sure it was fully loaded. It was. She dug around in the backpack and found two extra magazines which she stuffed in the front part of her bathing suit top. The flimsy shorts she had on wouldn't hold a magazine or—

Kate turned just in time to see Reload bolt. "Nooo, Reload, no."

Reload, who had been sitting patiently, dashed out from behind the sand dune, bolting toward where Nico was being held.

Kate could only stare in worried bewilderment as Reload scooted around the sand dunes and headed out into the wide open space of the blacktop.

Legs gobbling distance, the big dog didn't flinch when the first shot went high above his head.

Kate brought her Glock up to a shooting position. She aimed at the man and fired. The shot went wild.

The man whipped his head around trying to find where the shot came from.

Kate fired again, distracting the man. The brief muzzle flash caught his attention and he swiveled his rifle in her direction. He aimed and—

Nico catapulted over and swung his legs at the man holding him hostage, catching him in the crook behind his knee. The man buckled and fell backward. He got off a bad shot, and before he could shoot again, Reload had run up on the man and clamped down on his hand. He shook it with wild abandon as if he was shaking prey.

The man kicked Reload, but the big dog was undeterred.

Nico sprang up and wrestled the rifle out of the man's hand. An instant later, he put a bullet through the man's brain.

Another shot rang out and Nico ducked. He grabbed Reload by the collar and forced him down.

Someone was shooting at the helicopter, or at the men inside.

Nico scanned the dunes for Kate. His gaze went to a tall clump of grass high atop a dune. He frantically waved Kate to stay away, hoping she had seen him.

Crouching, Nico ducked under the helicopter, and spying a set of legs, he took aim at an ankle. The man screamed and fell. Another shot and the man went silent.

There was only one left. Afraid Reload might get shot, Nico got the dog's attention and said, "Kate. Find Kate."

Reload's eyes blazed at the mention of Kate's name.

"Go. Find Kate." Nico swept his arm in the direction where he had last seen Kate.

Reload dashed away from the helicopter and ran toward where Kate was hiding, tucked away between the dunes.

Once Reload was out of harm's way, Nico stood and hugged the outside of the helicopter, inching closer to the door.

"Don't shoot," a voice quavered from inside the cockpit.

Nico wasn't sure if it was a girl or male's voice. Not wanting to take a chance on an ambush, he ordered, "Drop your weapons and put your hands where I can see them."

A pair of slender hands appeared from around the helicopter door. "Don't shoot."

A moment later, a scared, gangly teenager wearing a baseball cap, worn jeans, and a man's shirt tentatively emerged. The teen hopped out of the helicopter to be greeted by the deadly end of the rifle.

Nico was taken aback by how young the teenager was. Then it dawned on him the teen was a girl.

"Don't hurt me," she said.

Nico eyed the girl with suspicion. He had been fooled before by a harmless looking old man. He wasn't about to let a waif of a girl lure him into complacency.

"Turn around," Nico ordered, "and put your hands on the helicopter."

"What for?"

"Do it," Nico growled.

The girl complied, her back to Nico. He took a step toward her and patted her down on her back, legs, under her arms, and when he put his hand on the front pocket of her jeans, his hand came into contact with a hard object.

"What's this?" Not expecting an answer, he reached into the pocket and pulled out a knife. "You can face me now." Nico flicked open the knife. "I told you to drop your weapons. That meant all of them."

"I don't have any guns."

The girl trembled, her shoulders were slumped, her eyes downcast, and before Nico could say anything else, she burst out crying.

Undeterred by the show of emotion, Nico coolly asked, "What's your name?"

The girl sobbed and hiccupped. "Haley," she squeaked. She sniffled and ran her fingers beneath her eyes. "Can I have my knife back? It's my daddy's knife."

"Where's your dad?"

Haley burst out crying again. Nico stood there unsure what to do. Dealing with crying teen girls was out of his comfort zone. "Where's your dad?" he repeated.

"Those men killed him. He had come to rescue me, and they shot him. That one there," she flicked her eyes to the man she was talking about. "Is he dead?"

"Quite dead."

Haley went over to the man and kicked him.

"I'm sorry about your dad." Nico studied the girl, wondering if she was telling the truth. Bewildered, he asked, "If they killed your dad, then what are you doing with them?"

"They kidnapped me."

"Don't lie to me!"

"I'm not. I promise. They kept me tied up most of the time."

The girl had some spunk left in her. Good.

"Have they hurt you?"

"No."

"Where's the rest of your family?"

"I'm not sure. I'm hoping they're still in Corpus. I had come to the beach with a couple of my friends, and after the electricity stopped, we weren't sure what to do. Cars weren't working, so we spent the night in our car on the beach."

"Where are your friends?"

Haley dropped her gaze to the ground. "Dead."

Nico didn't want to pry anymore regarding the fate of her friends. He pretty much knew anyway. "Corpus isn't that far. Why didn't you walk home?"

"I tried. But the bridge over the Intracoastal Canal had been taken control of by some gang and they wouldn't let anyone pass unless they paid a whole bunch of money." Haley's gaze dropped to the ground. "They said I could pay them another way if I wanted to get across." She took a hesitant peek at Nico.

"Did you?"

"No." Her answer was steadfast. "I ran away after that. Nobody would help me. I've been stuck on Padre ever since."

Kate and Reload walked up then. "What's going on? And who's this? Was she the one shooting at us?"

"No. The dead guys were the ones shooting."

Reload padded over to one of the dead men and sniffed the body. He ran his nose along the pants, sniffed the hands, moved across the body then to the face. He growled.

"It's okay, Reload," Kate said reassuringly. "They can't hurt us."

"Haley, are you hungry?" Nico asked.

"Yes."

"Kate, can you get her something to eat and drink?"

"Sure." Kate dug around in her backpack, found a candy bar and half a bottle of water. She offered it to the girl. Reload sat on his haunches and watched the girl eat.

"Stay here," Nico said to Haley. Taking Kate by the elbow, he guided her to the other side of the helicopter. Once they were out of earshot, Nico said, "We can't leave her here."

"I know." Kate looked up at Nico. "But we can't take her with us either. I don't want my parents to be responsible for another person."

"I'm not asking you to."

CHAPTER 3

Nico ran a hand over his beard, thinking. "I can take you home."

"You can?" Haley was beyond happy.

"Can you find your house from the air?"

"I'm sure I can. Just follow the road into town and hang a left at Everhart. I'll let you know which one it is. We're in one of the subdivisions, south of there."

"Hop in. Kate, you and Reload can sit in the back." While Nico was sure this girl wasn't a threat, it paid to be cautious. If she was in the front seat, he could keep an eye on her.

After everyone was secured in their seats, Nico powered up the helicopter, and fifteen minutes later he had set the helicopter down in the middle of a wide street leading to the subdivision where the girl lived.

"Thank you so much," Haley said, trying to be heard above the roar of the helicopter wash. "How can I ever repay you?"

"No need to. If you find someone else who needs help, then pay it forward."

"I will," Haley said.

"Wait," Nico said. "Here's your knife back."

Exiting the helicopter, Haley closed the door, waved good-bye again, then, with her shoulders hunched over she sprinted to a safe distance away from the helicopter.

Nico waited until she disappeared around a corner house.

"That was nice for you to take her home," Kate said.

Nico nodded. "She was a survivor. I like to help those kinds of people. The world needs more of them. Good riddance to the creeps who kidnapped her."

Nico took the controls of the helicopter and guided it to cruising altitude, following the interstate through town, then guided the helicopter past the ship channel and the harbor bridge. Several big ships were docked at the channel, no doubt unable to sail anywhere. A few aluminum fishing boats were specks on the bay, and whitecaps formed on the choppy gray waters.

For the next hour they flew in silence, each keeping to private thoughts. Kate's mind wandered to her parents and what they would do when they saw her. She thought about her oldest brother Chandler, and to the next oldest, Luke. It had been a long time since she had seen anyone in her family, and she wondered what it would be like to return home. She glanced at Nico and put a hand on his arm.

He nodded. "Don't worry, everything will be fine."

A lot had happened since Nico had walked into the bar at the Minor Hotel. When Kate first set eyes on him, she knew he was the one for her. She had fought the attraction, afraid to have someone else ripped from her life after what had happened to her fiancé. In the beginning, she felt she was not honoring Ben's memory by having Nico in her life, until she realized the life she had planned with Ben no longer existed. She had to make a new life, and Nico was part of that. He was different. There were no pretenses or false promises, only the promise he'd be there for her. He had accepted her dog without protest from Reload, and that meant a lot to Kate. Reload was a good judge of character, and had accepted Nico from the beginning. Okay, maybe there was a growl or two, but, if Reload hadn't liked Nico, he would have made it clear. The two were now bonded. Make that three.

Kate leaned her head against the window. The land segued from coastal marshes and bays to the flat farmland of cotton and corn. Palm trees became fewer. Woodland thickets and tall oaks dotted the land below in the hazy air. The warm cabin of the chopper and the noise and vibrating window lulled her to close her eyes, and she drifted off to sleep.

* * *

"Kate, wake up," Nico said. He nudged her leg. "We're here at the 360 Bridge."

"Hmm?"

"We're almost there. You need to direct me to where your parents live."

Kate yawned and rubbed her eyes. "I must have fallen asleep."

"You did. I didn't want to wake you until the last minute."

"I appreciate that. I needed the sleep."

"How do we get there?"

Kate's eyes scanned the city. They were flying over the 360 Bridge, which crossed the winding Colorado River. Fishing boats sat idle on the river. A man glanced skyward and waved at them. Limestone cliffs loomed high over one side of the Colorado, while on the other side, the land sloped gently to the river.

"Stay with the highway then turn left at FM 2222. Take another left at the second stoplight. Follow the street until it dead ends."

"Is there a place to land?"

Kate mentally imaged the street grid leading to her parent's house. "Probably at the intersection. You can land there, then we'll walk the rest of the way."

Minutes later Nico set the helicopter down where Kate indicated. He powered down the chopper and waited until the blades stopped rotating.

"How are you doing?" Nico asked.

"A little nervous." Kate chewed on a ragged hangnail. "You?"

"I'm fine. Let's take what we need and leave the camping equipment here. I'll come back for it later."

CHAPTER 4

Austin, Texas
Chandler household

William Chandler, better known as Uncle Billy, was sitting under the shade of a pecan tree at the John Chandler household. The previous evening, Uncle Billy had tied a six pack of Buckhorn beer to the dock and lowered it to a deep part of the river, hoping the beer would be cool by morning.

He had done his chores for the morning, including pulling weeds in the garden, and making sure the fence around the garden didn't have any holes in it. Rabbits were a constant problem, but not so much lately. People ate whatever they could find.

The two-story homestead house sat on the banks of the Colorado River, built beyond the one hundred year flood plain. The Big View neighborhood where the Chandlers lived was known for its large lots and extra large houses, where it was common for BMWs and Range Rovers to sit in the driveway.

The Chandler house was a throwback to a different era and looked out of place among the newly built, modern mansions.

So be it, Uncle Billy thought.

All the money the dot.com crowd had made was now about as useful as a tin shed in a hailstorm.

After Uncle Billy polished off his second beer of the day, he retrieved a rag from the tool shed and used it to wipe down his prized possession, a two door, V-8 engine 1972 Gran Torino he found abandoned upriver. What fool would abandon a beauty like that was beyond Uncle Billy's understanding. The car had a few dings and scraped paint. Who cared? Not Uncle Billy. When he found the car, he figured he could clean off the mud, give it a good coat of wax, put a quilt over the back seat to hide the ripped upholstery, and there you go. Almost as good as new.

The day he found the car, he and his nephew Luke had been out scouting for anything of value they might trade. Recent rains had flooded the river, and floods tended to push down all sorts of flotsam, some of it useful, and while they didn't find much of anything that day, it did lead them to the car.

Uncle Billy and Luke checked for any type of message indicating the owner would be back, and after they had thoroughly searched the car, Uncle Billy decided to hotwire it.

"Isn't that stealing?" Luke asked.

"Me? A thief?" Uncle Billy scowled and pretended to be offended Luke would say such a statement. "I'm only borrowing it so I can return it to its rightful owner."

"You expect me to believe that?"

"You can believe what you want to." Uncle Billy ran his hand along the contours of the car, down the fender, along the tire rims, admiring the style of the old car. "Yes, sir. A beautiful car is like a beautiful woman. Treat her right and she'll purr, treat her wrong and the claws come out."

Luke rolled his eyes. "You're hopeless."

"Maybe so, but I know what I like, and I like this, and I'm gonna have it."

"When are you gonna teach me to hotwire a car? Haven't you already showed Kate how to?"

"She's a quick learner. She likes cars, so yeah, I taught her. That's what a good uncle does."

"Teaches their nieces how to steal cars? You're something else."

"I'm the coolest uncle around too, don't forget that." Uncle Billy opened the driver's side door and removed the plastic cover on the steering column. "I think I can do this." He pulled a bundle of wires out, and let them dangle to the side. Taking the colored wires, he removed about a half inch of insulation then twisted them together.

Nothing happened.

"Think the car's dead?" Luke asked.

"Don't know. Let's check the engine."

Uncle Billy popped the hood and checked the connections. "I think all it needs is a good battery."

"Where can we get one?"

Uncle Billy pondered Luke's question. "Stay here with the car. I'll be back in thirty minutes."

True to his word, Uncle Billy came back, lugging a car battery. "Don't ask me where I got it," he said.

"I can only imagine," Luke replied.

Uncle Billy installed the battery, tried twisting the wires together again, and the engine roared to life. "Nothing like a V-8 engine. Hop in, Luke." He turned the car around, glanced at Luke sitting in the passenger seat, and said, "Hold on."

The tires spun, the car fishtailed, and Uncle Billy raced it down the dirt road. "Whoowhee!" He glanced at Luke, who was desperately trying to snap the seatbelt into place. "Told ya she'd purr."

* * *

Uncle Billy sat back in the chair, clasped his hands above his head, and stretched as he listened to a pair of chattering birds high in the top of one of the pecan trees. He waved to a kayaker on the river. "You catch any fish?"

"No," the man replied.

If Uncle Billy was on the river and had caught fish he wouldn't tell anybody where he'd found them either.

He polished off his third beer of the day, and as he crumpled the can, he caught the sound of a helicopter. He spotted it coming in south of the river, and tracked it across the treetops. When he couldn't see it anymore, he hobbled around to the front of the house to get a better look.

The chopper glided over the houses then came in for a smooth landing, setting down in the middle of the street. Uncle Billy figured it was probably one of the homeowners of the adjacent multi-million dollar houses. Still, curiosity got the best of him, so he waited to see who was in the chopper.

Once the blades stopped spinning, a man exited the chopper, stretched, and checked his surroundings. The man saw Uncle Billy, studied him for a moment, and waved.

Uncle Billy didn't recognize the man as being one of the homeowners, and wondered what he was doing in the neighborhood. The man appeared to be on the up and up, but in the current state of the world, one could never be too cautious. Uncle Billy raised his hand and waved.

The man looped around to the other side of the chopper and opened the door. A large dog hopped out, followed by a young woman. Uncle Billy shaded his eyes from the sun-glint trying to get a better look. He observed the man say something to the woman, then took the dog's leash, directing the dog to step aside.

Uncle Billy noted the familiar way the woman moved, confident and self-assured in her surroundings, like she had lived here all her life. She was mid-twenties, sandy blonde hair, about the same size as...

"Kate!" he yelled. "Kate, is that you?"

The woman searched for whoever had called her, then spotted Uncle Billy. There was a moment of hesitation, and then the biggest smile spread across her young face. She dropped the dog's leash and ran to her uncle.

Kate smashed into Uncle Billy and embraced him. He scooped Kate up and twirled her around once then set her down. He put his hands on her shoulders and stood her at arm's length. "Kate, I'm so glad to see you. We thought we'd never see you again. You look..." he searched for the right description, "...happy."

"I am."

"Let's get you in the house. Your mom will be so glad to see you."

"Wait," Kate said. "There's somebody else I'd like you to meet." She called Nico over.

Lugging a backpack, Nico extended a hand to Uncle Billy. "I'm Nico Bell."

"Uncle Billy. That's what everybody calls me."

"I've heard a lot about you."

"No doubt all good?"

"Of course, Uncle Billy!" Kate blurted. She teasingly knuckle punched him in the arm.

Nico said to Kate, "You go on in. I need to get a couple of things from the chopper."

After Nico was out of earshot, Uncle Billy leaned into Kate. "Are you two, uh, a couple?"

"We are."

"Does he treat you good?"

"He does."

"Then that's all I need to know, because if he didn't I'd whip his ass a good one and slap him into next week."

Kate jokingly elbowed Uncle Billy then put an arm around his waist. They walked toward the house, Reload following behind.

Coming to the house, Kate stopped and took it in, recalling the last time she had been here. The big fight with her mother had resulted in Kate packing a bag and storming out the house while her mother pleaded with her to stay. When Kate left, she had slammed the front door shut. Recalling the sound it made, and the force she used to slam it, she winced. It had rattled the windows in the front of the house. She had said hurtful words to her mother, and now regretted them.

"Is Mom still mad at me?" Kate asked, her voice tinged with a mixture of anxiety and hope.

"Not anymore. Whatever was said between you two happened a lifetime ago, Kate," Uncle Billy said. "I'm old enough to know we only get one stab at this life. Live it how you want to, not how someone else says you should. I know your mother and you had your differences in the past. Let it go. By the looks of it, you've done a lot of growing up since you were last here. Am I right?"

"For someone who pretends he's a backwoods good 'ol boy, you sure are smart."

"I take that as a compliment. Let's go on in."

CHAPTER 5

"Tatiana," Uncle Billy yelled. "We have a guest." He shut the front door and asked Kate not to say anything, wanting it to be a surprise. He took Kate by the elbow and guided her into the kitchen.

Tatiana had been in the kitchen inventorying food, trying to think of clever ways to use canned tuna, or rather ways to disguise it. Due to dwindling food supplies, protein such as fish or meat was limited to three meals a week. The unexpected company gave her a brief reprieve from her mundane task, so, with a smile on her face, she called back, "Who is it?" It took her a brief nanosecond to understand her daughter had come home. With open arms, she went to Kate and hugged her. Unable to contain her emotions, rivulets of tears flowed easily down her cheeks.

"Don't cry, Mom," Kate squeaked. "I'll start crying too."

"Let me see you," Tatiana said. "I've prayed every night you'd come home." She clasped her hands together. "My prayers were answered."

"Mom, there's something I've been wanting to tell you for a long time. I'm sorry for what I said, and for—"

"It's all forgotten. None of it matters." Tatiana brushed a strand of hair out of Kate's face in a gesture of motherly love. "What matters is that you're home safe. Can I get you anything? Are you hungry? When did you eat last? What have you—"

"Tatiana," Uncle Billy cut in, "there's another guest coming."

"There is? Who?"

Before Tatiana could continue the line of questioning, the front door swung open.

Nico took a quick sweep of the house, noting the flow of the rooms and the placement of the furniture. As common in old houses, each room had a separate purpose from the formal dining room and living room, to the den and kitchen. Traffic flow appeared to be in a circular pattern. It wasn't that Nico appreciated architecture, the observation was something to be filed away in his memory in case there was an emergency. He also noted the heavy mahogany china cabinet and table—bullet stopping furniture. It was old, heavy, and sturdy. His type of furniture.

Nico stepped into the foyer, wiped his shoes on the mat, and sensed the surprised atmosphere. "Am I interrupting something?"

"Not at all," Kate said. She rushed over to Nico and put her arm around him. "Mom, this is Nico, or should I say Nikolai Belyahov."

"Definitely Russian," Tatiana commented. "I'm Tatiana. Nice to meet you."

"*Rad poznakomit'sya*," Nico replied.

"You speak without an accent. Kate, you must tell me more about Nico."

Kate began to protest when Tatiana addressed Nico. "Do you mind if I steal my daughter for a little while? I haven't seen her in a long time."

"Not at all. Is there someplace where I can put my things?"

"Since we have a full house, use Kate's room."

"Mom!"

"Oh, don't give me that," Tatiana protested. "You're not going to do anything here you haven't already done."

The heat rose in Kate's cheeks and all she wanted to do was shrink away and hide somewhere.

"Uncle Billy, while I'm catching up with Kate, would you show Nico around, and also let John and Luke know Kate's back?"

"Sure," Uncle Billy said. "Come on, Nico. I'll show you

around."

Tatiana whisked Kate into the kitchen and prepared her a snack. They had a lot of catching up to do, and, while the big elephant in the room wouldn't go away regarding how long Kate would be staying, Tatiana decided to keep the conversation light. Serious issues would have to wait.

Without making their survival dramatic, nor retelling Nico's near escape with death the previous day, Kate gave a capsulized version of the time she had been gone, strategically leaving out the part about Ben. Like most children, even grown ones, Kate preferred to keep her mother on a need to know basis. As of now, she didn't need to know all the particulars.

Uncle Billy took Nico to the backyard and offered him a can of Buckhorn beer. "It's not as cold as I'd like it to be, but it's better than no beer at all."

"I'll drink to that," Nico said. "How has the family been getting along?"

"Okay enough. About a week ago, an old couple who lived a few houses up the street committed suicide when their prescriptions ran out. That's what the note said. The neighbors got together and we buried them in the backyard. While I was there I heard talk of some rumors coming from East Texas."

"What kind of rumors?" Nico took a swallow of beer.

"One of our neighbors who just made it back home from Louisiana said he saw big government trucks carrying drill pipe in East Texas."

"Interesting."

"Chandler – that's Kate's oldest brother, said before the EMP struck, he had gone back to East Texas to work on a drilling rig where his former boss said a job would be waiting when his tour was over. Apparently, he had some girl trouble, so instead of coming home, he got stuck in East Texas. That's where he met Amanda."

"Who's Amanda?" Nico asked.

"Chandler's girlfriend. I'll explain later." Uncle Billy shrugged. "It appears the government is drilling for oil while the people starve. That's not right."

Nico cast a disbelieving look. "That doesn't make sense."

"I don't know what to think of it," Uncle Billy said. "Something is going on though, that's for sure. Let's take a walk and find Kate's dad and brother."

"Luke's his name, right?"

"Yes, Luke is the middle brother and Chandler is the oldest of the three." Uncle Billy paused long enough to take the last swig of beer. "We all call him Chandler instead of Chris."

"Why is that?"

"When he was in school, there were four other kids in his class named Chris, including one girl. There was so much confusion, he made everyone call him by his last name. It stuck and we've been calling him Chandler ever since. Anyway, he left last week with his girlfriend to go back to her grandpa's place in East Texas."

"It's too bad I missed him. From what Kate said, he's a great guy."

"He is," Uncle Billy confirmed. He crumpled the beer can then tossed it into a barrel.

"So why'd they go back to East Texas?"

"Amanda inherited her grandfather's ranch." Uncle Billy waved off any questions. "It's a long story. I'll tell you later. Want to see my best fishing spot?"

"Sure."

Uncle Billy guided Nico to an unusual feature in the river where the water had eroded a small cave in the bank. He said the catfish liked that shady spot the best. "I've tried noodling, but those fish are smart and fast. Besides, I don't like putting my hands where I can't see them." Afterwards, he gave Nico a tour around the place, including the tool shed, the garden, and the pecan tree where Amanda rescued Chandler from the python.

"A python? Here? You gotta be kidding me." Nico stifled a laugh. "I thought those things only lived in Florida."

"Not anymore. Amanda killed the python right where we're standing. Chandler skinned the snake and decided to have a pair of boots made from the skin. Then we grilled the son-of-a bitch. It was tasty too. Like chicken, only better. Tatiana served it with picante sauce. Let me tell you it was delicious. The menu lately has consisted of a lot of canned tuna. You can have my portion tonight if you want. I still have some extra padding so it won't hurt me if I skip a meal." Uncle Billy grabbed a handful of fat on each side of his waistline to make his point. "I knew my spare tire would come in handy one day."

Nico wasn't sure what to say other than, "Is that your car?"

Uncle Billy scratched his chin, stalling and wondering how to dodge the question without lying. "For the time being it is. Wanna see it?"

"Of course."

Parked under the shade of a pecan tree, Uncle Billy's prized possession sat idle.

"Is this the same kind of car that was in the Clint Eastwood movie?" Nico snapped his fingers trying to remember the name of the movie. "*Gran Torino* was the name, right?"

"Sure was," Uncle Billy. "This one's not as shiny and clean as the beauty in the movie, but she's still purdy."

"Is she for sale?"

Uncle Billy coughed two pathetic fake coughs. "Uh, well, I'm only borrowing it for the time being."

"Right." Nico understood the subtlety of what Uncle Billy was trying to convey, and decided not to press the matter any further.

"Several months ago we took possession of a bright red Chevy, but decided Chandler could use it to haul Cowboy back to East Texas."

"Cowboy? Who's he?"

"A horse Chandler and Amanda borrowed to get here."

A perplexed frown spread across Nico's face.

"The long and short of it is, they borrowed the horse from Holly and Dillon, who are in East Texas, rode him here, and since Chandler had promised to return the horse, we decided the fastest and safest way was to use a trailer." Uncle Billy took a breath. "When the weather became warm enough, we hooked up a horse trailer to the Chevy."

"Why didn't you just let Amanda take the Chevy to drive there herself?"

"Chandler didn't want her traveling by herself. Besides, they are a couple. He said he also wanted to try to find his old boss at the drilling site where he had been working before his military tour."

"There's a lot of oil in East Texas," Nico said.

"Right, and Chandler wanted to make sure when the grid boots back up he'd be one of the first to start working again. It's also possible Amanda's ranch is sitting atop a big oil and gas field. Before the grid went down, some landmen from a big oil company stopped by to talk to her grandfather about extending a lease on the place. In case they come back, Chandler wanted to be there for her to make sure she got fair treatment and didn't sign anything she didn't want to. She's very young and a little naïve from what Chandler has told us. Amanda mentioned there had been a lot of seismic activity the previous year. We're guessing there's the possibility of a huge oil or gas field under all that pasture land and pine trees."

"Interesting." Nico mulled over what he had learned. "From everything I've heard about Chandler, he's a solid guy. I'd like to meet him some day."

Uncle Billy spotted two men walking down the road. "Speaking of meeting, here comes John and Luke."

After a round of handshakes and standard greetings, and upon learning his only daughter had come home, John excused himself and headed to the house. He had been worried sick about Kate as much as his wife had been. Hugs and more tears followed and John listened to every word Kate was saying. She provided the same rendition of her time in San Antonio to her father as she did to her mother. John sat silent as Kate told him about Nico, how they met, and about her dog Reload, who had already made friends with Tatiana, understanding the kitchen was where the food was and that she was in charge of the kitchen.

While John and Tatiana were captivated by their daughter's travails, reveling in the sound of her voice, Luke and Nico were out back talking. They exchanged tales of hardship from lack of food to sanitation issues, then the conversation naturally turned to guns – a topic each was enthusiastic about.

"I hear you and your brother are excellent snipers. What do you use?" Nico was genuinely interested in the answer since he did not have long range training because his bosses had felt it was unnecessary.

"I use a .338 Lapua with either 250 or 300 grain bullets," Luke replied. "Chandler is a formally trained sniper who still uses a .308 and has had combat experience with everything up to and including a .50 caliber Browning machine gun. How about you?"

"My long range shooting has been limited to three hundred yards, mostly with M-4 carbines. Every once in a while someone would show up with a LaRue loaded with Black Hills MK 262 MOD

1, and we would take turns shooting it out to six hundred yards. We never did any formal sniper training, so I couldn't tell you how many windage clicks are required for a fifteen mile per hour crosswind," Nico said.

"Chandler is a true Marine sniper who will share his expertise with serious students. He has a set of range cards that will take you out to incredible distances. We are talking two thousand yards plus for some calibers."

"Luke, how did you learn?" Nico had a feeling Luke was being too modest.

"My mother. She was taught by her mother, a Soviet sniper from WWII. Her mother ran a gun shop at a shooting range, and Mom did test targets for customized guns. She taught me when I showed an interest, and Chandler brought home tips from his time in the service." Luke was clearly proud of the story. "How did you learn about shooting?"

"I was in law enforcement and volunteered to take the Glock Armorer's course when no one else stepped forward. I would do an undercover assignment and then work in the armory in between trials. When the department was testing a new gun, I was always front and center. I got to shoot a full auto FN P90 equipped with a suppressor and a brass bag that could take up to seventy-five rounds. The P90's fifty round magazines really impressed the SWAT guys, but the department only bought a few. It was great fun playing with all sorts of exotic guns." Nico was grinning ear to ear, recalling the memories.

Luke and Nico had hit it off immediately and before they knew it, Tatiana was calling them in for dinner.

CHAPTER 6

East Texas
Holly Hudson's Ranch

The Double H Ranch, a five hundred acre spread in East Texas owned by Holly Hudson, was now home to Dillon Stockdale, his daughter Cassie, her fiancé Ryan Manning, Dillon's dog Buster, one horse, and one cat who spent most of its waking time hiding in various places in the house, while avoiding the mountain lion rug near the front door. Considering the other cat had met its demise in the jaws of a mountain lion, it was decided the cat could stay in the house.

Cowboy was Holly's horse, and was in a pen near the barn. After the shootout at the University of Texas Tower, Chandler had confiscated Zack's car, a cherry red Chevy. With Uncle Billy's help, they hooked up a trailer assembly, and, keeping to his word, Chandler returned Cowboy to Holly. Amanda had come with him, and after they delivered Cowboy to Holly's ranch, they set up house at the property she had inherited from her grandfather.

The previous day at the Double H there had been a flurry of activity as Dillon and Ryan set up tables and chairs outside under the shade of towering pines. Several rows of chairs were placed on either side of a short walkway which led to the base of a large pine tree.

Due to the shortage of chairs, Dillon had improvised and used as many canvas hunting stools he could find in the garage. Paper pinwheels hung from strings attached to the lower branches of the pine tree, and a swing attached to an oak tree was decorated with wild flowers and greenery. A few old barrels had been donated, turned upside down to be used as rustic cocktail tables. Mason jars used for canning had been filled with water, and right before the ceremony was to begin, wildflowers would be placed in the jars.

A wedding was about to get underway, and though Ryan couldn't give Cassie all the bells and whistles of a church wedding and reception, he thought this one would be more memorable.

"How are you doing?" Dillon asked.

"Nervous," Ryan said. "Weren't you when you got married?"

"It was a long time ago. I've forgotten what it was like."

"Aren't you and Holly going to tie the knot?"

"We haven't discussed it."

"Considering what you've been through, I just thought you'd want to—"

"It's different when you're older. Young love is different. Everything is new. You want to make it official, throw a big party, go on a honeymoon. I've already been through all that with my first wife, God rest her soul. Holly and I don't need a piece of paper for confirmation of our commitment to each other. Don't get me wrong, I want you and Cassie to get married, and I couldn't ask for a better son-in-law."

"Thanks," Ryan said. He was about to say something else when the sound of tires on gravel commanded his attention.

Larry Monroe and his wife Sarah arrived in style riding their dirt bikes. Larry owned property behind the Double H Ranch, and a hardware store in town. Dillon strolled over to Larry and Sarah. Larry hopped off his dirt bike and dropped the kickstand into the dirt. He removed his helmet and set it on the seat.

"You're the first to arrive," Dillon said extending a hand to shake. "I wasn't sure you'd be able to make it."

Larry nervously glanced around, his gaze bouncing from the house to the barn then back to Dillon, like something from a pinball machine.

"You okay?" Dillon asked as he too looked around, thinking he had missed something Larry had spotted. "Is something wrong?"

There was no reply.

"Larry? Are you okay?"

"Oh, sure, yeah." Larry scratched the side of his nose and diverted his eyes.

Dillon chalked up Larry's odd behavior and lack of eye contact to possibly too much imbibing, because Larry was known to drink a lot. Some people were obviously nervous in social settings, so Dillon figured it would account for his skittishness. Holly had warned Dillon that Larry was *one of those neighbors*, meaning he was known to be somewhat eccentric. His wife was quite normal, though, so nobody could figure how those two had stayed together.

"I hope we didn't get here too early," Sarah said. "It's kinda hard to tell time these days. The invitation said to come before sunset."

"It's fine, Sarah," Dillon said. "You're right on time. Larry, can I get you anything?"

"Not at the moment." Larry had his hands in his pocket, jiggling something.

Dillon came within a cat's whisker of asking Larry if he was playing pocket pool, then decided not to in front of his wife. Some people weren't the joking kind.

"Honey," Larry said. "You should probably go on in the house. I'm sure Cassie and Holly are in there."

"Oh, I get the hint. I'll head on in and let you men talk in private." She patted Larry on the shoulder.

After Sarah was out of earshot, Dillon asked, "Is something bothering you, Larry. Anything you need to talk about?"

"What? No."

"I thought since you asked your wife to leave—"

"Nothing like that. I thought Sarah might like to see Cassie get ready. You know how women are before weddings." Larry poked Dillon in the side.

"I guess so." Dillon flashed a perplexed expression toward Larry, and wanted to know what was going on, but he had other things on his mind, so he let it go for now.

While the men talked outside, Sarah went over to the house. The steps leading to the porch creaked as she walked up them. Opening the screen door, she peeked inside and glanced around. A sofa with a colorful quilt draped over it sat to the side. Two chairs were placed on each end of the sofa. Several fashion magazines dating to when the world was still normal were open on a coffee table. A light breeze ruffled the curtains.

Sarah stepped inside, taking care to avoid the rug made from a mountain lion. Larry had told her Dillon killed a mountain lion some months back and had made a rug out of the skin. Fortunately, the head was gone. She guessed a taxidermist was unavailable to make the eyes and tongue presentable. Just as well.

"Holly? Cassie? It's me, Sarah Monroe."

"We're up here," Holly called out. "Come on upstairs."

Sarah placed her backpack near the front door then proceeded to the second floor. Cassie and Holly were talking in one of the bedrooms while getting ready.

"Everyone," Holly said, "this is Sarah Monroe. I think you already know Cassie and Amanda." They nodded in Sarah's direction. "But I don't think you know Dorothy and her daughter, Anna."

"Nice to meet you," Sarah said.

"You too." Dorothy smiled pleasantly.

Sarah stepped over to Cassie. "You are absolutely lovely. Your make-up and hair are perfect. But why are you still in jeans and a T-shirt?"

"Holly is making a last minute alteration to the dress. Apparently I've gained a few pounds since I tried it on last." Cassie patted her belly. Sarah understood the subtle gesture.

"You're expecting, aren't you?"

"I am."

"Does your father know?"

Holly put down the sewing needle. "He knows and he's very happy. Morning sickness is a dead giveaway. That, and the fact Ryan has been hovering over Cassie and making sure she gets enough sleep and plenty to eat."

"I guess I should have told him," Cassie said. "It's kinda embarrassing. I didn't want him to be disappointed in me."

"Cassie, your father is extremely proud of you. Don't ever forget that. I assure you once the baby is born, Dillon will be a doting grandfather."

Sarah went over to the window and pushed aside the curtains. Several other couples from nearby ranches had arrived and were milling around the makeshift cocktail tables. Dillon handed out beer, while Ryan made small talk with one of the recently arrived guests.

"How many people are you expecting," Sarah asked.

"Not many," Cassie said. "About fifteen to twenty people. There aren't that many left around here. When Ryan and I made the rounds to the ranches we discovered several had been abandoned."

Sarah peered out the window at a bright red Chevy rolling into the yard. "There comes the couple you were telling me about.'

Cassie went to the window. "That's Chandler and Amanda. They are the ones who brought Cowboy back. I'm so glad they made it. Can you go down and tell Amanda to come on upstairs?"

"Sure." Sarah excused herself and walked down the staircase.

"Well, Cassie," Holly said. "If all the guests are here then you should probably get dressed."

Cassie was gazing wistfully at the pair of boots she had on, and hadn't even heard Holly ask her a question.

Holly put a hand on Cassie's shoulder. "What's wrong? Are you feeling okay?"

"What? Oh, I'm okay. I was just thinking I wished we had a camera."

"I know. Don't be sad, because your memories will always remain here," Holly said, tapping her heart. "Those will never fade."

"Cassie!" Amanda rushed into the room. She went to her friend and hugged her. "I can't believe you're getting married. You didn't even tell me. Chandler found the invitation tucked into the front door."

"You weren't home when we delivered it," Cassie explained. "We couldn't wait. I'm sorry."

"Don't be. This is your happy day. I'm so excited for you." Amanda's eyes swept over the room. "Is that your dress?"

Cassie nodded.

"It's gorgeous. Aren't you going to get dressed? I'll help you get—"

"Shhh. Do you hear that?" Cassie asked.

A faint pulsing vibration of choppy thrumming became louder until the windows in the bedroom shook, keeping rhythm to the thunder of spinning blades.

UNDEFEATED WORLD

The women stood awestruck, each peering out the window, searching for the helicopter making the unmistakable sound.

"A helicopter?" Sarah commented in surprised confusion. She lowered her head to get a better look at the massive aircraft. "That's like something out of the movie *Black Hawk Down*. Perplexed, she asked, "Who was invited that has a military heli—"

Gunfire shattered the peaceful scene of the bride and her attendants. Shards of glass and splintered wood peppered the room and the women. Surprised at the unfettered hostility and unsure what to do, Sarah stood frozen. Without hesitation Holly, Amanda, and Cassie dropped to the floor and covered their heads with their arms. Dorothy jerked her daughter down and stayed next to her. Keeping low, they crawled away from the window to the inner hallway where they huddled together. Holly put a protective arm over Cassie.

"Sarah," Holly whispered, "get down. You need to get down. Come over here."

Another volley of high-powered gunfire erupted, and the dinging of bullets thumped the walls.

Holly ducked and covered her head.

A visceral scream came from outside.

"Sarah!" Holly called more urgently. "Get down."

When there was no response, Holly peeked around the doorframe. Sarah was face down on the floor, her arms splayed outwards, her hair covering her face. A puddle of blood had formed around her head, while a viscous crimson river trailed along one of the grooves in the old wood floor, snaking closer to where the three were huddled.

Holly's eyes flicked to Cassie's wedding dress hanging on the door. Her lacy white dress had been splattered with Sarah's blood. She recoiled away from the sight and leaned her back against the wall, steepling her fingers together in supplication, and clasped her hands to her mouth. Her heart beat rapidly, and she flinched at the sound of sporadic gunfire.

A yell from outside was cut off by a round. There was an eerie silence until she recognized Dillon's voice, yet his words were unclear. She strained her ears, listening to an English response with an odd accent, and her mind searched for the country of origin.

Finally it came to her.

It was Russian.

"Cassie, Amanda, we have to get out of here," she said.

"What about Sarah?" Cassie asked.

Holly shook her head. "There's nothing we can do for her. It's only us now, and we need to leave. Now."

CHAPTER 7

Dillon, Chandler, Ryan, Larry, and several other guests had listened with growing curiosity to the distant methodical whumping of the helicopter blades. Unable to discern which direction it was coming from and thinking it would probably make a wide swing to skirt the ranch, the men hadn't acted adversely to it.

Recent chatter of military helicopters flying around the county without incident had made the rounds of the rural neighbors. When the chopper made an appearance over the tree line, circling to the back of the ranch, then to the front, there had been no need for concern.

Dillon observed Larry take the back of his hand and brush away sweat beading his forehead. Larry nervously scratched the side of his head and mumbled, "I gotta take a leak." The last Dillon saw of Larry, he had ducked behind a pine tree several yards away.

"Not so close!" Dillon yelled.

Larry poked his head around the tree, zipped up his pants, then found a more suitable tree to hide behind while he relieved himself.

Dillon shook his head. "He's a strange duck."

"Yeah," Chandler muttered. "He's as nervous as a buck during hunting season."

Although Dillon agreed, he said, "Forget about it. No telling what's going on with him."

Dillon and Chandler were deep in conversation near the tables, ribbing each other about wearing their best Western wear of blue jeans, a long sleeved shirt, bolo necktie with braided leather cords tipped in silver dangling down the front, and boots, per requests of the ladies. Earlier, Dillon had snuck some of the best whiskey out of the house and hid it behind a tree. When Chandler arrived, Dillon had poured him a drink.

"I haven't tasted anything this good since I met up with some SASS members on the 360 Bridge in Austin," Chandler said.

"So where'd you get those boots?" Dillon asked. Taking a closer look at Chandler's boots, he asked, "Is that snakeskin?"

Chandler nodded. "Yup. It's from a python that attacked me. I barely escaped with my life. Amanda ended up shooting it in the head. Good thinking on her part."

"Whatd'ya mean? For saving you?"

"That too," Chandler said, chuckling. "I mean, she didn't damage the snakeskin with the shot." He tossed back a swallow of the smooth whiskey.

"Who made them for you?" Dillon asked.

"A boot maker in Austin. Since I didn't have any money, and credit cards aren't worth the plastic they're made from, I paid the boot maker with an old Colt .45 single action. My Uncle Billy told me if I cleaned the gun for him, I could have it. I traded it for the boots."

"Excellent." Dillon polished off the last of his drink. "Can I get you another one?"

"I don't want to drink all your good stuff. Let's save it for the toast for Ryan and Cassie after they say 'I do.' Ryan is holding up the best he can, but I can tell he's nervous. Have you seen how much he's sweating?"

"I noticed, but didn't want to say anything."

"It's not that hot and he can't stop sweating. Not exactly like there's any AC for him to cool down in. Speaking of electricity, have you heard anything?"

Dillon shook his head. "No. Not a thing. We still have the light switches turned on in case the electricity magically boots back up, so we'll know. I've turned off the breakers for the AC unit and other electricity hogging appliances. What about you? Have you heard anything?"

"Not really," Chandler admitted. "The only thing Amanda and I have been doing is securing the gates to her ranch and fortifying the house. Her Grandpa Hardy did a good job inside, but outside he definitely let some things slide once he got sick. We haven't taken time to talk to any of the neighbors. They probably don't even know she's back. There's no mail, no phones, or any type of communication. We don't go out after dark either. Besides, there might be another mountain lion around here, and after the tangle I had with the python, I certainly don't want to meet up with a mountain lion like you did."

"Don't blame you. It does make for a good story and the hide makes a nice rug. The cat won't go near it," Dillon said laughing. "Look who's coming."

"Who is it?"

"The pastor. I guess it's time to get things rolling. Let's round up the guests and get them seated. Where's Larry? Did he go inside?"

"Last I saw, he had ducked behind the tree over there." Chandler nodded to where he had seen Larry disappear to. "Let's not worry about it." Raising his voice, he said, "I'll help you—"

The loud whirling of a military chopper flying low and fast drowned out Chandler's voice, and he and Dillon studied the chopper with growing curiosity. Treetops whipped violently in the backwash, tablecloths billowing in the rush of air.

"What in the hell is going on?" Chandler yelled over the sound of the helicopter. "Is that a Russi—"

Gunfire peppered the house, shattering windows and sending splintered wood flying. The men ducked and covered their heads, scrambling for cover. Chandler's high-powered LaRue was at his house, and the Glock he had with him was no match for the firepower pinning them down.

Rounds blasted the stately pine trees, sending bark and hot, sticky sap in all directions.

Someone screamed.

Dillon watched helplessly as the chopper's firepower continued its assault on the house and the wedding guests. He steeled himself for the inevitable searing burn of a round blasting through his body, and said a silent prayer to keep Holly and Cassie safe. He bargained with God to take his life to spare Holly and Cassie.

The gunfire abruptly stopped.

Chandler slid his hand under his belly and reached for his Glock. His heart was beating at breakneck speed, his senses on full alert.

"Don't," Dillon whispered. "If they wanted us dead, we'd be dead."

Several soldiers in full military gear exited the hovering helicopter by rappelling down ropes. They shot a volley across the tables and chairs then secured the area by forming a circle.

The helicopter maneuvered to an open area near the house, where the pilot expertly set the chopper on the hard ground, and powered it down.

The door slid open, and Colonel Mikhail Burkov, Commander of Operation Spindletop, exited the helicopter. He stood with his back straight, shoulders squared, and carried the unmistakable air of military authority.

He took in the surroundings and casually strolled closer to the house. The country home was similar to the pictures in textbooks when he had studied at Suvorov Military School, the Russian equivalent of West Point.

A wide porch wrapped around the front and sides of the house. There were long windows suitable for taking advantage of cross breezes, and a crawlspace under the first floor was camouflaged with white lattice work. A gorgeous country house by any standards. Not all that good from a tactical standpoint with all the windows and doors, but the second story provided an advantage of a 360 degree view over the land.

Burkov had excelled in military tactics, athletics, and had mastered English. A graduate program studying English in the United States had increased his knowledge of America, its language, and people.

The quaint house with a nearby barn and meager garden would be suitable for the lower working class, and not particularly for Burkov as he considered himself to be a connoisseur of the finer things in life. He preferred the ballet to movies, enjoyed eating in the finest white-tabled restaurants which attracted a certain breed of woman. He detested these backwoods Americans and the crude lifestyle they lived. Uneducated beer-drinking heathens. What was the American word these types of people were called? His mind searched for it.

Rednecks. That was it. *Rednecks.*

Two soldiers in Russian urban camouflage uniforms and body armor flanked the colonel. Their eyes were fixed straight ahead and each carried an AK 74 rifle.

A man dressed in civilian clothes followed several steps behind the Colonel. His most distinguishing feature was a scar running down the side of his face. The soldiers asked no questions why the man had come along, and they knew to keep their distance from Petya Ruslan. There had been rumors of what he was capable of doing, especially of making people disappear without a trace. He was loathed…and feared.

Colonel Burkov snapped his fingers and motioned for Ruslan to follow him while the two soldiers stayed behind. They walked into the house and Burkov took note of the hide inside the front door. It had been made in a hurry and showed no refinements of a talented furrier, providing more cause for him detesting the Americans and their crude ways. The magnificent animal that produced the hide should have commanded top dollar and been treated with respect. A pair of gloves made from the hide would have been appropriate for the cold Russian winters, not the ungodly heat and humidity assaulting Burkov. Sweat stained his shirt and he cursed his assignment.

His thoughts took him to his motherland, and the cool arctic air brushing the mountains and the mighty Ural River. Oh, how he wished he was in Russia walking among his people who had endured war and famine, and who had become stronger in spite of hardship.

Regardless of the dismal land and murky rivers, or any type of discomfort he would endure, Burkov stood straighter because his loyalty to the motherland was unfettered. He was proud of his Mother Russia, and despised the Americans who were soft and had shown no resistance. Let them try to live through the unimaginable horror of starvation during the siege of Leningrad in WWII.

"Ruslan, I've seen enough. Come."

The big man opened the door for Burkov. Before he exited,

UNDEFEATED WORLD

Burkov wiped his boots on the mountain lion hide, leaving it askew. As Ruslan was closing the door, he hesitated. He scoffed at the quaint country home and of the people who lived there who had been easily conquered. Fools. In a show of contempt, he kicked the hide across the room.

CHAPTER 8

"Well, what do we have here?" Burkov asked as he inspected the men and women lying on the ground. He cast a smug glower at each one.

While the Russian troops had their AK 74s trained on the captured Americans, a timid voice called out, "Don't hurt me. I'm unarmed." Larry Monroe peeked around the pine tree where he had been hiding. He held open his jacket to show he had no hidden weapons. "Don't shoot." He emerged with his hands in the air.

Burkov locked eyes with Monroe then ordered, "Get down."

Larry scrambled to where Dillon was, kneeled, then lowered himself flat on the ground. Dillon glowered at him with a look that sent shivers through the man who had excused himself moments before the military helicopter made an appearance.

"Who is the owner of this property?" Burkov asked. Long shadows danced across the land, and somewhere a bird sang a lonely melody.

After an intense few seconds of silence, Burkov studied the captives. There were several able-bodied men of varying ages scattered about. Two elderly men were side by side, flanked by a frail, white-haired woman. Burkov strolled over to the woman. He grabbed her arm and yanked her up. She cried out in protest.

"Who is the owner of this property?"

Still no answer.

Burkov unholstered his pistol and shoved it to the woman's temple, making her head tilt to the side. "If I ask again, I will put a bullet through her head."

"I am the owner," Dillon announced. He was on the ground, his face mashed into the prickly grass.

The woman stood shaking, her eyes darting around.

Burkov whipped his head in the direction of the voice. "Stand up and make yourself known."

Dillon pushed himself up from the ground, and brushed the dirt and leaves off his Sunday best clothes. He defiantly faced Burkov. "I am Dillon Stockdale. I am the owner of this property. It is private property. You are trespassing, and I am advising you to leave."

Colonel Burkov provided an equally defiant glare, then broke out in laughter. "You? Advising me and telling us to leave? That's the funniest statement I've heard." Burkov addressed his soldiers. "Do you agree?"

Muddled laugher followed.

"I do not think you are qualified to advise me. Were you in the military?"

"I am a citizen of the United States of America. This is private property and I am the rightful owner."

"Not anymore." Burkov strolled over to Dillon and stood facing him, eye to eye. Dillon didn't budge. "Let's get something straight. Russia is now in control of this area. We make the rules and we decide who owns the land. This," Burkov made a sweeping hand gesture to the house and land, "is mine. I shall do with it what I want to."

"What do you want with us?" Dillon asked.

"I need all able-bodied men," Burkov said without hesitation.

"Why?"

"Do you see my men questioning me? If they did, they'd get this." Burkov grabbed an AK 74 from one of the soldiers and came so close to Dillon he saw the evil in Burkov's eyes. Burkov aimed the AK at Dillon's chest.

Though Dillon's heart was beating at breakneck speed, he decided if he was going to die, he would face it head on and not back down to these Russian thugs. He stood his ground.

In a lightning fast motion, Burkov pivoted the high-powered rifle so the deadly end was facing away from Dillon then forcefully jabbed the butt into Dillon's stomach. Dillon doubled over and clutched his mid-section, grunted, and fell backward.

Although Chandler's first instinct was to help Dillon, common sense dictated otherwise. He could only helplessly witness the cruel tactics of the Russian Colonel. Dillon fell close to Chandler, who willed him with his eyes to stay down and to keep quiet.

Dillon blinked long and slowly to indicate he understood.

When Chandler got the chance, he'd tell Dillon to keep his cool and to let the Russians think they were in charge. While the Russians may have beat them this time, Chandler had other ideas. With growing hatred, he watched Burkov inspect each person. The Russian Colonel nodded at each man pinned on the ground, and when he got to the elderly woman who was still standing, Burkov asked, "Which of these fine gentlemen is your husband?"

The woman hesitated, then feebly pointed to her husband.

"Him?"

She nodded.

"You," Burkov said. "Come here."

An elderly man stood and joined his wife. He put his arm around her in an attempt to show solidarity. He gently squeezed her in a loving gesture to tell her it would be alright, and that he would protect her to the end.

"Let this be a lesson to all of you," Burkov said. "If you defy or question me, this will be the result." Burkov handed the AK 74 to a nearby soldier then withdrew a semi-automatic Makarov pistol from his waist holster, and without hesitation or indecision, fired two shots: one into the man's temple, the other into his wife. They were dead before they hit the ground.

One of the wedding guests gasped. Others kept their eyes closed in horror, their faces mashed into the hard ground. Dillon and Chandler kept their eyes on Burkov.

"Let me be perfectly clear," Burkov said. Using his foot, he nudged the elderly man, confirming he was dead. In a show of superiority Burkov put one foot on the man's shoulder as if this was his trophy. "The decision to live or die is yours. Follow my orders, and you will live. Fight back or disobey, and there will be no second chances. As you will find out, I can also exhibit acts of selfless altruism. Though Dillon Stockdale questioned me, and while I should have executed him, I instead showed mercy upon him. Once we are finished here, we will return to Russia, and you may return to your peasant lifestyle for which I have no desire. Are there any questions?" After a few beats of silence, he said, "Good. A truck will be here to take you to your destination. There is one thing, though I am curious about."

Burkov strolled to where Dillon was, and told him to stand on his feet. "Obviously, from the decorations, a wedding was about to begin, and since you are owner of this place, I am assuming your daughter was to be married. Am I correct?"

Dillon sent Burkov a good old fashioned eye-piercing glare. If eyes could talk, he'd be telling the Russian he'd be a dead man soon.

"Silence indicates guilt, which is good enough for me. May I ask where the bride and her mother are?"

The ease with which Burkov spoke, and the underlying meanings infuriated Dillon. "My wife is dead," Dillon said indignantly. "She died over two years ago from a brain aneurism."

Burkov dipped his chin. "Please accept my sincerest apologies."

While there was nothing sincere about Burkov, regardless, Dillon played along with his pretend cordialness. "Accepted," Dillon said through a clenched jaw.

"Is the bride not in the house? I would like to meet her."

Thinking quickly on his feet and needing to divert attention away from the women in the house, Dillon casually explained. "There was a delay in the wedding. Something about last minute items were needed. My daughter and her attendants made a run into town. They should have come back by now."

"What did they need?" Burkov asked, suspicious of Dillon's answer.

Dillon shrugged, and tried to be as casual as possible. "You know how it is when the ladies talk. I put them on a filter. I vaguely recall them talking about flowers and ribbons."

Burkov tapped the air. "A filter? Ah, I understand. They talk, you nod, but don't hear anything."

"Right."

Burkov laughed. "Well, Mr. Stockdale, I think you and I could have gotten along or had a beer if we had known each other during a different time. It is obvious you are a man of your word and of standing. What was your profession, if you don't mind me asking?"

Dillon did mind the question, and if he got the chance to be alone with Burkov, a beer would be the last thing on his mind. What he'd like to do was send a Spyderco knife deep into Burkov's spine. "I was an Assistant District Attorney."

"I am familiar with the American judicial system. Upholding the law and prosecuting criminals suits you. Am I right to observe you are a man of honor and truth?"

"Yes." The line of questioning and observations was becoming worrisome to Dillon. Burkov obviously wasn't making small talk, so what his intentions were was anybody's guess.

"Let me understand. The house is empty? Yes?" Burkov paced among the men, studying them for their reactions.

"That is correct."

"Forgive me since I need to be certain." Burkov turned to the big Russian in civilian clothes. Petya Ruslan took a step forward from where he had been standing in the shadows. "Petya, take Andrey Koshkin with you and search the house. If you find anyone, shoot them. Man, woman, or child."

A breath caught in Dillon's chest, which he prayed to the Almighty had not been noticed. He concentrated on keeping his breathing calm and even, and to keep his rising and falling chest from betraying him. He considered rushing Burkov, then thought better of it when his eyes caught several rifles pointed at him. There was nothing to be done except to live. If he died, there was nothing more to be done. Live, and he could fight another day. He dipped his chin and closed his eyes, silently praying the Almighty would keep Cassie, Holly, and Amanda safe, and to give them the strength they would need in the face of hostility. Let them be calm, let them hide if necessary, or give them the fortitude to fight if that was the only choice they had. He prayed for strength and absolute cunning to outwit his enemies; he prayed for his own calmness, and for those around him.

In the waning light, the dark corners and shadows of the house would provide camouflage. Dillon respected the dark. Yet he recognized these soldiers were also aware darkness was a friend and not foe.

* * *

Ruslan jerked his head and motioned for Andrey Koshkin to follow him. While Andrey carried the standard accoutrements of Russian military soldiers, Ruslan carried a large hunting knife in a scabbard attached to his belt. He preferred to kill in close quarters, without using the luxury of a rifle from a distance. He had been trained in knife fighting by the best, and didn't hesitate to overpower his prey.

Killing was personal to Petya Ruslan, and he was good at it.

The rumbling of a truck along the dirt road leading to the house broke the silence, and it was not clear if it was a Russian military truck. Burkov swiveled to the direction of the road and motioned for several soldiers to stand ready in case the truck was not theirs.

The rumbling became louder, indicating a heavy truck was nearing, and during the lull in security, a wedding guest catapulted up and sprinted to the cover of the pine trees.

Ruslan, who was opening the front door of the house, swiveled around. He saw the American man disappear into the brushy forest.

Burkov thrust an angry arm in the direction of the escapee. "Ruslan, find him!" he yelled. "Kill him."

The big Russian took off running.

Andrey Koshkin was standing on the porch awaiting instruction. Burkov nodded for Andrey to begin the search without waiting on Ruslan. Andrey pushed open the front door and stepped into the house and quietly shut the door.

The tidy house had the usual American furnishings, not that he was familiar with the style, yet he appreciated the homey atmosphere. Framed prints of American landscapes hung on the walls. A family picture of a man, woman, and older child sat on an end table, and Andrey ran a finger over the frame. Various magazines lay open. He went to the fireplace mantle and inspected more pictures. For a moment, a tinge of homesickness washed over him, and he briefly recalled his long dead parents and sister.

In the quiet room, his thoughts took him to the car accident that had claimed the lives of his parents and sister on that cold winter day. He had only been a child when it happened and had been shuffled from relative to relative, feeling like a third wheel, and on his eighteenth birthday, he was given his walking papers. Without a home, he had joined the Russian military, hoping to find a substitute family. He had never found it, and though he had made friends and had gained the respect of his commanders, he was now early thirties, and longed for the home he never had.

The anti-American propaganda the Russian people were subjected to was quite different than what he had experienced once he set foot on American soil. These weren't bad people, and a lot of them had similar characteristics like Andrey. Tall, brown-haired, skin tones the same as his, yet the mingling of different cultures was apparent.

The reverie was short lived when he heard a faint noise, like someone was shifting positions. Was it his imagination? The wind? The normal creaking an old house made? Whatever it was, he needed to investigate it.

He methodically searched each room on the first floor. The living area contained no obvious hiding places, yet he looked under the furniture and behind a large mahogany buffet, a piece he surmised was an antique. Studying the size of the buffet, and the fact it could hide a small adult, he opened a cabinet door and shined a flashlight in. Nothing of use except a few pieces of silverware. He pushed those around to find empty envelopes, pictures, and other various useless household items. Closing the door, he went to the kitchen and opened cabinet doors, then searched the pantry and refrigerator.

Andrey moved deeper into the house, checking closets and under beds, and when he came to the staircase, he glanced upward to the landing. If he were to get shot, the time would be when he was on the stairs. He could either quietly move to the second floor, carefully putting his weight on each wooden step, or he could surge forward, hoping to take anyone by surprise.

He decided a stealthy approach was best. He tested the first step and put his weight on it, waiting for it to creak. Satisfied the step was solid, he crept along the stairs, hugging the wall. He held his AK 74 in a ready position, and when he came to the second floor landing, he ducked his head around the corner to check each hallway.

It was empty, yet a shiver captured him. For a brief moment he thought he was being watched. The unfamiliar surroundings were his enemy, and if there was an escape route or outside stairs, he surmised the occupants had already escaped. From what he had heard the man who was being questioned by Burkov say, several women were probably in the house. Briefings on American culture had indicated the citizens living in the country were well armed. In his inspection of the house, he had found a rifle behind one of the doors and a handgun in a drawer along with ammo, not exactly what he would consider well-armed.

Whoever lived here was indeed armed, though no match for Russian military arms. If someone was in the house, they were well hidden and quiet.

Andrey needed to be careful. Women could shoot just as well as men.

He let his nose dictate where he needed to go next. He caught the unmistakable smell of blood so thick he tasted metal and swallowed down the sour bile rising in his throat. He inched down the hallway and came to a door that was ajar. He pushed it open with the end of his rifle to find a woman dead on the floor, surrounded by a pool of blood, no doubt a casualty of the first volley of fire.

She was middle aged, dressed for the occasion, but Andrey suspected she was not the mother of the bride or a close relative.

His attention shifted to the shattered window and to the glass shards blown into the room with a force tremendous enough to embed them in the wall.

A white wedding dress splattered with blood hung askew on a hanger.

Andrey stepped into the room and gave it a onceover. The sparsely furnished room had a bed, a dresser with a mirror, and a quick peek determined men's and women's shoes were under the bed. A stuffed animal surrounded by pillows was on the bed.

This was the bride's room. The men's shoes probably accounted for them moving in together after the wedding.

Carefully, Andrey stepped to the closet, stood to the side, and turned the brass doorknob. It squeaked open. His heart beat fast and he dreaded what he might find. The closet was a jumble of clothes and shoes, and a plethora of useless stuff. He breathed a sigh of relief. Satisfied the room was empty, he stepped into the hallway. Two other bedrooms needed to be searched, so he started there.

Finding both empty, he decided the house was vacant.

Just as Andrey decided to leave, he heard the sound of shifting weight.

Someone was here.

The sound had come from behind him, yet he was sure he had searched all the rooms. He walked along the wooden floor, taking his time as he searched the wood-paneled walls. Every foot or so, he pressed his hand against the wall to test the strength, gauging if the panels felt like the others.

He came to the end of the hallway where there was a window. He took a peek of the front lawn where the wedding party was being held captive. A brief moment of regret hit him hard and fast, knowing the lives of the Americans meant absolutely nothing to Colonel Burkov.

Still, Andrey was a soldier and he had a mission to accomplish.

As he was about to leave, the warping of the paneled wall caught his attention. Squinting, he tried to understand what was different about it, and he let his eyes focus on the patterns of the wood.

There, he understood now.

It was the break in the pattern that clued him this wasn't a wall.

It was a facade of a hidden room.

CHAPTER 9

"Holly, what are we going to do?" Cassie asked. Her features, glowing minutes earlier in the knowledge she was about to be married to the man she loved, were now contorted in anguish.

"Let me think," Holly said.

They had been huddling in the hallway taking cover from the bullets that had blown through the walls. Dorothy and her daughter Anna waited for guidance.

"Do we take a stand?" Cassie asked. "I can get my dad's rifle. There are pistols for everyone to use too."

"I can also help," Amanda chimed in.

"No," Holly said firmly. "Our weapons are no match for theirs. "The best thing for us to do is to hide and stay quiet so we can live another day to fight. With any luck, Dillon has said something to throw them off."

"Where should we hide?" Amanda asked. "Should we split up? Or make a run for it?"

"There's no time. The house has probably been surrounded by now," Holly said. Her mind raced, thinking of alternatives. She recalled the remodeling of the house and how the newer part of the house was built so the old house could be incorporated into it. Her father specifically had the wooden floor constructed so it could hide valuables under the wood. People walking over it had no idea weapons were stored there. There must be something else. What had her father said about the second story? She closed her eyes, her mind whirling, trying to recall the conversation. Holly's eyes popped open. "I remember now. There's a hidden closet in the hallway near the window."

Crawling on her hands and knees, Holly ran the pads of her fingers over the wall as if she was playing a piano. She focused on the sound the wood made on each stroke. There it was–a break in the pattern. She pushed on a plank and a camouflaged paneled door swung inward. Tucked between the closet of two bedrooms was a space large enough to hold several grown men, or in their case four women and one child.

"Quickly," Holly said, motioning with her hand. "Everybody in here."

The women shuffled in single file into the dark space. Once everyone was in, Holly closed the door, throwing the space into pitch black darkness. "Shhh," she whispered. "Don't move. Don't make a sound."

Cassie was pressed against the back of the space, Amanda in front of her. Dorothy was standing straight against the wall, and in the haste to get in the hidden space, Anna was leaning against Holly. There was no time to switch places. Holly put a protective arm around Anna.

Holly listened with growing apprehension as the soldier moved through the house. Doors opened and closed, the creaking of footsteps grew closer. Whoever was searching for them had found something of interest. Holly's heart beat fast and hard, and she held her breath, listening to a hand searching the wall.

Another creak of the floor, and this time it was nearer.

After a long silence, a flashlight clicked on, and the beam bounced from top to bottom.

Her eyes, now acclimated to the darkness, focused upon the sliver of light bending through the cracks in the panels.

The hidden door suddenly swung open.

Upon seeing the group of women, Andrey Koshkin relaxed his

posture and lowered the barrel of the AK to the floor. He shined the flashlight beam on each of the four women, and when the beam fell to Anna, he let out a surprised huff.

He hadn't signed up to kill children. A child thrust into the world of international politics, a child who hadn't had time to grow up, a child whose fate he held, a child the same age as his sister was when she died.

If you find anyone, kill them.

Burkov's command and his nonchalant attitude at killing sent shivers up Andrey's spine.

Holly put a hand to her eyes to shield them from the blinding light. Peering through her splayed fingers, she caught a glimpse of a soldier dressed in full military garb. He had on a helmet, body armor, camo fatigues, and heavy boots. Holly expected to be executed at any moment so in a show of defiance she threw back her shoulders and dropped her hands from her face. She stared straight at the soldier. If she was to die, he'd have to look her in the eyes.

Anna was trembling so much, Holly's dress fluttered. Holly tugged the little girl closer to her and put a hand around Anna's shoulders to try to calm her.

Anna's mother whispered, "Please don't."

Holly studied the soldier's face, the shape of his jaw, his eyes, and she wondered why he was transfixed on Anna, as if she reminded him of someone. Perhaps he had a daughter in Russia. Whatever it was, the soldier gazed upon Anna with fatherly love. She wondered if she should say something or not, then decided the best offense was to stay quiet, especially since the AK could dispatch them all in a matter of seconds.

She concentrated on lowering her heart rate, knowing if it beat any faster, she might pass out.

The soldier lowered the flashlight and put his finger to his mouth. "Shhh," he whispered, nodding his head in silent communication. "Shhh. I go now."

As silently as he found them, he exited in equal silence.

Holly swallowed and exhaled the breath she had been holding. She pushed Anna behind her in an attempt to shield her from the volley of bullets that was sure to come.

A long second went by, then another, and Holly strained to listen.

Hurried footsteps upon stairs echoed in the silence. A slamming door, then more footsteps running down front porch stairs.

Anna cried and reached to her mother, and Holly relaxed her face for a moment. They had made it for now. They had been discovered, and by the grace of God had been shown mercy. Holly vowed not to forget the soldier.

* * *

Andrey took the porch stairs two at a time, and hit the ground running. He came to Colonel Burkov and saluted him.

"At ease."

Andrey dropped his hand to his side.

"What did you find?" Burkov asked.

"Nothing, sir. The house was empty."

"Any sign of the women?"

"Yes sir. I found the wedding dress hanging in the bedroom. Wedding decorations were scattered on the bed. No sign of the bride, her mother, or anyone else." Andrey kept his sentences short and concise, skipping any further embellishment of the story which might give fodder to Burkov to question him further. Andrey fixed his gaze upon the bark of a pine tree, focusing on sap leaking down the side. Concentrating on something of inconsequential value helped provide Andrey the focus he needed. He had seen the consequences of others lying to Burkov. Some disappeared, while others had been forced into hard labor.

Burkov clasped his hands behind his back and strolled over to Dillon. "It appears you were telling the truth. I thank you for that. Truth is always the best policy, regardless of the cost to life or property."

"I am a defender of the truth," Dillon replied. His sharp jaw line and narrow eyes indicated his anger.

"Of course." Burkov dipped his chin and ignored the signals Dillon had sent. "I admire that. I am also a defender of truth and of Russia. We are a great country, greater and older than yours. Centuries older with abundant natural resources. We are rich in arts and history."

"A land you took from others," Dillon said.

Burkov laughed, but not with mirth. "I am well versed in Indian

Wars and how America stole their land. Were they not the first Americans?"

"The Indians conquered the land from others, as others had taken from those before them."

Burkov's irritation was mounting. He was not used to clever bantering or challenges to his intellect from underlings. On the other hand, Burkov found meeting someone with equal intellect refreshing.

"Point taken. Perhaps we can talk about this subject further sometime. Over dinner, even. If you will excuse me now." Burkov walked past the soldiers, past the helicopter, and the truck. This was such a simple ranch with one house, a barn, a corral for the horses. He strolled over to where Cowboy was and admired him. He was a fine animal, strong, with a good coat and markings.

During his time in America, Burkov had been fascinated with cowboy movies starring John Wayne, James Stewart, Clint Eastwood, names he remembered. American cinema at its finest. A time when men were men, and women were women, when differences were settled with a gun. A simple time with simple people, and even simpler results.

Burkov strolled over to the corral and put his foot on the lower rung. His mind wandered to the movies. *True Grit* and *The Searchers* came to mind, with imagery of horses and wide open spaces, smoky saloons and good whiskey, jovial piano music. But foremost, the horses. Burkov had always wanted a horse. He spied Cowboy at the far end of the corral, and called to him.

From a distance, Cowboy eyed the strange man. His nostrils flared and his dark eyes widened as Cowboy used the visual and auditory cues presented to him. One of his ears moved to better understand the strange sounds the man made, foreign, sharp sounds Cowboy had not heard before. The man's body language indicated one of authority, moving with ease and purpose, the voice strong and deep, yet Cowboy didn't immediately respond to the verbalizations.

Cowboy tossed his head and snorted, and refused to go to the stranger who called to him with increasing levels of garbled sounds. Angry shouts and hand waving followed until another man entered the picture, and from his body posture, Cowboy recognized him as being subservient.

While Cowboy didn't understand the situation, it was obvious the men were communicating, and Cowboy studied the interaction. The subordinate hurried away then returned minutes later with someone Cowboy knew and trusted.

Cowboy's eyes brightened and he trotted over to Dillon, lowered his head, waiting for a scratch. Dillon rubbed the horse along the flat part of his head between his nose and eyes while talking to him in a soothing tone.

"What is his name?" Burkov asked.

"Cowboy."

"Hmm. Cowboy. Does he understand his name?"

"Yes," Dillon said. He moved his hand to Cowboy's ears, twirling them between his fingers.

"I've always wanted a horse," Burkov said. He reached to Cowboy to pat him, only to have Cowboy move out of reach.

"I wouldn't do that. He'll bite."

"A spirited animal. I like that." Burkov pivoted to Andrey. "Take the American and get whatever you need for the horse. We will attach the trailer to the truck and take the horse with us."

"He's not for sale," Dillon said.

The suddenness of which Burkov spun around to face Dillon startled him.

"I didn't ask if he was," Burkov answered tersely. "Do you think I would leave the horse here? To starve to death?" Burkov's face scrunched in disbelief, annoyed his intentions were being questioned. "That would be cruel and inhuman. What kind of man do you think I am?"

Dillon knew what kind of the man the Russian was. He'd seen it in the courtroom when defendants thought they were untouchable by the law. What Dillon really wanted to do was prosecute the SOB in an American courtroom. He imagined Burkov with his pompous attitude being forced to sit complacently in front of a judge. Yeah, it was best to stay quiet and let the Russian talk so Dillon could glean all the information he could.

"I am fond of animals and have always wanted a horse since I was a child. This one will do. This is Texas," Burkov said opening his arms wide, "the grand land of cowboys and Indians. I want to experience the Wild West like John Wayne did in the movies. Perhaps I'll ride Cowboy." Burkov put a finger to his cheek. "Yes,

I think I will. Andrey, take him and get whatever the horse needs."

Dillon glared at Burkov, seething that Holly's beloved horse would be in the hands of the Russian Colonel.

Burkov went back to where the wedding party was being held.

Andrey motioned with his AK, indicating Dillon had to move. He followed Dillon into the barn, and supervised Dillon gathering Cowboy's food, saddle, and other items the horse needed.

The cavernous barn built from virgin timber had farm relics of a bygone era scattered around, including an old tractor. Hay had been stacked three bales high in the corner. A plethora of tools were hanging on pegs on a wall. Numerous boxes caved in from weight and weakened by the elements leaned at a precarious angle. The scent of animals living in the barn came full and strong and Andrey sneezed. A rusted metal container with a spout garnered his attention. He walked over to it, picked it up, and shook it. The lid to the spout was long gone, and an old red shotgun shell had been used to cap the spout. Andrey removed the makeshift cap and sniffed the contents. Some sort of fuel. He put the cap back on.

Once Dillon had gathered the necessary items for Cowboy, he reluctantly coaxed the horse over to the trailer Chandler had used to transport him from Austin to East Texas.

As Dillon was leading Cowboy into the trailer, the military truck came rumbling over. After the trailer was secured, Dillon was told to get in the back with the others.

Outgunned and outnumbered, Dillon reluctantly joined the imprisoned wedding guests where there was standing room only. He made his way to Chandler and stood next to him.

Chandler leaned into Dillon and whispered, "Where did Holly and Amanda go?"

Dillon's eyes bounced over to Larry, who had gone AWOL moments before the Russians appeared. Larry had his arms crossed, his head bowed, but his eyes were wide open. Dillon knew the man was listening. Dillon shook his head and mouthed, "Don't talk." He flicked his eyes to Larry.

Chandler leaned back and nodded he understood.

Burkov came to the side of the military truck. "Dillon, is there anything of value you would like to retrieve from the house?"

"No."

"Anything sentimental, perhaps?"

"No."

"Good. Then you won't mind if we torch it."

When Dillon opened his mouth to protest, Chandler used his fist to put pressure on Dillon's back. Under his breath, and without moving his lips, he whispered, "Don't."

Burkov barked, "Andrey! Since you searched the house, it should be your honor to torch it. We have an extra can of petrol in the truck."

"No need to use our supply, Colonel. I found a can of petrol in the barn."

"Very well. Do what you need to do."

Dark, low clouds, heavy with rain, appeared on the horizon. A gust of wind blew leaves around, and Burkov scowled. He made a forward motion with his hand, toward the helicopter already powering up, indicating it was time to go.

Ruslan, who had disappeared into the woods hunting the escapee, emerged. Burkov noted the deepening crimson stain on his pocket. "You better get that taken care of," Burkov said. "You're bleeding."

Ruslan grunted. "Do you think I'm so incompetent I'd be injured by a sniveling coward?"

"You've got blood on your shirt."

"It's not my blood." Ruslan reached into his shirt pocket, and with his index and thumb pinching together, he slowly pulled out what appeared to be animal fur attached to recently removed skin.

Burkov squinted at the item, recognizing it as a human scalp with hair. He made a grunt of disgust. "You're a savage."

"One who does your dirty work."

"Keep it out of sight." Hurrying toward the helicopter, Burkov shouted, "Let's go!" trying to project his voice over the roar of the helicopter. "Andrey, once you're finished, catch a ride in the truck. They have already started for the gate. I'll be sure they don't leave you." Burkov cast a glance at the sky and the thunderous clouds rolling in. "You'd better hurry because it will be dark soon. Rain is coming. Go now."

"Yes Sir."

Burkov ducked his head and sprinted to the helicopter. He stepped into the chopper and sat next to the pilot, while Ruslan pushed his way inside. Once the other men were in, Burkov instructed the pilot to take off.

Andrey jogged to the barn and took his time retrieving the can of fuel. Coming back to the house, he gauged which would be the best place to spread the fuel, while getting the most benefit.

The driver of the truck poked his head out the window and yelled angrily at Andrey to hurry up. "Rain is coming! Hurry or we'll leave you here." Andrey sneered while the truck rumbled slowly along the dirt road leading to the gate. The Americans were standing in the back of the truck, helpless, Cowboy was in the trailer.

Andrey was as helpless as the Americans, knowing disobeying Burkov was out of the question. He removed the shotgun shell from the spout and flung it away. He stepped closer to the house and splashed the fuel in places where the fire would cause the most damage.

CHAPTER 10

"Do you think it's safe to come out?" Cassie asked.

The dark, closed space was becoming more claustrophobic with the hot breath and increasingly warm bodies of the women huddled together. Holly had on a dress she had saved for the special occasion and open-toed sandals. The back of her dress was stained with perspiration. Amanda had chosen to wear her best pair of dark wash jeans and a sandy toned jacket over a light colored blouse. She was hot as well. She had tried earlier to remove her jacket, but in the cramped space, and, since she lacked the magical escape powers of Harry Houdini, she decided she'd have to wait.

Cassie's eyes had grown accustomed to the dark interior, and the outlines of the other women who had taken shelter in the hidden closet were visible. They hadn't moved in an hour, and with each passing minute their muscles cramped more. Dorothy had managed to sit down, and if she bent her legs at just the right angle, it allowed Anna to lay curled across her.

"Holly," Cassie said more urgently, "is it safe to go out?"

"I think so," Holly replied. "I haven't heard anything since the helicopter left."

"We might as well take a chance," Amanda chimed in. "It's getting hard to breathe in here. I thought I heard thunder a few minutes ago."

"I heard it too," Cassie said.

Holly nodded, then with great trepidation and caution, she opened the door. Fresh air whooshed in, and the women took a collective breath. It was dark in this early evening hour, and when Holly glanced at the window at the end of the hallway, a strange glow worried her.

She inhaled two short breaths through her nostrils. "Do you smell something?"

Cassie cocked her head, searching for the odor. "Like smoke?"

"Yes." Holly stepped over to the window at the end of the second story hallway and peered out. Her mouth dropped open at flames licking the porch. "The house! They've set fire to the house!" Holly whipped around and barked orders. "Dorothy, take Anna and go out the back door. Hide if you need to. Cassie, you and Amanda come with me."

The three women sprinted downstairs and threw open the front door. Dry spots in the yard smoldered and the vegetables Holly had planted in the former flowerbed had been reduced to blackened, wilted stalks. The ligustrum was ablaze, the porch steps charred by growing flames, yet the house had not been touched by the inferno.

Holly sprang into action.

Taking a garden hoe propped against the side of the house, she used all her strength and swung it at the base of the five foot tall bush. Repeatedly she heaved the blade of the hoe into the ligustrum's base until it fell.

Cassie and Amanda had dashed to the barn, then felt their way around until they found shovels. Racing back to the house, they joined Holly, and worked together to put out the remaining flames by shoveling dirt onto the fire. Using the blade of the hoe, Holly hooked it around a branch and dragged it across the lawn and onto the dirt road, away from the house and the other trees.

Sweat poured off her forehead and dripped into her eyes, stinging them. She used the sleeve of her dress to wipe her eyes dry.

Dorothy had filled a gallon jug with water and as she was about to pour it on a stubborn hot spot, Holly waved her off. Panting, her faced reddened from the heat and exertion, she said, "I need a drink of water." She drank greedily, then passed the jug to Cassie and Amanda.

After extinguishing the remaining hot spots, the four women and Anna sat down on the porch steps to regroup. Cassie sat in a slouched position, her elbows resting on her knees, her hands cradling her cheeks trying to ward off defeat. Her thoughts went to Ryan, and she prayed he would be okay. She couldn't imagine life without him or trying to raise a child by herself, and while she had her dad and Holly to help, there was no replacing a father.

It was quiet, and lingering trails of smoke filled the air. Lightning illuminated the sky far in the distance, followed by rumbling thunder.

A sprinkling of rain fell upon the land and puffs of dust rose.

"Are you okay?" Amanda put an arm around Cassie to comfort her.

Cassie nodded.

"You shouldn't be exerting yourself like this. It might harm the baby. I don't think it's good to get too hot."

"I'm fine." Cassie straightened up and surveyed the damage. "I guess we were lucky. The fire could have been much worse. We could have all been killed."

"I've been thinking about that," Holly said.

"What do you mean?"

"Whoever set the fire poured the accelerant in a manner so the house would not catch fire."

"How would you know?" Cassie asked. Gentle raindrops tapped Cassie on her cheeks and she reached to dry her face.

"Several years ago, I was the defense attorney in an arson case." Holly reached to a blade of grass and pulled it loose. She broke off a piece and started shredding it. "I learned a lot about how fires start, about how to look where the accelerant had been poured to start it, about burn patterns, all of it. I can tell you, if they had wanted the house to burn, it would have. All it did was to create a lot of smoke, which is probably what was intended. Green foliage creates a lot of smoke. From a distance, it would appear the house was on fire, and the smell can travel for miles."

"What about all the damage to the porch?" Amanda asked. "Wasn't that intentional?"

"It's only superficial and looks much worse than it is," Holly explained, shrugging. "The structure is intact. The heat from the bushes caused the paint to peel, that's all. It will only need a good scraping and new paint."

"Do you think it was the same guy that found us?"

Holly reached to her face and pushed hair out of her eyes. "I believe so."

"Why would he do that?" Amanda asked.

"I don't know."

"Did you get his name?"

Holly shook her head. "After he left all I heard was a bunch of garbled Russian. I don't even know one word of Russian. I know a little Spanish, which obviously won't do us any good. Whoever he is," Holly pondered, "he's a friend, and I bet this wasn't the last we'll see of him."

"What do you want to do with the couple over there?" Dorothy called out. She had left the group and walked over to where an elderly man and woman lay dead in the front yard.

"We'll worry about that in the morning," Holly said. "We'll also need to get the dead woman out of Cassie's bedroom. That can wait until morning too."

"What happened to our guys? My dad, Ryan, Chandler…they're all gone. Do you think they're…" Cassie hung her head, unable to finish the sentence.

"Is Mr. Stockdale dead?" Anna asked in a way only a child could, too young to comprehend the finality of death. Her worried gaze bounced from Holly to her mother then back to Holly, searching for an answer. "He can't be. He's been like a father to me. I've never met my own father because he left when I was born." Anna dipped her chin, and sniffled.

Dorothy brought her daughter closer to her. "Don't worry, Anna. I'm sure Dillon is okay. He told me if he could have had another daughter, he would have wanted her to be just like you."

Anna met her mother's eyes. "He said that?"

"He did." Dorothy smoothed Anna's hair. "He's told me that several times."

Anna hiccupped. "Okay."

Holly gazed upon Cassie with her own motherly love, then to Amanda and Dorothy, who had their eyes trained on her.

They were all waiting for leadership, and it was up to Holly to provide it.

This was her courtroom. This was her chance to use her skills, but this time, she was the prosecutor, and the Russians were the ones on trial.

Rising from the porch step, Holly stepped onto the lawn where she stood facing the group. Little Anna, so petite, clinging to her mother; Amanda, a young woman who exhibited incredible strength and fortitude in times of adversity; and Cassie, about to be married with the additional burden of carrying another life, all waited for Holly's sage wisdom.

Holly took a deep breath. She stood defiant and strong. "The important thing is that we are alive. We are together. This is our land, our country, where we were born. It's where our forefathers fought for the right to own land, to escape the tyranny of whatever government they were fleeing from. They rose against a better-armed opponent, used guerrilla tactics when needed, endured hunger when they had no food. They united, fought, and won. It's what we need to do now.

"In the morning, we will bury the dead, assess our supplies, and make a plan. Whatever the Russians want, belongs to us, and we are not going to allow them to take it. This is our land, and if it is necessary, we will fight to the death for it. Don't ever forget that. They have surprised us, but let them know we will unleash the full wrath of our fury on them, and of our determination to take back our homeland."

Holly took a breath.

"So dry your tears. There is no more time for crying. We have work to do, and we will start first thing in the morning." Holly's attention was diverted to the sky, darkened with low clouds, and a cool downdraft rushed in. "I think it's time we go in."

Cassie swiped under both eyes, sniffled once, and stood. "Before we do, I want to say something." Holly sat down and gave Cassie the stage. "I met a brave man in Louisiana last year who said he lived his life by the three Fs. His name was Garrett, and he said, and I quote, '*I live my life by the three Fs: faith, family, and firearms.*'" She paused for effect to let that sink in. "And now, this is me speaking. For faith, our heavenly Father will protect and guide us to do what we need to. For family," Cassie nodded at each person, pronouncing each name slowly, "Holly, Amanda, Dorothy, Anna. You are my family now. Each one of us will need to give the other strength and the willpower to persevere. For firearms, we are armed and I am not afraid to use them. A gun in our hands is just as deadly as in a man's hands. Remember that."

Amanda stood. "To faith."

Dorothy stood. "To family."

Cassie said, "To firearms."

"What about me?" Anna asked. "I want to help too."

Cassie laughed. "You're too little."

"I may be small for my age, but I can still help."

"No doubt you will," Cassie commented.

"I helped my mom when she was sick. I went to the pharmacy all by myself and that's when I met your dad and when I helped him find antibiotics for Holly."

"You were very brave to do that," Holly said.

"I also found your dog."

Cassie furrowed her brow. "Speaking of dogs, has anyone seen Buster?"

CHAPTER 11

Buster dashed through the thick brush and piney woods of East Texas, dodging over streambeds and gopher mounds, a black missile streaking through the land, unaware of the painful stickers embedded in his tender paws. He ran with the ease of a greyhound, legs stretching out and gobbling distance, away from the wailing of bullets hurting his ears; away from the whining helicopter blasting hot air, and flinging sand in his face.

Away from the brutal death he witnessed of an elderly couple who had been in the wrong place at the wrong time.

He panted hard and fast from running, his lungs expanding to compensate for his body's increasing need for oxygen.

He ran past the pecan orchard and past the deer blind nestled in a stand of young oaks where he had accompanied Dillon. A flickering memory of Dillon hammering nails into cedar posts came to him.

His senses were overloaded with memories of changing images and confusing odors.

The zing of bullets hitting the trees, the acrid odor of gunpowder, the resulting sickening thump of metal obliterating flesh and skin, and the crumpling bodies was too much for his canine mind to bear, so he ran, afraid to look back. Afraid to face the fate surely bestowed on Dillon and Cassie. He had failed in his duty to protect them from intruders, so like the coward who ran, Buster ran.

Fight or flight.

He had chosen flight, a trait unbecoming to a dog of his stature.

When he came to the fence line marking the back boundary of Holly's sprawling ranch, a place he had grown to know as home, Buster hesitated. In the waning light, darkened with rain and clouds, he trembled, a spasm gripping his muscles from head to tail. His ears flopped on his head. His soulful eyes, usually alert and keen as he walked by Dillon's side showed the strain of anxiety and indecision. To return to Dillon meant facing the exploding sounds and images, and his inability to protect his pack.

The land was abundant with oaks and pines, teeming with quail and turkey. A nearby doe hid in a thicket. A rabbit was tucked low into a clump of grass, brown eyes wide open, lying perfectly still, camouflaged even from the eyes of a coyote or a hawk.

A pang of indecision came to him. Go home where he could be assaulted by foreign sounds and images, or run into the unknown and dark places of the unfamiliar?

A shiver captured him, and another dark cloud rolled in over the land.

Thunder rumbled in the distance.

A bolt of lightning flashed. A yellow-white streak zigzagged angrily from the sky.

Raindrops, big as silver dollars, hit the dry land, bringing with it the peculiar smell of fresh rain.

Buster blinked his eyes as rain pelted him.

Another low rumble.

The land shook and Buster shivered in response.

Electricity filled the air, and the dark ruff of his back stood on end. Confusion set in and he trembled.

Then an ear-splitting crack of white lightning shook him to his core when it hit a nearby tall pine.

He shook, paralyzed by the sensory overload.

Splinters of hot sap and smoking pine bark exploded off the tree, and a powerful explosive wave raced down the inner core.

It was more than Buster could handle. He took off running, dodging brush and fallen logs. He leapt over a fire ant mound and dashed through thorny cactus. He wove through a stand of saplings as if he was on an obstacle course racing to the finish line.

Deeper he ran into the land, away from civilization, away from the unnatural sounds and piercing screams.

He splashed around the edge of a stock pond, then came to a herd of cows milling under a large oak where they had taken cover from the rain. A massive bull lifted its snout and tasted the air, searching for the meaning of the scent wafting on an air current. Emerging from the middle of the herd, the bull spotted Buster, who was similar in size to coyotes who could easily kill a newborn calf. The bull snorted once, lowered its head, and charged Buster.

The dog stood frozen as the thundering bull trampled the land. Closer the bull came, and right when it lowered its massive head with horns as lethal as a razor sharp blade, Buster took off running.

Another crack of lightning and rumbling thunder propelled him to run faster, deeper into uncharted land and unfamiliar sights.

Buster ran until he could run no more. His fur was soaked, paws bleeding from splinters and thorns. Exhausted, he stopped and huddled next to a large pine where he took stock of his surroundings. He was lost, scared, and was far away from his home. He was on the edge of a pasture lined by thick woods and animal trails.

Tall pines loomed dark, and Buster detected no human scents. A familiar shaped building caught his eye and he squinted through the misty rain. It was a barn, similar to the one on Holly's ranch. Buster perked up his ears at the prospect humans could be near.

Deciding the barn needed further investigating, he trotted a few steps then stopped.

He heard something.

It was the sound of a human voice, calling out, searching. A voice so faint and indiscernible, Buster was unsure if it was male or female. With great trepidation, he trotted over the uneven pasture land until he came to the barn. A door was ajar. He went to it and nosed it open. It was dry inside, musty smelling, yet containing the same familiar odors of the barn he had become accustomed to.

He lifted his snout in the air, tasting it. Several rats had left their mark on an eave high in the barn. A raccoon had been in earlier, deposited scat, then left, and the odor of an owl's nest drifted in the air. He listened for the voice and tried to identify the human scent. It had been from a man who worked the land whose body smelled of honest sweat, yet the scent was unfamiliar. Whoever had been here was now gone. Deciding it was safe, Buster cautiously went deeper into the barn and padded to a pile of loose dry hay. He scratched at it a few times, twirled, then pillowed into it, and curled into a ball. He tucked his head close to his body and exhaled once. His eyes became heavy and he closed them, lulled to sleep by nature's metronome of rain pattering on the tin roof.

CHAPTER 12

Austin, Texas
Chandler Household

"Tatiana, that was an excellent meal," Nico said. "I never knew tuna casserole tasted so good." He dabbed the corners of his mouth with a napkin, folded it, and placed it on the table.

"You're welcome." Tatiana scooted back from her chair and reached across the table to bus the plates.

"Kate and I will do that. I insist." Rising, Nico reached for the plates Tatiana had in her hands. "We'll clear the table."

"I can't ask you to do that. You're company."

"Mom," Kate said, "let us clear the table. Nico doesn't mind doing dishes."

"Really?" Tatiana asked dubiously.

"It's true," Nico confirmed. "I do a lot of dishes." He glanced at Kate and winked.

"If that's the case, then be my guest. Please scrape off any leftovers and give them to Reload. After you're finished, I'll get dessert."

Sitting around the table, John, Uncle Billy, and Luke discussed minor issues while Kate and Nico cleared the dishes. Tatiana was busy setting out plates for dessert. "We'll reuse forks if that's okay with everyone."

After Kate and Nico sat down, Tatiana waltzed in holding a pecan pie. "Pecans were picked from our trees, and I've been saving sugar and other ingredients for a special occasion. This certainly qualifies as special." She smiled and set the pie on the table, cutting it into eight slices. "Who wants the first piece?"

"Me, me!" Uncle Billy chimed in. He patted his rotund belly, stifled a belch, then with gusto, dug into the piece of pie on his plate as if it was his last meal. "This is delicious," he said, stabbing his fork into the piece of pie. He scarfed down the last bite while chewing with his mouth open. Afterward he licked his fork clean. "That was absolutely delicious."

"Thank you," Tatiana said demurely, horrified by Uncle Billy's table manners, especially since they had company. Nico's table manners, on the other hand, were quite agreeable. He obviously hadn't been raised in a barn. She shook her head. How Uncle Billy and her husband John had come from the same parents, Tatiana would never understand. She decided to change the subject. "Kate, I'm so glad you've come home. How long will you stay?"

Kate glanced at Nico. He bobbed his head indicating it was okay for her to tell everyone. "Mom, I'm not sure how to say this…" Kate glanced down at the table briefly, then lifted her eyes. "I'm not staying. Nico and I will be leaving, possibly tomorrow."

"What? But you just got here." Tatiana knitted her brow, showing deep lines. She set down the fork on the plate with a clink. "You can't leave. You and Nico can stay as long as you want to. I've been worried sick about you, Kate. We didn't know what had happened to you, or if you were hurt. I won't allow—"

"Tatiana!" John said, his voice stern. "Remember what happened last time."

Tatiana opened her mouth to reply to her husband then thought it would be better not to. She dropped her gaze and put her hands in her lap.

The dinner table went quiet without so much as a clink of a utensil on a dish, a cough, or a sniffle, and even Uncle Billy went silent.

Nico was the first to speak, but instead of speaking in English, he spoke in Russian. What he had to say was better said so others couldn't understand it.

"Tatiana, there's something I'd like you to know."

"You speak Russian very well."

Nico acknowledged her compliment with a dip of his chin. "I nearly died yesterday. Has Kate told you that?"

"I didn't know." Tatiana's eyes bounced to Kate, trying to discern if she had understood anything that had been said. Satisfied Kate didn't understand enough Russian, other than a few words and polite phrases, Tatiana said, "Please continue."

"Kate saved my life. She dragged me out of the water when I was having an allergic reaction to a sting. I would have drowned if she had not risked her life to save mine."

Tatiana snuck a peek at Kate, whose gaze was firmly planted on the table.

Nico understood the subtlety of Tatiana's questioning gaze. "Before I go on, does anyone besides you and I understand Russian?"

Tatiana didn't answer immediately. She took a few moments to study both her children. Kate picked at a ragged cuticle and showed no sign of understanding the conversation, or having mastered the intricacies of the Russian language. Luke sat silent too, twirling a fork. She motioned for Nico to continue.

"When I was somewhere between life and death, I thought about Kate, and how sorry I would be if I was not in her life. It was a wakeup call for me. Because of her I am changing my life.

"I want you to know I love your daughter. She's changed a lot over these past few months into the person you knew she has been all along. She's strong, she showed incredible bravery when we were under attack at the Alamo, and she didn't waver on tough decisions she had to make.

"I also want you to know she talked a lot about you and how you were her role model, and while she may have butted heads with you, it never meant she stopped loving you or respecting you. I know about the fight between you two when she left home, and what was said. She didn't want to come home because she was afraid of what you would say to her."

"But," Tatiana protested, "I would never—"

"I know," Nico interrupted, "but she didn't know how you

would react. She had to leave home to understand a lot of issues. And if she hasn't told you, then I'm going to. You have done an excellent job of raising her. In fact, all of your children. They are fine people. You and your husband should be proud."

"We are."

"The biggest compliment a child can give their parents is when they become their own person. When they can be on their own. You have done that. Do you understand?"

"I'm trying."

"Let her go with open arms. Wish her luck, and one day I guarantee we will be back with a surprise."

Tatiana's eyes widened and her voice rose in excitement. "A surprise? Is she expecting?"

"No."

"Oh." The disappointment in Tatiana's voice was palpable, and while the others at the table showed no signs of understanding the conversation, they did understand whatever was being said was profound and personal. "I've always wanted to be a grandmother."

"If I have anything to do with it, you will be," Nico said. "I plan to ask her to marry me. I'm asking you now, may I have your daughter's hand in marriage?"

"Yes. Of course." Tatiana spoke cheerfully. "I will speak for my husband that we wish you a long and happy life together. And pray you will be fruitful."

Nico stifled a laugh at her last comment, and while he wanted to say something clever about being fruitful, he decided a simple acknowledgement would suffice. This was his future mother-in-law after all. "Thank you. There's one thing though."

"What's that?"

"Please keep it a secret."

"I will. I promise," Tatiana said. "You have my word." She scooted her chair back and stood. Changing to speaking in English, she asked, "Who would like more pie?"

"I do," Uncle Billy said. He picked up his plate, licked it, and said, "You can put it right here."

After Tatiana excused herself to the kitchen, Uncle Billy poked Nico in the side and asked, "So what did you say to her? I've never seen her in such a good mood."

"Yeah, Nico," Kate said, raising an eyebrow. "Tell us." She

leaned forward expectantly.

His gaze steady on Kate's, Nico said, "I can't. It was said in confidence, so don't bother asking me or your mom." His tone was serious and indicated a rather firm warning not to bother asking anymore questions.

Kate had only once experienced that particular demeanor of Nico's. Understanding what he meant, she crossed her arms over her chest and sat back in the chair, her eyes blazing.

"Well," Uncle Billy said, taking two forks in his hand and thumping them on the table to get everyone's attention, "if there's one thing I know, it's that Russians can keep a secret. Who cares when there's more pie. Let's eat!"

CHAPTER 13

The night passed slowly, and Kate had been restless. Around midnight or later, she wasn't quite sure what time it was since clocks had stopped working, she wandered downstairs to the kitchen. Reload padded alongside her.

Kate was surprised to see her mother sitting at the kitchen table, lit by candlelight, reading a book. "Mom? What are you doing here? You can't sleep either?"

Tatiana dog-eared the page, closed it, and set the paperback on the table. She removed her reading glasses and rubbed her eyes. "I'm too wound up to sleep."

"What are you reading?"

"Nothing. Just something to pass the time."

Kate noticed the book had been set front cover down so she couldn't see exactly what kind of book it was. "Can I get you a glass of wine? I read somewhere that wine affects the same part of the brain that anxiety drugs do to make you relax."

Tatiana laughed. "I would need an entire case of wine for that."

"I know where Uncle Billy keeps his hidden stash," Kate said.

"There's a bottle with your name on it right over there in the—"

Tatiana waved her off. "I'd have one heck of a headache in the morning if I drank an entire bottle. Besides, we're getting low on Advil, so I'll pass. Thank you, though."

Kate sat down at the table opposite her mother. Reload squeezed under the table and sat down at Kate's bare feet. He sensed the tension between the two women, and while Reload didn't understand their relationship, he did understand they acted familiar around each other in the way they talked and their body language. While the verbalizations meant nothing to him, he recognized the tone of the words being spoken. Kate needed him.

Reload nudged her feet with his warm nose until Kate wiggled her toes enough to massage his ears.

After an uncomfortable few seconds of utter silence, Kate asked, "Are you still angry at me?"

Tatiana shook her head. "Not anymore. I was for a long time, but the longer you were gone, the more I realized the only thing I cared about was your safety."

"I'm sorry for not calling you when I was in San Antonio."

"It doesn't matter. Your father was able to track you down at the Minor Hotel, and we had decided to go get you and bring you back when—"

"How'd you know where I was?"

"A credit card company contacted us to confirm how long you had lived here. You used this as your previous address on the application form."

Kate shrugged. "I needed a new credit card after you and dad cut off the one you had given me."

"We thought if you didn't have any money, you'd come back."

"Mom, you should know me better than that."

"I know. You're quite self-sufficient. We were at our wit's end and didn't know what else to do. We were about to travel to San Antonio to get you when the EMP struck."

"I'm glad you were delayed."

"Why?"

"Because of Nico. Otherwise, I would have never have gotten to know him."

"Tell me about him."

"There's not much to know other than he's a decent guy, and he helped me get over what I had been through."

"What was that?" Tatiana's motherly concern had taken over, and all the previous disagreements she had with Kate didn't mean anything anymore. She studied her daughter, who had changed from the angry buck-the-system girl to a woman who understood life, including its disappointments and exhilarating moments. "I know something bad must have happened. Please tell me."

Kate explained how when she first got to San Antonio, she visited the Alamo, which was where she met Ben. She gave a brief rundown on their life and how he had been killed in an armed robbery at a bank. As she spoke, her chest tightened at the images of Ben dying, and from her inability to help.

Tatiana reached over and put a hand on Kate. She gently squeezed her arm. "It's okay. I'm your mother. There's nothing you can't tell me."

Taking a deep breath, Kate explained she had a hard time coping after Ben died, which led to her being diagnosed with severe anxiety and borderline post traumatic stress syndrome. She recounted how she found Reload starving in the alley behind the Minor Hotel, and after gaining his trust, she rescued him, then had him qualify as a service dog.

Reload was alert, ears cocked, listening to Kate's tight words and he sensed her angst. Rising, he gently rested his muzzle on her thigh. Her hand naturally gravitated to him and she petted him in long strokes starting at his head, down along the ruff of his back, taking in handfuls of fur. She massaged Reload's ears, then stroked him between his eyes and up to the flat part of his head. When she stopped talking about Ben, she unconsciously withdrew her hand, and when she began talking about Nico, Reload sensed her anxiety dissipating. He lowered himself to the floor and placed his snout on her foot.

"Nico and I spent the winter alone at the hotel."

"Just the two of you?"

"Yes."

"Didn't you get bored?" Tatiana asked. She couldn't imagine staying the entire winter in one place with only one other person.

"Not at all. Nico and I have a lot in common and never ran out of things to talk about. He's an interesting guy and has lots of stories to tell, especially about border patrol work. We also work well together as a team." Kate took a breath. "We left because we were running low on supplies...and because it was time for me to come home."

"You know you can stay here for as long as you need to," Tatiana offered quietly. She put her elbows on the table and rested her hands in supplication.

"Thanks, Mom, but I can't. Nico and I are leaving tomorrow."

"Do you mind if I ask why?"

"He inherited property in East Texas. He thinks the house is still okay, and he stocked it with non-perishable food the last time he was there. He said grocery shopping is no fun when you're trying to get to your destination."

Tatiana didn't acknowledge Kate's last statement about grocery shopping. In a worried voice, she said, "His house might have been ransacked by now. Or maybe someone is squatting in it."

Kate let out a sigh. "If someone is there, he'll throw them out. He learned a lot working in border patrol."

"I have no doubt he is a capable man. Do you know where in East Texas his property is located?"

"Not really. You'd have to ask him about it."

"I wonder if it's close to where your older brother is?"

"Chandler is in East Texas?" Kate's voice intonation rose in surprise. "I haven't seen him in so long."

Tatiana scooted her chair away from the table and opened one of the kitchen drawers. Rifling through it, she found what she needed. Coming back to the kitchen table, she shook open the Texas roadside map and laid it out flat.

"Your brother is there," she said, tapping the eastern part of the map, close to the Louisiana border. "Near the town of Hemphill."

Kate leaned into the map. "Never heard of the place."

"Your brother knows all about it. For a sleepy little Texas town, there sure was a lot going on there. Chandler mentioned the reason he had gone back there after his deployment was over, was for a couple of reasons. One, he had a girlfriend, and two, he was going to work on a drilling rig. There's a lot of oil in East Texas."

"That's what I've heard," Kate said.

Tatiana folded the map in half so the east side of the state was on top. "This is where Dillon and Holly live."

"Who?" Kate asked.

"Dillon and Holly. They're friends of Chandler's, and if I know my son, he's probably at their house helping them out." Tatiana addressed her daughter. "Kate, I've got work to do. Go on back to bed. I'm going to trace this, and in the morning I'll give it to Nico. If it's not out of the way from where you'll be going tomorrow, you can stop by. I'll make a goodie bag for everyone, then you can give it to Chandler and the others. They'll be so glad to see you. I wish I could be there."

Kate yawned. "Okay, thanks, Mom. See you in the morning."

"One more thing. Can you put this book in the bookshelf?" Tatiana asked, handing the paperback to Kate.

"Sure." Kate took the book, flipped it over, curious what it was and wondering what her mother was reading in the middle of the night. Kate laughed when she read the title. *The Willful Child.*

No doubt about it, Kate had been the willful child.

* * *

Early morning snuck up with low beams of the day's first sunlight filtering into Kate's room through the open window, casting the night aside. A breeze fluttered the sheer curtains, and a rooster crowed at a nearby house.

Kate rolled over on her back, yawned, stretched, and became aware of the weight on the mattress next to her. She blinked open her eyes to find Reload had wiggled in between her and Nico, who was snoring softly. She briefly considered waking Nico, then decided he needed as much sleep as he could get, so she threw the light cover off her. Reload lifted his head, his eyes fixed on Kate.

"Shhh," she said, putting a finger to her lips. "Stay."

Nico woke and groggily asked, "What are you doing? Come back to bed. We can catch a few more winks."

"I'm going to take a shower. Go back to sleep."

Nico scratched the stubble on his chin. "Okay. Don't use all the water. I think I'll shower after you're done."

Kate sat on the bed, and ran a finger over Nico's chest. She teasingly said, "I thought you were going to say you'd join me."

Nico propped himself up with an elbow. "Umm, have you seen the shower?"

"On second thought, you're right. There isn't much privacy."

"Be safe, and take a gun with you."

"In the shower? It'll get wet and then it'll rust."

Nico yawned and put his head back on the pillow. "Okay. Be careful."

Kate slipped on a pair of shorts and didn't bother to change the T-shirt she had been sleeping in. Checking herself in the mirror, she ran her fingers through her hair then headed downstairs, deciding she needed a trip to the outhouse. Uncle Billy, John, and Luke had made an outhouse by digging a 4x5 hole, topped with a foundation which supported the wood structure. Openings for two windows had been cut on the insistence of Tatiana. She found several stained glass windows in the old shed which would allow some light in the outhouse while providing privacy. It was located on the other side of the fence line, away from the orchard. It was quite rustic, and partially made using reclaimed wood collected from a recent flood on the Colorado River. A bowl of wood ashes was available to sprinkle in the hole after each use to encourage faster decomposition.

The outdoor shower had been constructed using flotsam and surplus boards from a neighbor's fence built before the grid went down. Before the neighbors had abandoned the house, they told Tatiana she could use whatever she needed. Uncle Billy had built the shower similar to how a fence was built with posts and runners to nail the boards into place. About eighteen inches of open space was left at the bottom so feet and knees could be seen, but everything else was covered up once the shower was occupied. A big cistern placed on a platform on top of the shower structure collected rainwater, and a pulley system had been rigged so when water was needed, all that had to be done was to pull on the cord.

A spasmodic shiver ran down Kate's back, and she briefly considered waiting to shower until she and Nico had settled in at his place in East Texas. Then again, she wasn't sure of the water situation at Nico's. She decided the best course of action was to bathe quickly.

She hastily grabbed a towel, a bar of soap, and shampoo from the upstairs bathroom, then quietly tiptoed downstairs.

CHAPTER 14

Stepping into the outdoor shower, Kate pulled the door shut and placed her towel over the top. There were two shelves for soap and shampoo, and other items such as a washcloth or a razor. A mirror was attached to one of the boards. The slatted wood floor had been constructed so water would flow through the cracks and onto the ground.

It was quiet and the neighborhood had not yet woken in the early morning hour, and as Kate removed her clothing, she had time to reflect on the previous day's events and how she and her mother had come to an understanding. A great load had been lifted off her shoulders when Tatiana had given her blessing to Kate and Nico on their decision to go to East Texas. Kate now saw her parents as people with their own dreams and faults, and she recognized the hard work her parents had done in providing a home and a safe haven for Kate and her brothers to grow up in.

She had a lot to be thankful for. She bowed her head and took the quiet opportunity to say a prayer of thanks. Afterward, she lifted her head and mouthed *Amen*.

She pulled the cord and a rush of cold water showered over her. Goose pimples prickled her skin and she shivered. She squirted shampoo in her wet hair, massaged it in, then soaped the rest of her body. She gritted her teeth and steeled herself for the shower of cold water she'd have to endure. This cold water was much worse than jumping into a swimming pool at the start of the summer season, and Kate was so focused on enduring the frigid shower she didn't notice the door had opened.

Gathering the courage to douse herself with more water for a good rinse, she pulled the cord, and a miniature tsunami of water splashed over her. Her muscles tensed and she shivered again.

Kate had her eyes shut tight as she ran her fingers through her hair untangling it. Two freezing cold minutes later, and two more drenchings of rainwater, she was satisfied all the soap was out of her hair. She ran her hands over her face, smoothed her hair, and blinked the remaining water out of her eyes. She reached for her towel only to find it missing, and when she turned around to find the door wide open a squeak of surprise escaped her lips.

In an instant, her face morphed from shock to horror to the scolding look of a mother who had caught her child's hand in the cookie jar.

Oliver, a ten-year old boy, who lived two houses down the street, was standing outside the shower, holding the door open with one hand and Kate's towel in the other. His eyes were big, and he grinned wide and mischievous, knowing his hands *were* in the cookie jar.

"You little twerp," Kate blurted. She covered herself with her hands the best she could then slammed the door shut. Peeking through the slats, she snapped, "Give me my towel."

"Come and get it," Oliver said. He wiggled the towel for emphasis so Kate could see it.

Kate opened the door a slit and thrust an arm out as far as she could, but Oliver stepped away just far enough to be out of reach. "I swear I'm gonna tan your hide if you don't give me my towel! If you don't I'll tell your mother."

Oliver snickered. "If you want your towel, you have to come and get it."

"Where are my clothes?"

"I put them on the picnic table. I didn't want them to get dirty."

Oliver tried to sound as innocent as possible. He moved over to the table and gathered her clothes. "Here they are."

Kate was so angry she had forgotten how cold she was, and she mulled over her choices. Scream and scare the entire household that something was terribly wrong? Stay in the shower until someone came to give her some clothes? Or take her chances and run after the little twerp? If she decided on option one, someone might come out of the house guns blazing and that certainly wouldn't end well. Option two wasn't exactly a good idea because she'd freeze waiting. There was option three, but if she took off running after Oliver, the entire neighborhood might see her so that was definitely out of the question. Perhaps she should just streak into the house, giving Oliver an eyeful while she ran. On the other hand, if she surprised Oliver she might be able to—

Oliver squealed like a piglet caught for the roasting pan.

Kate peeked through the slats and cracked a big, satisfied smile. Nico somehow had managed to sneak up on Oliver. He held the kid by the waist, and propped him on his hip. Oliver kicked and squealed. "Let me go! I'm going to tell my mother."

"I don't think so," Nico said with a hint of delight in his voice.

"I will!" Oliver pounded his fists on Nico's thighs.

Nico released his hold on Oliver, set him down, and before Oliver could run away, Nico gripped him tight by the arm.

"You're hurting me."

"Stop whining like a little girl. Tell Kate you're sorry."

Oliver shook his head.

"Okay. Your choice." Nico jerked Oliver away from the shower and took a few steps toward his home.

"I'm sorry," Oliver finally said.

Nico whisked Oliver to where he stood in front of the shower. "I'm going to let go of you. If you try to run away, I'll tell your mother what you've been doing."

"Please don't tell my mother."

"If you do as I say, I won't. Put the towel and Kate's clothes back where you found them.

Sullenly, Oliver did as he was told. Once Kate had dressed, she exited the shower, and put her hands on her hips.

"Tell Kate you're sorry *again*," Nico said.

Oliver eyes bounced from Kate then to the ground. "I'm sorry," he mumbled.

Kate said nothing, only stared daggers at the kid.

"Don't do that again," Nico said.

"Okay, I won't." Oliver rubbed the toe of his sneakers into the dirt.

"Let's go over there." Nico jerked his head to a picnic table. "I want to talk to you."

Out of earshot of Kate, Nico kneeled to where he was about eye level with Oliver. He cupped his hand and whispered into Oliver's ear. Whatever was being said was something that kept Oliver's attention.

"Go on home." Nico gave Oliver a slap on the butt, sending him scurrying.

"What did you say to him?" Kate asked, walking over to Nico.

"I gave him some advice."

"What was it?"

"I told him to stop being a little pervert, then I told him to do what all little boys do."

"What's that?"

"Look at magazines that belong to their friends' fathers. He said he already asked his friends and they couldn't find any, so I told him where he could."

"Where's that?"

Nico bobbed his head in the direction of the tool shed.

"The tool shed?" Kate repeated incredulously. "That's where Uncle Billy keeps all his junk."

"Right, Kate. Including an entire stack of *Playboy* magazines."

Kate put a hand to her mouth and stifled a laugh. "Recent ones?"

"No. From the 70s or 80s. All in good condition. Your uncle takes care of his prized possessions."

"How would you know?"

"How do you think?"

Kate scoffed.

"I told Oliver he needed to offer to help out your mom or dad, like doing yard work or other odd jobs where he might need tools from the tool shed. Because that way, he could look at the magazines without being discovered. I told him it was our secret and I gave him strict instructions not to steal any magazines otherwise I'd arrest him and throw him in jail."

"He believed you?" Kate asked.

"Yeah, especially after I showed him my Border Patrol badge. He was quite impressed."

"I still can't believe that about Uncle Billy."

"From what Luke told me, your uncle was quite the ladies' man back in the day, and the more I get to know Uncle Billy, the more I like him. Luke told me about the shootout at the tower, and how Uncle Billy came through for everyone. He's a real stand up kind of guy, the kind who has your back in a dark alley. Don't underestimate someone due to their appearance, Kate. While your uncle seems harmless and soft on the outside, he's a warrior on the inside. He'd give his life to protect you. Just like I would."

Kate wrapped her arms around Nico. "I know you would." She paused a moment. "There's one thing I don't quite understand."

"What?"

"What made you get out of bed?"

"Reload needed to go outside to do his business."

Kate acknowledged the explanation. "Where is Reload?"

"I'm not sure. The moment I opened the door he hightailed it over to the neighbor's yard. More than likely to leave a present."

Kate chuckled. "Fortunately there are a lot of leaves on the ground, so you won't be able to tell what's a leaf and what isn't."

Nico huffed in exasperation. "Dogs." He shook his head. "Let's go back inside and get our things together. The chopper is already fueled up, so all we need to do is to say goodbye and get going. In a few hours, and with any luck, we'll be in East Texas and talking with your brother Chandler."

* * *

The time had come for Kate and Nico to say goodbye. Nico was already sitting in the pilot seat of the helicopter, while Reload was in the back. Nico had the map Tatiana had traced for him, set out so he could follow the roads to where Holly and Dillon were, which was where Chandler and Amanda would probably be. Tatiana wasn't quite sure of the directions to Amanda's ranch, but estimated it wouldn't be far from where Nico and Kate were traveling.

Tatiana had packed them enough food to last for several days, including dog food for Reload, which Uncle Billy had traded for with a neighbor whose dog had recently died.

"This should get you through," Tatiana said, handing a paper bag to Kate. The backwash of the helicopter blew Tatiana's hair around her face. She wrapped her hands around her hair, putting it in a ponytail. "I packed some dried fruit and pecans, a few cans of tuna, half a loaf of homemade bread that's a little hard as of now, but if you're hungry it won't matter. There are two jars of wild mustang grape jelly I made myself, which are a little tart. I found a chocolate bar I had been saving, and—"

"Thanks, Mom," Kate cut in. "Nico and I can't thank you enough for all you've done." She tilted her head indicating it was time to say goodbye. "I have to go."

"I know you do," Tatiana said.

Kate hugged her mom, then said goodbye to her dad. She told Luke she and Nico would be back, and when they did come back, he and Nico could go hunting or fishing together. Finally, she addressed Uncle Billy.

"I'm going to miss you too, Uncle Billy."

"You're my favorite niece."

Kate laughed. "That's a no brainer because I'm your only niece."

"Even if you weren't, you'd still be my favorite. Take care, Kate." Uncle Billy gently brushed hair out of her face. "No goodbyes, okay? What did we used to say when we didn't want to say goodbye?"

"Later gator."

"Roger dodger."

Kate waved to her family, ducked her head, and sprinted to the helicopter. She climbed in and shut the door without looking at Nico.

"You okay?" Nico asked. He sensed she wasn't, but asked anyway to give Kate an opportunity to say what she needed to say.

"Good enough," Kate replied. Her face was red and eyes teary. She blinked several times. "Let's get going."

"Everything will be okay. Don't worry." Nico patted her on her leg. "We'll be there before you know it."

Kate swallowed a lump in her throat and nodded. Her eyes flicked once to Nico and she patted his hand. As the helicopter gained altitude Kate took one last look at her family and waved, knowing change was difficult, but necessary.

CHAPTER 15

East Texas
Holly Hudson's Ranch

"Think those are deep enough?" Holly asked. She stepped back from the empty graves she had been digging, and leaned the shovel against a tree. The bodies of the elderly married couple killed when the Russians attacked had been lying on the ground nearby, along with Sarah Monroe still in her blood-splattered dress. Earlier, Holly had covered their faces with burlap sacks she had found stored in the barn. Flies had buzzed the bodies, and she noticed several crawl under the burlap.

Holly peeled off her canvas work gloves one finger at a time, and set them on the ground. Sweat poured off her brow and she wiped it away with the back of her hand. She had on an old T-shirt, ragged jeans, and a wide belt holding a holstered Glock and two magazines. She vowed she'd never be caught unarmed again.

Anna offered Holly bottled water. She thanked Anna then guzzled the entire bottle.

Cassie was armed and stood to the side, holding an approximately nine pound AK in a sling across her chest so as not to fatigue her arms. She had been forbidden by Ryan to do any hard manual labor or to stress her muscles considering she was with child. He explained if her body temperature rose too much, it could harm the baby.

Dorothy, who was not proficient in handling firearms, stood next to Cassie helping her with guard duty. She had a pair of binoculars around her neck, and would intermittently scan the sky for any sign of another helicopter.

Amanda was standing in the shade trying to stay cool. She was just as hot and sweaty as Holly, seeing they had been digging for hours. "It's deep enough so the animals can't get to them. I'll help you move the bodies." She scrunched her nose. "They are already starting to smell."

Holly donned her gloves. "Amanda, be sure to put your gloves back on. We don't need to be handling dead bodies with our bare hands." Holly rubbed her temples, trying to ward off a headache. If Dillon was here, he could work his magic by massaging away the nagging headache. Her thoughts briefly took her to Dillon, and she wondered how he was doing. Knowing him, he and the others were already formulating an escape plan. "Anna, where are the masks I gave you to hold?"

"Right here," Anna said. She dug around in her pink backpack decorated with a picture of a cartoon kitty. She pushed around several bags of high protein nuts, two packs of gummies she was saving for an emergency, a change of clothes, and her favorite doll. Retrieving the masks, she handed them to Holly and Amanda.

Continuing the gruesome task, Holly and Amanda worked together to place the bodies in the side-by-side graves. During the move, the burlap sack fell off the elderly woman's face. The mottled skin and dead eyes were swarming with flies, and Amanda gagged at the grisly sight. She recoiled in disgust and breathed through her mouth. The stench of the bodies was something she'd never forget.

"Are you okay?" Holly asked.

It took a moment for Amanda to compose herself. "I'll be alright. It's bringing back memories of my grandpa."

"If you can't do this, I can handle it myself," Holly offered.

"Just give me a moment."

Anna made a move to put the sack back on, but Holly said, "Stay back, Anna. You don't need to see this."

98

"I'm braver than you think I am," Anna said defiantly.

"I'm sure you're indeed brave, but you're only ten and you don't need to see things like this."

"I've seen a dead body before, haven't I, Mom?"

"She's right," Dorothy added. "She's been to a funeral."

"This is different," Holly said. "Much different."

"I'm not afraid either." The little girl picked up the burlap sack and tossed it on the woman's face.

Once the bodies had been placed in the graves, Holly and Amanda worked to shovel dirt over them. Anna and Dorothy pitched in by scooping handfuls of dirt into the graves. Cassie had been told to stay back.

Holly shoveled the last of the dirt on top and patted it down with the shovel. Digging the graves had been hard work, and had taken longer than expected. It was hot standing in the shade, and the humidity was only making things worse. Amanda looked like she was about to pass out, but not once did she complain.

It was quiet and still in the early afternoon hour, and the sun beat down hot on the land. The woodland animals had taken shelter in the shade of the trees or in their burrows, away from the heat. The sprinkling of rain the night before added to the rising humidity. A lone cloud drifted in the sky, casting a shadow when it moved in front of the sun.

"Let's all bow our heads and say a prayer for these good people who were taken away from us too early," Holly said. "To let everyone know, I've noted their names and time and date of their deaths in our family bible. At some point, we'll need to contact their next of kin."

"Why in the bible?" Anna asked.

"That's how people used to record births, marriages, and deaths," Holly explained. "Before the time of the internet or any certified register, it was a way to record important dates. People don't use them as much as they used to, but I still have my family's bible dating back to the 1800s."

"Can you show me?" Anna's eyes were wide with wonderment. "I'd like to see it."

"Of course I'll show you. First let's pray."

The four women and one child stood in solemn silence, each keeping their thoughts private as they listened to the sounds of the country. The wind whistled through the trees and a cicada chirped. A symphony of buzzing cicadas filled the air, reaching an unusually loud crescendo before falling quiet in unison as if a conductor had lowered a baton signifying the end of the musical piece.

Holly said, "Amen," took a big breath, then sighed heavily, as if she was expelling all the stress of the morning out of her body. She straightened her back and rolled her shoulders to work out a tight muscle that had been bothering her while digging. When the cicadas became quiet, she said, "I think that was a nice send off. The cicadas sang better than any choir I've ever heard."

Dorothy said, "I'll take the shovels to the barn. Holly, you and Amanda have done enough work."

"Thank you. Let's go in and rest. I think we all need it."

"I'm not tired," Anna said. "I can stay up and be the lookout. I'll yell if I see anything."

"Okay, sweetie," Holly said. "As long as it's okay with your mother."

"You have to stay on the porch, okay?" Dorothy said.

Anna grumpily nodded.

As the group left, Cassie stopped in mid-stride. "Wait."

"Why?" Holly asked.

"Shhh. Don't you hear that?" Cassie cocked her head, trying to discern which direction the sound was coming from.

The rhythmic thumping came closer, louder, until it was obvious what was making the sound.

"Another helicopter!" Holly shouted. "Take cover behind the trees!"

The women scattered into the dark woodland canopy, thick with vines and underbrush. Cassie dropped to the ground carpeted in a thick layer of pine needles. She stretched out and propped her AK on a fallen log to steady it for accurate shots.

Holly crouched behind another tree and pulled her Glock out of the holster. She pulled the slide back a bit and checked to make sure a round was chambered. It was, so she let the slide ride back into place.

Amanda had her own Glock and held it in both hands, peeking from around the massive girth of a bullet-stopping oak.

Dorothy and Anna took cover behind the trunk of a large pine tree located deeper in the woods. Dorothy wrapped her arms around

Anna's head to protect her. They remained motionless, melting into the shadows of the woods.

Holly, Amanda, and Cassie were equally camouflaged in their working clothes, stained with honest ranch work and the subtle colors of the outdoors of dried leaves and grass woven into the fabric.

"Don't anyone make a move or make a noise. And don't shoot unless we are shot at first. Whoever it is doesn't know we are here. Let's try to keep it that way."

* * *

"Are you sure this is the right place?" Kate asked.

Concentrating on maneuvering the helicopter for a smooth landing near Holly's ranch house, Nico didn't answer.

While the helicopter hovered over the landing spot, Kate scanned the ground, searching for any sign the ranch was occupied. Perhaps clothes hanging on the line, children's toys, a freshly tilled garden. A strange sensation came over her and she shuddered. "Nico, I don't like the feel of this place. Something is wrong. I don't see anybody. Let's leave. It might be the wrong ranch."

Nico set the chopper on the ground and powered it down. He waited for the blades to come to a stop then shook open the map to double check the location.

"This is definitely the right place." Nico surveyed the land and adjacent buildings, noting the chairs and makeshift tables. "Kate, there's nothing to worry about. I bet Holly and Dillon are out somewhere or preparing for whatever party was planned. Besides, the house, the barn, and the pump house are exactly where Chandler told your mom they would be. Your brother was quite thorough in the directions and landmarks. Kate, I think your nerves are getting the best of you. It's been a rough several days."

Kate accepted Nico's observations. "You're right. I'm still jumpy from all that has happened."

She opened the door, stepped out, and helped Reload exit the helicopter.

The big dog stayed close to Kate and eyed the unfamiliar surroundings. He lifted his snout in the air, tasting the land and the nearby animals. A horse was pastured nearby, while another one had recently walked the same spot where Reload stood. Other scents of a strange culture were noticeable from dried sweat lingering on the ground. Reload put his nose to the ground, trying to understand the people and what they meant.

Reload's acute senses indicated some type of conflict had taken place recently.

Grass mashed down from heavy boots told the tale of many men who stood in this same place. Gunpowder residue lingering on the grass indicated weapons had been fired. Men carrying weapons had been clothed in uniforms stiffened from a cleaning solvent. A man with a commanding presence had walked among the crowd of men who had stood rigidly when the man came through.

Charred grass and timbers lined the porch, rimmed with some type of accelerant indicating a fire had been set, and the amount of footprints and dampness of the ground told the rest of the tale.

Reload huffed the ground, taking in the jumble of humanity and testosterone laced scents, and men who captured and took what they wanted.

Reload's attention was interrupted by a strange scent wafting on an air current, and his mind whirled trying to identify the odd odor. It was similar to the odor of the humans who had been killed at the Alamo shootout, and Reload tried to make sense of what it meant. The odor was not repulsive, only one he had filed away in his mind for future use. An earthy, pungent odor of freshly dug dirt mingled with and covered the lifeless human scent.

He sniffed the air again.

Nearby, several females hid among the trees, and Reload's eyes gravitated to the direction where they were. He did not recognize any of the human scents, yet he understood the meanings of flight or fight the humans were experiencing. The ruff on Reload's back bristled and he growled low in his throat.

"What's wrong, boy?" Kate asked. Her eyes tracked in the direction Reload had zeroed in on, a dark thicket of brush and large trees where the light was low and shadows long. She searched the woods for movement where none should be, and a sensation she was being watched gripped her again.

Nico folded the map and stuffed it in the pilot seat. Stepping out of the chopper he yelled, "Hello! Anybody here?"

There was no answer.

"We need to go," Kate said. "Now." She whistled for Reload, who loped over to her in several long strides. Kneeling next to Reload, she held him by the collar. The big dog hadn't taken his eyes off the woods. "Something's wrong, Nico. Reload is acting odd. I think people are hiding behind the trees over there."

"Stay here. I'll investigate." Nico unholstered his Glock and took a few strides toward the trees then stopped. "Is anybody there?" When there was no answer, he motioned for Kate to stay behind.

As he took another step toward the trees, a voice called out. "That's far enough. Drop your weapon."

Nico froze then slowly backed up a few steps to put distance between him and the threat. While he knew the person who had ordered him to drop his weapon was a woman, he needed to be careful. He had seen plenty of proficient female shooters.

Firearms were the big equalizer.

Taking a chance, he yelled, "Holly, is that you?"

No answer.

"I'm Nico Bell and I have Kate Chandler with me. We are looking for Holly Hudson's ranch and we were told Kate's brother Chandler might be here. Or perhaps you know where he is. Is he here?"

The female answered. "I'm coming out. I've got an AK aimed square at your chest, so if you're lying, you'll be a goner." Earlier, Cassie had handed the AK to Holly.

With growing curiosity, Nico watched a form emerge from the woods. She was carrying an AK, and as promised, it was aimed directly at him. He noted her finger was resting on the trigger. While she'd have to make a concerted decision to shoot the weapon, it made him quite nervous knowing it wasn't all that difficult to pull a five pound trigger.

"I am Holly Hudson."

"I'm Nico Bell. I'm former Border Patrol, and I'd appreciate it if you would lower your weapon."

Holly eyed the big man for a moment, and several long seconds later, she lowered the AK. She approached Nico and extended a hand to shake. "Who did you say was with you?"

"Kate," Nico called. "Come on out."

Tentatively, Kate peeked around the helicopter and eyed Holly. She stepped over to Nico and stood next to him. "I'm Kate Chandler, and I'm trying to find my brother."

"Chris Chandler is your brother?"

"Yes."

Holly's shoulders shrunk.

"Is something wrong?" Kate asked.

"I don't know how to tell you this."

"Tell me what?" Kate cast a perplexed and worried look at Holly. "Is he…" Kate trailed off, unable to say the obvious. "Is he okay?"

"I don't know." Holly said. "I hope so. He was captured yesterday."

"Captured?" Kate glanced at Nico, who was as bewildered as she was. "By whom?"

"Russians. We were attacked yesterday."

Kate's eyes flicked to Nico then back to Holly.

"Why?"

"I don't know. It's been a long morning. Let's all go in and I'll explain what I do know." Holly put the tips of her index finger and thumb to the corners of her mouth, and blew a sharp whistle in the direction from where she had emerged. "Come on out!" she yelled.

Slowly, emerging shadows in the woods took shape in the form of three women and one child, and Kate briefly wondered why the survivors had been reduced to hiding in the woods. Whatever had happened to cause them to act the way they did, had to have been profoundly disturbing, and she fought her response to run away. Then she saw the graves and the charred porch wood. Whatever happened had to have been bad.

"Amanda," Holly said, "this is Chandler's sister, Kate."

"I've heard a lot of good things about you, Amanda," Kate said. "My mom and dad were so happy Chandler found you. Don't worry about him. He can take care of himself."

"I hope so," Amanda said. "Is that your dog?"

Kate nodded. "His name is Reload."

"He looks protective." She eyed Reload warily, wondering if he was friendly or not.

"He is."

"I have a dog. His name is Nipper. He's at my grandpa's…I mean my house. He has plenty of food and water, and a doggie door, so he's alright."

Dorothy hung back from the conversation. Her eyes bounced around, and she rarely made eye contact with anyone except for the girl, which Kate figured was her daughter. The tenseness of the situation must have affected her, making her a loose cannon in all this. Considering Kate had fought alongside men at the Alamo siege, she wasn't prepared for Dorothy's modest demeanor.

Call it women's intuition or female radar, but whatever it was Kate sensed all was not right with this group of women. She sized up people quickly, a trait she learned and nurtured while bartending.

First impressions were rarely wrong.

Reload approached Kate, leaned into her, and nudged her hand with his muzzle until she responded. The big dog sensed she was experiencing rapid heartbeats, shallow breathing, and damp palms.

Reload observed body posture and voice intonation, allowing him to gather all the information he needed about the humans interacting. The unknown woman was experiencing distress along with the others who were cautiously staying close to the woodland edge. Nico's stance and unwavering eye contact with the woman indicated he was on high alert and preoccupied with her, and unable to help Kate. Reload acted according to how he had been taught. He stayed close to Kate and nudged her until she stroked him on the flat part of his head.

Kate's hand absentmindedly fell to Reload. She scratched his head, then his neck where she took in a handful of fur and loose skin, massaging her dog, letting her fingers thread through his rough fur. The simple contact with her dog, one who accepted her on all terms, gave her the strength she needed at the moment. She resisted the urge to run away and hide; to go where she was safe. She was a survivor, and she'd be damned if she would shrink away again from anybody or any situation.

To hide and live to fight another day was one thing, but to hide for the sake of hiding like a coward, well, Kate wouldn't do that.

If needed, she'd fight alongside these brave women. Descending from a WWII woman sniper made Kate stand taller. It was in her blood. Her genes.

If the Russians were behind this attack on her homeland, she would fight to help reclaim it. Several generations removed from her ancestral homeland was enough for Kate to be fiercely loyal to America. It was the land that shaped her and her brothers, and it was the land of the free and the home of the brave. If they were called upon to protect their land, where good people had lived and died for the right of their descendants to live free, then Kate vowed to do the same. She was an American through and through.

For the time being, however, she decided to keep that bit of intel about her family history to herself, and the fact Nico had deep ties to Russia. She needed to be sure everyone was on the same page.

Spies could be anywhere.

CHAPTER 16

Dillon, Chandler, Ryan, and the other men attending the wedding had been trucked to the local high school, which had been commandeered by the Russians and transformed into a prisoner camp.

Dillon and several others, including Larry Monroe, were ordered out of the truck. Ryan and Chandler were told to remain seated, while armed guards had weapons trained on them. A guard barked orders in Russian, and when the meaning was not understood, he aimed an AK at Dillon, Larry, and three other men, and motioned for them to walk single file into the compound.

From the moment Dillon had been captured, escape was foremost on his mind. Walking into the compound, he reminded himself to memorize the number of steps from the gate to the closest building. Twenty steps.

There were several noisy generators thrumming, which accounted for the lights at the compound. He gauged the height of the guard tower, and the estimated trajectory of a shot, in the dire circumstance he'd be on the receiving end of one of their shots should he decide to make a run for it.

Dillon's low center of gravity and powerful legs were built for short bursts of speed. If long distance running was required, he'd be out of luck.

The guards carried the Russian AK 74 rifles with a folding stock and a sling looped over their necks, allowing them to effortlessly fire the weapon by sweeping down on the safety. If a long shot was needed, pressing the button on the rear of the receiver then swinging the stock to the locked position, were the only two motions needed. The sleek automatic was an impressive firearm by any standard, and the guards handled them like they knew what they were doing.

The perimeter was cordoned off with a ten foot tall electrified chain link fence topped with four strings of razor wire.

Though the prisoners were forbidden to talk, Dillon's mind whirled as he took in the compound layout and number of guards. He was especially interested in how they interacted. Were they alert and cautious, or bored and careless? Guard duty was a never-ending fight against boredom, requiring hours of repetitive monotony that would easily dull even the sharpest of minds, leading to carelessness and perhaps an opportunity for escape.

Dillon's mind, on the other hand, was ever active and he constantly searched for subtle meanings found in a laugh or in body posture. Silent communication told a lot about who was the Alpha or the Beta dog, or the ones who would fold at the first sign of trouble.

One guard, if he could be called that, was standing on the sidewalk and leaning casually on the building as he watched the men walk by, zeroing in on Dillon. Contempt spread across his face at the Americans who had been captured so easily. They hadn't even put up a fight.

Dillon pegged him immediately as an Alpha dog.

The man outweighed Dillon by fifty pounds and had several inches on him. He stared at Dillon with cold, black eyes. His arms were massive, and he had the power of a bull elephant, uncaring about who or what had to be trampled if needed. The man was older than the fresh-faced soldiers full of boyish charm, barely old enough to be called men. The guard was not an officer either. What was he? What was his purpose? He would be the one to watch. Dillon pegged him as one who could kill without remorse.

Dillon recognized him as one of the Russians involved in the attack the previous day. He obviously reported to the Colonel, yet Dillon wasn't sure about the man's purpose other than added muscle for the Colonel.

Dillon challenged the man with unwavering resolve until a guard stuck a barrel between his shoulder blades, shuffling him along.

The group was roughly shoved inside one of the classrooms containing twenty bare cots in four rows set side by side. Several men had already claimed their spots. Some were ranchers, others shopkeepers, and all were husbands or fathers, brothers or uncles.

The classroom had a thin strip of windows near the ceiling running along the outside wall, left open to allow air circulation and light to filter into the cramped space. Escape through the windows was out of the question. Perhaps a child could wiggle out, but not a grown man.

Larry Monroe followed behind Dillon the way a clumsy Labrador puppy would follow an owner, tripping over feet, waiting for attention.

Dillon selected a cot near a wall, which afforded some protection and a view of the door. Whenever he was in a restaurant or other public place, he made sure to choose a seat where he could see the front door. If there was a threat, he wanted to be the first to see it.

Larry claimed a nearby cot. Dillon recognized the local game warden, Jeremy Brown, a big man who had been a running back during his college days. His nickname had been "Lawn Mower" which, over the course of his athletic days was shortened to "Mower" for his ability to mow down his opponents. While time and age had softened the man, he was still a warrior, and one who Dillon surmised could be counted on when the going got tough. Unsure if he should acknowledge the former game warden, Dillon decided to let Jeremy take the lead.

Once the guards closed the door and bolted it, Jeremy was the first to greet the new detainees. "Dillon Stockdale? Is that you?" He extended a hand for Dillon to shake.

"Jeremy? God, it's good to see a familiar face." Dillon slapped him on the shoulder.

"What'dya do with the mountain lion you killed?"

"Made it into a rug."

"You're a legend 'round these parts now."

109

"Didn't know that."

"What's happening on the outside?" Jeremy asked. "And what's up with your Sunday clothes?"

Dillon's formerly pressed jeans and white shirt he had saved for the special day were dirty and wrinkled. Sometime during the scuffle his bolo tie had disappeared. "My daughter was about to get married. We were setting up outside when they," Dillon jerked his head to the outside, "got us."

"How many?"

"About ten of us."

"Where are the others?" Jeremy asked.

"Not sure. Larry and I were marched in first, probably to separate us from the others."

"And your daughter? Is she…?"

Dillon wasn't quite sure to answer. He surveyed the room, searching for a hidden camera or mic possibly hidden in an air vent or light fixture. He didn't trust anyone other than Chandler and Ryan, and they had been taken elsewhere. While Jeremy was probably on the up and up, it was better not to take any chances. Larry? What to say, other than the guy was a nervous wreck. Dillon's eyes flicked to Larry, who had taken a seat on a cot near Dillon's. Sweat beaded his brow and his right hand quivered compulsively whenever it was at his side. His eyes darted around the room, yet never made eye contact with anyone. Dillon wondered if the Russians had somehow persuaded him to be a snitch on the Americans. Before the grid went down, he heard the bank was about to foreclose on Larry's hardware store. The man was swimming in debt, so it was a possibility, lending to the likelihood he might have been bought.

Jeremy repeated his question about Dillon's daughter.

"Not sure," Dillon said. "I didn't see her get captured, so I don't know what happened to her."

"Were there many women?"

"A few."

Jeremy ran a hand over his beard, showing a week's worth of growth. He lowered his voice and leaned in closer to Dillon. "Be careful what you tell people."

"Gotcha." Dillon's eyes flicked to Larry. He raised his voice. "I wonder how the Russians knew the exact time a gathering of able-bodied men would take place at the ranch?" Dillon paused. "Huh, Larry?"

"Why are you looking at me? I got captured along with everybody else." Larry was beginning to feel the pressure of the room, and of ten sets of eyes trained on him, watching his every move. He hadn't bargained for this, and he should have cut his losses on the hardware store and started over somewhere else where he wasn't known, where he could reinvent himself. Then the grid went down and his escape plan went the way of the dodo bird.

"Yeah, and you just *happened* to have excused yourself at the exact time the Russians attacked us."

"What's that supposed to mean?" Larry searched the room hoping to find some backup or a pair of sympathetic eyes. No luck on either count. He was on his own and didn't much like it.

"Coincidence? Or something else?"

Dillon's frustration mounted. His cool demeanor under fire was being put to the test by the false imprisonment in the cramped quarters and lack of information on what had happened to Cassie and Holly. Chandler and Ryan could take care of themselves, prisoners or not, but the women? If the Russians got ahold of them, Dillon wouldn't be able to protect them. He balled a fist and pounded his palm of his other hand like a baseball player pounding a mitt.

By now the other men in the room were listening intently to the conversation. Several had risen off their cots, arms folded, glaring at Larry.

"I don't like what you're insinuating," Larry said. His voice shook and he wiped his damp palms on his pants. "I got captured too. Remember?"

"Someone snitched on us, and from my experiences with snitches in the courtroom, you'd fit in well by the way you're acting. If I find out you're collaborating with the Russians, you're a dead man. I can guarantee it," Dillon said. He took a step toward Larry and challenged his space.

Larry leaned away from Dillon and looked for help. Crossed arms and glaring eyes indicated he wouldn't find any.

"Wait a minute," Jeremy said. "Let's all cool off and take a breather before things get out of hand. Remember, we're all in the same boat and we don't need to fight among ourselves. We need to present a united front against the Russians. If they divide us, then they win. Are we all on the same page?"

"I guess so," Dillon muttered. "I'm sorry, Larry." Dillon ran his fingers through his hair and down the back of his head. "I'm worried out of my mind about Cassie and Holly and Amanda. I guess I took my frustrations out on you."

"Don't you think I'm worried about my wife?" Larry asked. "She was upstairs with your girls and Amanda, so let's all hope they are okay." Larry made a conciliatory gesture to Dillon. "No hard feelings, alright?"

"Yeah. No hard feelings."

The men shook hands. Dillon's handshake was firm, while Larry offered a handshake as limp as a wet noodle. Dillon made a mental note of that. No way Larry could shoot straight with that kind of handshake. Holding a gun firmly was a prerequisite to good shooting.

Dillon wiped his hand on his pants.

A loud whistle akin to a locomotive reaching a busy crossing interrupted the tense moment. In a thick Russian accent, a voice came over the loudspeaker. "Attention. Attention. All prisoners are required to be in their rooms. Anyone caught outside the building will be shot on sight. There will be no second chances."

Moments later, the Russian anthem blared over the loudspeaker, and Dillon listened to it in amused detachment. If the Russians had pride in their anthem, well so did the Americans. In defiance, Dillon stood, placed his left hand over his heart, and began singing the Star-Spangled Banner. By the second stanza, others in the room joined in, and they sang loud and at times extremely off tune. Their vocal ability didn't matter. What mattered was their ability to group together and stay true to their homeland.

After the singing died down, someone said, "Hell, yeah! 'Merica!"

Another prisoner yelled, "That's right! 'Merica!"

The compound lights flickered off, plunging the building in darkness. The men fumbled around searching for their cots.

Without any lights, and nothing else to do, Dillon shook out the blanket on his cot and stretched out. He clasped his hands together and put them behind his head. Too wound up to sleep, he kept his eyes open until they grew accustomed to the dark while he listened to the noises of the complex.

Someone snored, followed by a cough, and more snoring.

A guard dog barked.

The air in the closed room became warm and thick with the musty smells of men who had been imprisoned too long without the benefit of bathing.

Dillon tried to gauge the time. It was possibly midnight, a guess he confirmed when he heard footsteps outside, followed by the guards talking. The change of guards happened at midnight, a fact he squirreled away in his memory for future use.

Dillon's eyelids became heavy and he had difficulty keeping his eyes open. His thoughts went to Holly and Cassie and he wondered what had happened to them. The last he remembered, was a soldier entering the house to search it. Tortuous minutes passed while Dillon waited for the soldier to emerge, and when he did, Dillon studied his face for any hint of what had transpired, but found none in his blank expression. If the soldier had discovered the women, they would have been executed as Burkov had ordered. Was Dillon's lie about the women having run an errand in town convincing enough so the soldier would have not thoroughly searched the house? But where could the women and a child hide in the house undetected?

The house was old, and had been remodeled by building around a water well. Could they have hidden in the well? It was feasible, yet unlikely, for if the water table was high enough, they could all drown. Dillon dismissed the idea.

His mind went over possible escape routes by windows or the back door, but the fact the soldier emerged without finding them was a good sign. Somewhere, somehow, they were safe.

"Pssst."

Dillon jerked open his eyes, listening.

"Pssst. You awake?" Jeremy asked in a low whisper.

"Yeah." Dillon answered in an equally low voice.

"Was anybody hurt when you were captured?"

"An elderly couple was executed in front of us."

Jeremy shook his head in disgust. "Burkov?"

"How'd you know?"

"He's a psychotic killer. Thinks he's John Wayne and this is the Old West."

"That explains why he took my horse."

"Hopefully to ride instead of eating him," Jeremy said without much thought or consequence.

"What?" Dillon propped himself up using his elbow. His disgust of thinking Cowboy could be slaughtered was evident. "Eat Cowboy? That's barbaric."

"Uh, sorry, I didn't mean to…"

Dillon didn't hear Jeremy's apology, all he could think about was Cowboy being shot and butchered. "I'll kill that son of a bitch before he does that to Holly's horse." Dillon shook his head. "Disgusting."

"As long as your horse…" Jeremy paused, "Cowboy's his name, right?"

Dillon nodded.

"As long as Cowboy lets Burkov ride him then nothing will happen."

"That might be a problem."

"How so?"

Dillon hung his head. "It would be impossible for Burkov to ride him. He's been trained to respond to certain commands, and I'm guessing a Russian dialect is horse proof."

"Let's hope if he does try to ride Cowboy, the horse will throw him. I'd like to see him break his neck."

"I've been meaning to ask you something," Dillon said.

"Shoot."

"How long have you been here?" Dillon asked.

"A week," Jeremy replied.

"Doing what?"

"Nothing. Absolutely nothing. They haven't told us a thing."

In the dark room, Dillon noticed Jeremy prop himself up to check if anyone was awake.

"One more thing," Jeremy said. "Remember what I told you, and be extra careful who you talk to. I'm pretty sure someone snitched on you."

* * *

Dillon tossed and turned during the night, worrying about Cassie and Holly. During the early morning hour he fell into a restless sleep full of vivid dreams. A particularly intense dream of his deceased wife jostled him out of his sleep. He woke to a throbbing head, his chest covered in a cold sweat, and he waited for the pounding headache to subside. He shivered and pulled the thin gray blanket over him.

Larry was in the cot next to him, mumbling about his wife and how sorry he was for what he had done. Dillon rolled on his side and faced Larry, watching his head thrash back and forth. Larry obviously was struggling with his actions, and Dillon wondered what he needed to apologize to his wife for.

Since his wife was with Cassie and Holly, she would probably be okay. In fact, she was probably back at home waiting for Larry.

The faintest hint of a summer breeze floated in through the open windows near the ceiling. Breathing in the fresh air, Dillon closed his eyes and visualized his former dream. He blocked out extraneous noises of shuffling bodies and the chirping crickets to concentrate.

A brief flash of his wife's essence came to him…her hair, the way the light touched her face, the way she moved. Her laughter. It was like she was trying to communicate to him, and he struggled to recall her words and the meaning of the dream. It wasn't so much what she had said, rather what she had been trying to convey. She had been his anchor in life, and it had taken him a long time to come to terms with her death. Yet life went on, and Dillon had considered himself fortunate to have been given a second chance to rebuild his family, and to possibly marry again. He closed his eyes, trying to remember what his wife had said in the dream.

You must live.

That was it. Amy was giving him the boost he needed to fight the imprisonment and any hardship he had to endure. The love and partnership he now shared with Holly was testament to his life with Amy. She was giving him permission to lead the life he had built with Holly.

You must live.

He had to live, and at that moment he channeled Amy's sage wisdom, and he vowed to make it back to Holly and Cassie, regardless of what he had to do, or who he had to stop. Or kill if he must.

With a newfound determination, and confident he could accomplish his goal, Dillon fell into a deep and satisfying sleep, exhausted by the previous day's events and the resulting turmoil.

CHAPTER 17

Colonel Mikhail Burkov was obviously in a foul mood. He sat alone in the principal's office, dimly lit to conserve as much generator fuel as possible. He cursed the unending problems with logistics and supply chains, and his well-thought out plan was experiencing cracks in its hardened veneer.

Unleashing an EMP on the United States had been his brainchild, which he'd carefully cultivated for several years, researching the effects it would have on the breakdown of society. Nature would take its course by thinning the population, leading the way for Russia to capture the spoils of war: black gold, Texas tea, ripe for the plucking in the biggest damn oil field the world had ever seen.

The plan was to cripple the United States, sneak in, secure the area in East Texas, suck dry the natural resources, and get out.

They'd strike so fast, the Americans wouldn't have time to react.

How hard could that be?

Harder than Burkov had expected.

He had planned for every imaginable contingency, except for the incompetency of his own people and an unforeseen international crisis brewing in the Persian Gulf, offshore the United Arab Emirates, a pathetic wasteland of sand and rock, yet filthy rich in oil and gas.

After Iraq had tried to invade Kuwait and failed, decades later their neighbor Iran decided to give it a try further down the coast. Oil was just as plentiful in the UAE as it was in Kuwait. It was no secret Russia and Iran were in cahoots with each other, and while there had been a copious amount of chatter about an invasion, the details had been kept under lock and key, a monumental accomplishment all by itself.

The coordinated attack went awry from the beginning. Iran had become impatient with Russia, and acted prematurely by invading the UAE before the planned attack on America, resulting in Russia attacking the United States before they were ready.

Ships set to carry oil field equipment and engineers, geologists, geophysicists, roustabouts, mud loggers, roughnecks, and a hundred more men and women of various oil and gas professions were diverted to the Gulf of Oman. Submarines scheduled to ghost the Texas coast in the deep waters of the Gulf of Mexico to provide additional muscle if needed, were redirected to the Middle East.

The powers-that-be gave the green light for the EMP attack on the US without consulting Burkov, further souring his already foul mood. He had been understaffed from the start, and the invasion had not gone well.

Russia should have done better.

Foremost on his mind was lack of discipline, not enough personnel, and promised military backup which never materialized. It was up to Burkov to secure the East Texas oil field all on his own. Latest intel indicated the Russian troops stationed along the Texas border were being met with resistance and guerilla style tactics offered by the fiercely independent Texans.

Damn rednecks.

Burkov kicked a trashcan across the room where it clattered against a wall, scattering papers and trash.

He had already lost too many good men. Burkov was one to meet challenges head on by embracing, even welcoming, the increased brain power and strategizing needed to overcome his adversaries. It kept him from becoming complacent. Since he wouldn't get the necessary troops to accomplish his goal, Burkov decided rounding up able-bodied men to work the oil field was his only choice. It was proving challenging, putting the Russians in unfamiliar territory by demoralizing their prisoners, then convincing them it was in their best interest to work for Russia.

The heat was becoming an issue too. The soldiers were accustomed to freezing temperatures, not the hotter 'n hell temperatures engulfing this godforsaken land, galvanized by a high pressure system sitting fat and happy above East Texas. Unfortunately, the rain shower the previous day only added to the miserable humidity instead of cooling the land.

Burkov had pleaded and made his case for self-cooling uniforms for the soldiers, only to meet incredible resistance from the bureaucrats who had no business being in charge. They sat in a temperature controlled environment with their big screen monitors and spreadsheets, working the numbers until they got the results they wanted.

Manipulating data was one of Burkov's specialties, so he knew when he had been beat. Questioning the decision by his superiors wouldn't bode well for his rise to the top. He had to be careful.

So not only was the world stage and the Russian bureaucracy against him, he now had farmers and ranchers nibbling away at the mighty power of Russia, picking off soldiers at random.

Burkov went to the broom closet and retrieved a rifle confiscated from one of the Texas snipers, now quite dead. He admired the .30-06 Winchester model 70 with a wooden stock, probably handed down from the previous generation. He shouldered it and peered through the 3-9x variable scope which he estimated was accurate to up to 400 yards depending on the proficiency of the shooter. He made a mental note to smuggle it home so he could keep it as a trophy.

It was humid and hot, unlike the cool summers where he was from. He longed for the green grass and clear lakes dotting the forest, and the snowcapped mountains of his homeland, a stark contrast to the mosquito and fire ant infested backwoods of East Texas.

This was God's country? Nothing here remotely reminded him of God or Heaven. Burkov scoffed at the expression he so often read about to describe the wide open spaces of America. If it was so celebrated, then why was he sweating profusely? He slipped a handkerchief from his back pocket and wiped the sweat beading on his forehead, cursing the ungodly heat and humidity. A mosquito buzzed his face and he slapped it away.

What he wanted was a five course candlelight dinner, topped off with a bottle of his favorite wine at his favorite restaurant. He'd have the company of a beautiful woman who would lavish her charms on him. He held a coveted position in the military, which didn't go unnoticed by the fairer sex. Burkov had been ruthless regarding whose hand he planned to ask for in marriage. When he returned to Russia, he planned to seriously court the daughter of his High Commander, a General he didn't particularly like. His daughter wasn't all that pleasant to look at, yet she could be the mother of his children, and could keep a nice house. More importantly, she would provide a direct avenue to the General.

Sacrifices were necessary to climb the ranks, and Burkov had his eye on the top prize. He opened the bottom drawer of the desk and retrieved a bottle of whiskey, unscrewed the top, and poured himself a drink in a shot glass.

His gaze went to the portrait of former President Ronald Reagan hanging on the wall opposite him. Reagan was seated in the Oval Office with the American flag propped behind him.

Burkov studied the picture for a long moment, then tossed back the shot of whiskey. It was a big flavored whiskey and dominated his mouth. He swallowed, breathed in, and recognized a smoky flavor and others he couldn't identify. It was a man's drink, and if Reagan was a drinking man, he would have liked whiskey. In fact, Burkov would have liked to have shared a drink with Reagan, to learn his secrets of why he was so revered.

He toasted to the picture. "To you old man, and to the America you thought was yours."

Burkov poured another shot, letting it fill his mouth as he felt the burn of the Kentucky bourbon. He kept staring at Reagan, and he swore the old man was staring right back at him.

"What do you want, old man?"

Another shot of whiskey later, Burkov became annoyed about why one of his subordinates hadn't taken down the picture. He certainly couldn't understand why Ronald Reagan was the most revered American president of modern times. The fact no one on his staff had removed the picture insinuated they had left it there for a reason. Burkov didn't trust anyone. He hadn't risen through the ranks on niceties. Quite the opposite.

He invented ruthlessness. Anyone who questioned him or knew his secrets met their maker under mysterious circumstances.

There had been whispers, but the more powerful he became, the less people whispered, knowing they might need a favor.

Burkov leaned back in the chair and put his boots on the desk. The office was full of display cases showcasing trophies, and Burkov mused this was how Americans educated their next generation. Football and baseball games, dance contests, pep rallies, booster club and PTA meetings, and if he knew the word *hogwash*, he would have used it to describe the American educational system.

Instead of promoting military superiority and pandering to whoever was offended, they should instead be grooming their leaders from an early age, like Burkov had been. He attended boarding school from the time he could remember, sleeping in sparse quarters, and forming alliances with the strongest boys in the class.

Burkov had been bullied as a young boy due to his small size and asthma attacks which his parents thought were brought on by cowardice. To toughen him up and to prepare him for military school, he had been sent to boarding school. The family name descended from a long line of Russian military heroes, thus their name required protection, and his parents would do anything to keep up appearances.

Burkov discovered not all his classmates were up to the same academic prowess as he was, so to reciprocate for being accepted into a cliquish group, he provided tutoring, but only at a cost to his classmates. In some cases, when his classmates had nothing to offer, he'd require something of theirs. A memento from home, a favorite sweater, a pair of clean socks. He'd sell the treasured memento for a profit, occasionally even back to its original owner, while learning a valuable lesson about nostalgia and the driving force it had on people's actions.

Burkov despised nostalgia. The good old times memorialized in movies of the past were gone, so progress could forge ahead, to claim its rightful place in history, and if Burkov had to destroy half of America and its citizens for Russia's progress, he'd do it.

Collateral damage was a fact of war.

A knock at the door interrupted his patriotic musings. Burkov replaced the whiskey bottle in the bottom drawer. He licked the tips of several fingers and patted down a few errant strands of hair.

"The door is open."

CHAPTER 18

Petya Ruslan entered.

"Shut the door," Burkov barked. "What do you want? Can't you see I'm busy?" He reached for some papers on the desk and straightened them.

Shutting the door, Ruslan walked in like he owned the place. His massive arms, barrel chest, and towering stature were more than enough to claim ownership wherever he went. He strolled over to the chair in front of the principal's desk, kicked it back, and sat down. He propped his feet on the desk with an unusually loud thud, and crossed them at the ankles.

Burkov's gaze went to Ruslan's mud-caked boots. A brief sneer escaped his lips, but he knew better than to correct Ruslan's abominable and offensive manners. From what little Burkov knew of Ruslan's background, manners and niceties weren't taught where he came from.

Burkov took a whiskbroom he had stashed near his desk, and using exaggerated strokes, he brushed away the dirt on the desk left by Ruslan's boots.

The big Russian wasn't amused. "Busy drinking? Give me what you have."

Burkov glared at Ruslan for a long moment. He hated the big man as much as he admired him. "Small talk was never in your repertoire of skills."

"My line of work doesn't require talking."

Or high level thinking Burkov wanted to say. He thought better of it since he needed Ruslan's help. Instead of exchanging barbs, he retrieved the whiskey bottle, and tossed it to Ruslan, who caught it deftly in one hand.

Ruslan removed the top and took one drink straight from the bottle, much to Burkov's annoyance.

"It's good," Ruslan said, savoring the aftertaste. He put the top back on.

"You might as well finish it." Burkov's icy tone indicated contempt.

Ruslan held the bottle at arm's length in front of his face. He studied it. Long and smooth, the color of the whiskey shone through the clear glass. While Ruslan enjoyed a good whiskey, he certainly didn't plan on getting drunk tonight, or any other night. In his line of work, a delayed action or muddled thinking resulted in dire consequences, namely death.

In the past he had formidable foes, worthy to be killed, and he'd also had pathetic foes, those who whimpered or begged for mercy like the computer geek whose car happened to break down on a deserted road. The so-called vacation the man had planned had been carefully crafted in advance in preparation for the hit. A convenient entry into a local contest had required Ruslan to bribe the sponsor of the contest. The result couldn't have been any better.

The only requirement was for the rube to travel along a rarely traveled road, one where he would have to drive a car. A taxi driver called to the man's residence had been persuaded to leave after Ruslan stuck a knife to his throat. Leave or die. The choice was quite simple, and the driver didn't need to be told twice. Ruslan admired the guy for his wise choice. Unnecessary killing was not to his liking.

Planning a killing was.

On the night it happened, Ruslan set out spike strips, causing the tires to go flat. After that, plunging the knife into the man's liver had been much too easy, and Ruslan longed for a worthy opponent, one who could test his skills, requiring Ruslan to keep *his* skills sharpened, which made him think of the Americans, and a few particularly worthy opponents.

"There are troublemakers in the group," Ruslan said. He leaned back in his chair.

"Who?"

Ruslan reached into his shirt pocket, retrieved three driver's licenses, and tossed them in front of Burkov.

Picking up the licenses, Burkov read the names slowly. "Dillon Stockdale, Chris Chandler, Ryan Manning." He cast a glance at Ruslan. "Where did you get these?"

"We confiscated the wallets of the prisoners."

"Interesting." Burkov stacked them neatly, as if he was handling a stack of cards, then placed them on the desk. "Get me the wallets of these three men." Burkov tapped the licenses. "Quickly."

Ruslan left without questioning why Burkov needed the wallets. Money had already been removed, not that the US currency was any good anymore, but some of the soldiers had never seen American dollars before, and asked to take them home as souvenirs. Ruslan had no need for the green bills, so as the soldiers rifled through the wallets, he didn't interfere.

Five minutes later Ruslan returned with three worn wallets, faded brown and curved, indicating the men had kept them in their back pockets for a long while.

"Which one belongs to Dillon Stockdale?"

Ruslan pointed to the wallet on the left.

Burkov opened the wallet and carefully thumbed the contents. There were various credit cards, notes scribbled on folded Post-it notes, a paperclip—which Burkov scolded Ruslan for overlooking—and most importantly, pictures.

Burkov removed a faded picture from Dillon's wallet. It appeared to be a high school graduation photograph, a rite of passage for American students. The girl had long hair, a wide smile worthy of a toothpaste commercial, clear skin, with similar eyes and bone structure her father. Written on the back was the name "Cassie." His daughter. Burkov searched the rest of the wallet, opening compartments and taking out the rest of the contents, checking for anything of personal value. Zero. His only connection appeared to be with his daughter, the one he said had been running an errand before the wedding.

"Bring Stockdale in here."

While Ruslan was gone, Burkov carefully replaced all items back in the wallet except for the picture. That would be his trump card. He thought about his good fortune of finding the picture. As he was folding the wallet and placing it on the desk, Ruslan shoved his prisoner in the room.

"Sit there," he said gruffly.

Dillon shot a death stare at Ruslan. He pulled the chair back and sat in it. Ruslan stood to the side and leaned against a wall.

"Pardon his manners," Burkov said to Dillon, bobbing his head at Ruslan. "I'm afraid he didn't have suitable schooling."

Dillon's hardened expression didn't change. "I'm going to kill him first." He nodded to Ruslan. "You'll be next."

At first Burkov was surprised at the audacity of such a statement, then he let out a long and hearty laugh. Ruslan didn't move or show any type of emotion.

"Kill him, then me?" Burkov repeated. "That's the funniest thing I've heard all day. You certainly are a comedian, Dillon. Do you mind if I call you Dillon? Perhaps when all this is over, you might consider a career on television. You'd have the audience rolling with laughter. I just know it."

Dillon wasn't amused by Burkov. "What do you want with me?"

Burkov's expression changed from jovial to serious in the time it took him to blink. He pushed the picture in front of Dillon, and kept his eyes trained on him.

Dillon glanced once at the picture, immediately recognizing Cassie's senior picture. She had fussed and fretted over what to wear, which earrings to choose, and she'd even had her make-up professionally done at a make-up counter at the mall. He had driven her to the photographer's studio and looked in amazement upon his only child as the camera clicked and whirled. Where had all the years gone? His little girl had grown up. It was a happier time when the world was sane, when he was at the pinnacle of his professional life. Cassie was heading to college, and it should have been a time to celebrate a new phase in their life, until Amy died. He shook off the remembrance.

"You took that from my wallet."

126

"That implies stealing. I don't steal."

"I suppose invading a country, confiscating land, killing, and taking prisoners is better than stealing?"

"Stealing is for the common thief. I am no thief. I remind you I am a Colonel in the Armed Forces of the Russian Federation. I am highly trained and educated, and—"

"So am I."

Burkov's jaw clenched when Dillon interrupted him, and he felt the beginning of an eye twitch. He despised how his body betrayed him when he was being challenged. That little nerdy kid never quite left his psyche regardless of how he tried to bury that part of his life. He rubbed his eye to hide the twitch which had materialized at an alarming pace. The boldness of the American showed no bounds.

Burkov envisioned his beloved homeland, a place of deep rivers and country pride, of beautiful women, military pageantry, warm food, music. The vast tundra, the forests, the sea. At last, a calmness washed over him. He held up the picture. "This is your daughter, Cassie, no? The one who was to be married?"

Dillon remained silent.

"I've always found silence indicates agreement, so I'll take that as a yes." Burkov studied Dillon's facial expressions.

The guy was good, Burkov would give him that, and if Ruslan wasn't around, Burkov would definitely be worried. While they were equally matched in strength, Burkov knew from past military mistakes never to underestimate the people who were being invaded.

"Your daughter is very beautiful. A woman of class and integrity, who I'm sure has been taught about the finer things in life. She's a woman I'd like to know." Burkov sensed he was getting under Dillon's skin. Good. When people lose their cool, they say things they regret, things Burkov needed to know. "Where is she?"

"How would I know?" Dillon retorted. "I've already told you, she and the other wedding attendants were on an errand when you attacked us."

"You say that with such vehemence."

"I don't know where she is. How could I? You burned down our home. If she came home, she and the others would have left to seek shelter somewhere else."

"Ah, yes, I forgot. What a shame to have destroyed such a quaint country home." Burkov lowered his chin. "Forgive me. It is getting late. Now if you'll excuse me, the guard outside the door will escort you back to your quarters."

After Dillon left, Ruslan, who had been observing the interaction, took a seat in the chair in front of the desk. "That was useless. You should have let me have a turn at interrogating him. I would have made him talk."

"He didn't know where his daughter is. That was plain to see."

"What do you want his daughter for?"

"To control him."

"She's dead. You burned the house down and they were probably in it."

"Did you see a body?"

"No. I didn't need to. The fire would have been too intense."

"They could have escaped."

"From that fire?" Ruslan scoffed at the suggestion.

"I need to find Dillon's daughter. If his daughter's life is in danger, Dillon will be putty in my hands. He's a natural leader, and I need him to convince the others to work."

Tired of Burkov's musings, Ruslan changed the subject. "What's the latest on the oil rig?"

"Not rig. Rigs. We need many rigs to drill as quickly as possible. The equipment is being shipped here as we speak." Burkov picked up a pencil and twirled it between his fingers. "We still don't have enough men to man all the rigs. Our extra troops are securing the area."

"What are you suggesting?" Ruslan asked.

"Isn't it about time you visited our informant? Find out what is known about Dillon's daughter, and where the next congregation of able-bodied men will be."

CHAPTER 19

For the past thirty minutes or so, Petya Ruslan had stood outside in the dark, hidden in the shadows of a massive pine tree in the dense East Texas woods near the town of Hemphill. His pupils became large and black as his eyes became accustomed to the low light. Though he had a working flashlight in his pocket, flicking it on would have alerted someone to his presence.

Darkened clouds floated across the moon, casting an eerie midnight blue light upon the land. Something scurried in the brush and Ruslan's eyes flicked to the movement. A raccoon waddled along a path, stopped, and lifted its nose at the odd odor of the man. The nocturnal animal couldn't see the statue of a man, but sensed his presence and the danger. The animal hastily chose another path.

Ruslan slunk away from the cover of the night, following the path he had carefully chosen the day before. Satisfied he hadn't been seen, he sprinted to the building. Ruslan removed a lock picking case from his inside pocket, and using the specialty tools he knew so well, he clicked open the locked door. The room was dark and smelled of several days of uninhabited human use. His eyes swept over the room and took in its contents. Nothing had been moved since the first time he had made a visit. The room was furnished with a table, a few chairs, a filing cabinet. Pictures hung askew on the walls. An LED lantern sat dark on the table.

He eased the door shut without making a sound. Hugging the wall, he slid to the window and glanced outside. It was dark and there was no movement. Not even a dog barked.

Good.

He hadn't been followed.

Taking the tilt wand of the blinds between his thumb and index finger, he twisted the flimsy plastic slats shut. The clacking of plastic on the window echoed in the sparsely furnished room. He stilled, listening for any movement or indication he had been heard.

Spying a chair, he picked it up and set it in a corner where the shadows were thick and heavy. His black clothes melted into the shadows.

The only fresh air the room had seen was when Ruslan opened the door and slid in without making a sound. A cat couldn't have made less noise. Once, when he had been in Mexico, the locals had nicknamed him *el gato*–the cat–for his ability to watch and wait unseen.

He waited.

Ruslan was good at waiting. The thrill of knowing his prey would be scared witless once he made his presence known excited him. Even more exciting was the knife he carried. His hand went to it and he felt the outline of it in the scabbard. Satisfied he was alone, he practiced withdrawing it and making mock plunges into soft flesh.

He estimated he had been waiting for over an hour. His ears searched the nighttime sounds for a clue his contact had appeared. Footsteps, a cough, or crickets suddenly quieting.

All normal.

Crickets chirped their nightly calls, a dog barked, then others joined in. A tree branch scraped the roof and Ruslan listened for any indication of movement. The turn of a doorknob, a door latch opening, breathing, or the automatic adrenaline rush flooding his body at the presence of his prey. Even his arm hair prickling. He hadn't yet experienced those; he only heard the vague night sounds he had become accustomed to.

Growing impatient, he pressed a button on the side of his watch. Glowing green numbers illuminated the hardened features of his face, the scar more ragged and ugly. His contact was an hour and a half late.

Ruslan quieted his thoughts.

In the darkness, he listened.

The hushed padding of approaching footsteps came closer, steadier, then halted.

He listened to a key being inserted into the lock, clicking it open. A rush of air followed and the person hurriedly shut the door. A big sigh followed as the person leaned against the door.

Whatever it was, perhaps the floor creaking, a sixth sense, or just dumb luck, the person asked in a shaky voice, "Who's there?"

"You're late," Ruslan said. Rising from the chair, he approached his contact. "Don't touch the lantern."

"I need some light. I can't see."

"You don't need to." Ruslan took the LED lantern and moved it out of reach.

"What do you want?"

"I need to ask you a few questions." Ruslan stepped closer and loomed threateningly over his contact, peering down into the eyes wide with fear; armpits perspiring heavily. He got a scent of sweat laced with primal terror. Fight or flight. Ruslan enjoyed making people sweat. Enjoyed making them uncomfortable. Fear made them easier to control and interrogate once the brain was engaged with surviving instead of evading questions.

"I'll tell you anything you want to know."

"I need to know about Cassie Stockdale."

"What do you want to know about her?" The voice was meek and quiet.

"Where is she?"

"I don't know."

With lightning fast speed, Ruslan grabbed his contact, exposing the neck in a vulnerable position. "I could slice you from ear to ear. Nobody would hear you scream because I would have cut your vocal cords."

Ruslan's contact didn't move, didn't make a sound, except for the hammering heartbeat racing at breakneck speed. His eyes were inches away from his contact's.

"Where is she?"

"I don't know."

"You know what happened. People talk. Is she still alive? Did she escape the fire? Her father must know, but he isn't talking."

Thinking quickly, and taking advantage of the lack of knowledge on Ruslan's part, the contact replied, "The last I heard was that Cassie and the other women were in the house. I swear to God I don't know what happened to her."

Ruslan grunted and threw the contact to the floor, who then curled into a protective ball. "You're useless. I should have never agreed to Burkov's wishes. He's a fool. If I find out you're lying to me, I'll come back and finish you off."

The contact didn't reply. Hands were wrapped tightly around knees, face buried, and chin tucked for protection from a rib-breaking kick sure to come at any moment.

"We need more men. When's the next gathering?"

"Two days from now at the courthouse."

"How many?"

"I don't know. Maybe ten or twenty."

"You'd better be right. What time?"

"I heard they are supposed to meet an hour after sunrise. It'll give people time to get there."

"Have you told anybody about our arrangement? Does anybody suspect?"

"What? No! I haven't told anybody. Nobody knows."

"They better not, or else I'll take this knife and slit your throat. Then I'll slit—"

"You bastard. I'll—"

"Do what? I could snap your arm if I wanted to."

"Go to Hell and stay there!"

Ruslan laughed deep and throaty at the American's impotent threats. He left as quietly as he appeared. He'd had enough of this American's uselessness, and when the time came, he'd come back to finish what he started. While the Russians needed the intel the American provided, Ruslan's utter contempt was obvious.

CHAPTER 20

At Holly's ranch, once niceties and cursory introductions were completed, Holly invited everyone to the house, including Reload. With Buster nowhere in sight, the house felt empty without a dog.

"Kate and I could leave and return tomorrow," Nico suggested.

"No," Holly said. "It's getting late and there is no need for you and Kate to wander around looking for your property."

"Holly," Dorothy said, "Do you mind if I borrow the truck and head into town?"

"What for?" Holly asked. "It's getting late, and you and Anna shouldn't be out at night. You're not armed, and even if I gave you a gun, I don't think you'd know how to use it."

"I was going to ask if Anna could stay here. I really need to get home and get my high blood pressure medicine. I'm not feeling well, and I know my blood pressure must be sky high. I haven't had this problem for a while, and I've got some leftover pills from last year stashed somewhere in the house."

"Anna can stay here. Let me get my things and I'll come with you."

"Oh, no. That's not necessary," Dorothy insisted. "I'll be fine, and I'll be back before you know it."

"I'm sure Nico could escort you." Holly gauged Nico's reaction, which indicated he was agreeable.

"Absolutely not," Dorothy said, shaking her head. "He's tired and I don't want to impose more than I already have."

"Okay, if you're sure." Holly wasn't convinced why Dorothy couldn't wait until the morning, and was uneasy about letting her borrow the truck, but if she needed medicine then there wasn't much choice. High blood pressure was a killer, and they needed to keep everyone alive. "If anyone approaches you, don't stop, just keep on going."

"I can do that. I'll be careful. Promise." Dorothy smiled pleasantly to reassure Holly.

"Alright. Let me get you the keys."

Holly went to the kitchen and dug around in a Tupperware container half full of flour where the keys were hidden. Holly took one end of the plastic baggie and pulled it out, careful not to spill any flour. She blew a puff of air on the baggie and wiped it clean. The keys were always hidden in case they were out working the land when an unwanted visitor showed up. Keeping keys on a peg by the front door worked perfectly fine during normal times, but this was anything but normal.

Once Dorothy left, Holly prepared a meal for everyone. They had quite a spread of food leftover from the wedding that was to have taken place the day before. Treats included smoked meat, just about every kind of canned vegetables, or fruit to choose from, including figs. A sleeve of crackers, which was now considered a delicacy, was on the menu. A dish of baklava with walnuts was still in the brown paper bag. Holly considered whoever brought the baklava had forward thinking, especially since the dessert didn't require refrigeration. Someone else had brought a jar of honey and enough pecans to feed guests at several weddings.

Kate offered the goody bag, but Holly told her to keep it since there was plenty of leftover food.

Holly sat down at the table and placed a napkin on her lap. "Nico, can you do the honors please?"

"Honors?" He raised his hands, palm side up. "I don't understand."

"The blessing."

"I'm not very good at that."

"It doesn't matter, just say whatever comes to your mind."

Nico took a glance around the table and cleared his throat. "Let us bow our heads. Heavenly Father, we thank You for this meal we are about to receive. We thank You for the blessings You have bestowed upon us. Allow Your strength to flow through Dillon, Ryan, and Chandler, who are not at this table. Lift up their spirits, and guide them for what they must endure. In Jesus' name, Amen."

"Thank you," Holly said. "That was nice."

Nico's tone changed from one of spiritual thankfulness to one of military precision. "Tell me exactly what happened yesterday."

Holly recounted how the Russian helicopter arrived minutes after the last guest had arrived. She told in detail about the number of soldiers who had jumped out of the helicopter, describing their uniforms and the types of weapons they carried. She recalled the bullets hitting the house and how she, Cassie, Amanda, Dorothy, and Anna had ducked and taken cover, except for one.

"What was her name?" Nico asked.

"Sarah Monroe."

"You mentioned her husband..." Nico snapped his fingers, trying to recall her husband's name.

"Larry Monroe."

"That's right. You mentioned Larry was taken prisoner too."

"He was."

"Does he know his wife is dead?"

"No. There's no way he could know."

"And you're pretty sure one of the guests was a snitch for the Russians?"

"What else could explain the timing of their arrival?" Holly asked. She placed her fork on the plate and sat back in her chair. "It couldn't have been dumb luck. The Russians must have been planning the attack on the US for months. Years probably, including the one on my ranch."

"I don't understand," Nico said. "They didn't want your land, they tried to burn down your house, but they didn't harm any of the able-bodied men. Correct?"

"They shot the elderly couple."

"Who did?"

"I'm not sure. We couldn't see what was happening at the time. We were hiding in the closet."

"Then a soldier found you, right?"

"Yes. He motioned for us to be quiet."

While Nico was forming his next question, Anna butted into the conversation. "He looked straight at me, like he recognized me."

"Had you met him before?" Nico asked.

Anna shook her head to indicate she had not.

"Curious. I wonder if he has a daughter your age. It would explain why he took pity on you. No father would do that to their child."

"I don't have a father." Anna dipped her chin to her chest, her hands fidgeting with the napkin in her lap. The corners of her mouth drooped in sadness.

Nico wasn't sure how to respond to the child's declaration. Needing to stay on track, he asked, "Would you recognize him if you saw him again?"

"I think we would all recognize him," Holly said. "He spared our lives."

"Then we have at least one American sympathizer on our side, and one traitor among us. The two don't cancel each other out."

Conversation at the table quieted at the mention of a traitor. Nico thought about possible reasons, and he suspected everyone at the table was deep in thought as well. Who could it be? And why would a citizen of the United States betray such a great country? Had the Russians waved dollars around? Or had a family member been threatened with harm?

Conversation during the next hour covered more mundane subjects and local gossip. Holly prepared hot tea for everyone, explaining, "We are almost out of coffee. I'm saving what's left for a special occasion. Who wants another serving of baklava?"

The front door burst open. Nico swiveled around, drew his pistol, and leveled it at the door.

Reload sat up, eyes alert and his muscles tensed, readied for action.

Dorothy entered. She wiped her shoes on the rug then shut the door. She took a step into the room and froze. Six pairs of eyes were fixed directly on her, and she gasped at the muzzles of several guns leveled in her direction. Frozen, her heart pounded at breakneck speed, and myriad thoughts bounced around in her head. Her mouth hung open in the shape of an *O*.

"Dorothy?" Holly said in a scolding tone.

As Nico and Holly holstered their guns, Dorothy let out an audible breath. "Y'all look like you've seen a ghost. What's going on?"

"Nothing," Holly said. "We were so absorbed in the conversation that we didn't hear you drive up. You startled us. That's all."

"Oh," Dorothy put a hand over her heart, patting it. "You gave me a terrible fright."

"Did you find what you needed?"

"Hmm? Find what?"

"Your medicine? Did you find it?"

"I did. Sorry, my heart is still in my throat." Dorothy patted her chest again. "I went blank there for a moment. I'm okay now."

"Come sit down at the table. I'll get you tea and dessert."

"Before you do," Dorothy said, "I have some information for you. I know why the Russians are here."

CHAPTER 21

Darkness had fallen on the East Texas land of piney woods and towering hardwoods. Nocturnal animals stirred, waiting for the sun to set, and for darkness to cover the land. Emerging from their hidden dens, the animals sniffed the air, checking for adversaries competing for territory or breeding rights.

Deep in the woods, a screech owl twilled its eerie call, silencing the forest. More joined in from nearby trees until the night air was heavy with owl songs. Long shadows danced in the moonlight.

Buster lay shivering in the barn where he had taken shelter. His eyes were big and he tentatively looked around, his mind retreating to memories causing him distress.

Earlier, explosive dings of rapid gunfire had assaulted his ears, confusing him, the noise an intolerable pox on his senses.

Frightened, he had bolted.

He ran until his lungs burned from exertion, until his legs gobbling mile after mile of rugged terrain became as wobbly as spaghetti, and when he had run himself to the point of exhaustion, he collapsed.

UNDEFEATED WORLD

He had slept fitfully, memories flooding his dreams. Gunpowder burned his sensitive nose. The reverberations of gunfire assaulted his hearing. He trembled at the *tap, tap, tap* of bullets on wood.

Glass shattering.

Screams.

Blinding flashes.

As he slept, he panted and yipped, his paws twitched, legs in motion, escaping from some perceived enemy.

Overwhelmed by memories, he rose from his makeshift bed of hay, and ventured out of the barn and into the darkness. He stood there for a while, hesitation gripping him into inaction.

A sudden noise startled him, and instinctively he bolted away from the barn, dashed into the woods, weaving his way through the brush where he stumbled upon a hollow log.

He lifted his snout, testing the air. Somewhere nearby was water. Letting his nose guide him, he crouched down and belly crawled into the log. A puddle of rainwater had formed in a depression in the log. Buster nosed it, tasting the wood, the moss, the sandy soils and moist carpet of leaves and pine needles. He lapped greedily until no water remained and his tongue grazed the soft bark.

For a moment Buster quelled his shivering body, cocked his ears to the pattering feet of an animal trotting along a hidden trail tamped down by countless trips of four-legged creatures. The animal slowed its walk, stopped, then scurried to other foraging grounds.

A bullfrog croaked and crickets chirped. An owl hooted long and lonely.

Time meant nothing.

The stars moved in the heavens.

The moon brightened then paled by passing clouds.

Buster lowered his head and put his head on his paws, fatigued from the dangers of the woods. His eyelids became heavy, and no longer able to keep them open, he fell into a deep slumber. Voices and laughter came to him. A warm home with a soft bed.

The gentle hand upon his fur.

A scent of perfume tickling his nose.

The aroma of sizzling meat on a grill, and smoke filling the air.

That was the essence of his home, where Dillon and Holly lived. Where Cassie and Ryan would live with their own family. Finally, Buster drifted off to sleep.

* * *

Morning came, soft and slow, the sun's rays threading through the canopy, bringing light and warming the land.

Buster opened his eyes a slit to unfamiliar territory and sounds. He stretched, and let his eyes absorb the low morning light.

A twig snapped and suddenly Buster was wide awake.

He remained motionless as footsteps approached. He sniffed the air and listened with eagerness at the sound of a baritone voice talking in soothing tones. Buster sniffed again and caught the unmistakable scent of another dog. The man was communicating with the dog and it was tracking Buster!

He searched for an escape route, but the opposite end of the log was blocked. Panic set in when he realized he was trapped.

He shivered and waited.

The man spoke in a calming tone, and this time Buster saw boots. They were work boots, scarred and stained from use and shaped to the contours of the man's foot. One sniff indicated he was a man who worked the land, who got dirty, slogging through manure and hay. It wasn't an unpleasant smell, only one Buster had smelled at Holly's ranch as he accompanied Dillon or Ryan on ranch chores.

Buster hesitantly thumped his tail.

A black nose appeared at the end of the hollow log. It was attached to a brown and white muzzle, the nose moist and interesting, twitching to gather information about Buster. It was a dog's nose, and Buster inched closer. This was a friendly dog, leashed and collared with a well-worn leather collar, female to be exact, and that bit of information excited Buster.

His tail thumped the sides of the log.

The female dog whimpered.

The man tugged his dog back. "Stay." Unsure what was in the log, the man knelt and cautiously peeked into the log. A pair of kind eyes and the weathered face of a man who had worked the land all his life peered back at him. "How long you been there?" the man asked. "Are you lost?"

The rising intonation of the man's voice alerted Buster to the fact the man was communicating with him, but the words were only garbled sounds similar to the words his owner made.

The man reached into his pocket and retrieved a crinkly package.

Untwisting it, he pulled a cracker out and placed it at the edge of the log.

Buster lifted his snout and tasted the air. His mouth watered, and hunger overcame fear. He belly-crawled to the edge, spied the cracker on the ground, and licked it into his mouth. He gobbled it greedily.

The man placed another cracker on the ground, a few inches away from the previous one. Again, Buster edged closer to get the cracker, and each time he retreated into the log. The scenario transpired over the next twenty minutes until Buster had to completely exit the log.

The man sat down and was eye level with Buster. His female dog, who he called Skippy, sat obediently to the side. The man held out a hand, palm side up, and offered it to Buster, who licked the cracker crumbs from his fingers. Gradually, Buster came to trust the man who showed no violent tendencies, only the offer of food and a gentle pat on the head.

The man reached into his pocket and retrieved a length of cord. He placed it over Buster's head then gently tightened it.

"Let's take you back to my house. The missus will get you something to eat."

Buster followed obediently behind, along with the other dog.

The man glanced at Buster. "You sure are off the beaten path. Not sure who you belong to, seeing I know most of the dogs around here. Did you run away? Someone dump you? Well, you can stay with me. I could use another hound dog. My boy, Gus..." The man became lost in reverie, remembering his favorite dog when he was still alive. As if Buster could understand the man, he said, "I still miss him. He reached to Buster and patted him on the head. "I think you'll be a good replacement."

CHAPTER 22

Dillon's eyes popped open, and it took him a second to register his location. The room was dark and crowded with warm bodies. Springs creaked on a cot. A heavy sigh and anxious shallow breathing emanating from one of his fellow prisoners alerted Dillon to the fact he wasn't the only one awake, and he was still imprisoned.

What had stirred him from a deep sleep? A noise? A sixth sense alerting him to imminent danger? Normally a deep sleeper, his current situation wasn't conducive to a good night's sleep. What time was it? How long had he been asleep?

While he lay awake, the first rays of the morning sun filtered into the room through the high windows. He surmised it must be early morning, perhaps an hour until sunrise according to the chirping birds, announcing the end of a long night.

Dillon furtively swung his legs off the cot. With his eyes accustomed to the low light, he crept to the teacher's desk and knelt behind it so his back was to the chalkboard. He slid open a drawer, inch by inch. It squeaked once. He popped his head above the desk to gauge if anyone had awakened. Whoever had been awake earlier had gone back to sleep.

So far, so good.

He peered into the drawer and pushed around its contents for anything useful. He found a box of erasers, a date stamp and an inkpad, dry-erase markers, crayons, a dull Sharpie, Post-it notes, and labels. He reached his hand to the back and felt around.

There! That was what he needed. A number 2 pencil. He touched the tip of it, confirming it had been recently sharpened. Excellent. It could easily put out an eye. Dillon placed the pencil in his waistband and fluffed his shirt so it wouldn't be seen.

Approaching footsteps echoed in the hallway, and his muscles tensed as the stampeding of soldiers came closer and grew louder. Instinctively, his hand reached for his Glock, only for him to remember he and the other prisoners had been stripped of weapons, including his knife, the same one he had used to kill the mountain lion. He normally kept it clipped to his back pocket for ease of use. If only he could get his hands on a knife then he'd find a way to escape.

Dillon's preferred knife was the assisted-opening Kershaw Nura with a three and a half inch blade, complemented by his back-up Kershaw Leek. Since his military service, he had developed an appreciation for good knives and valued razor sharpness at an affordable price. Many of his peers would drop big bucks for a big name knife, while Dillon bargain shopped for usable Kershaw knives.

He discovered a good hollow ground knife blade was easy to sharpen. Daily use of any knife made handling it as natural as tying shoelaces, and about as innocuous, while increasing speed and agility of the handler's full potential as a knife fighter.

The sound of a key unlocking the bolt of the classroom door electrified the already tense atmosphere, and a burst of adrenaline flooded Dillon's body. He shut the drawer and ran to his cot. Stretching out, he pushed the gray blanket to the floor. If the situation required quick movement, the blanket would encumber his actions.

He needed to be ready.

Dillon remained perfectly still on his cot, concentrating to control his breathing and rapidly beating heart.

Someone swung the door open and it hit the wall, hard. Several guards carrying AKs burst into the room. A glaring light flooded the room, wakening the prisoners, causing confusion. Dillon put his hand to his eyes to shield them from the blinding light.

A guard barked out orders in Russian to his comrades. Another shined a second searchlight into the room.

In broken English, the Americans were told to assemble single file against the chalkboard.

Dillon rose and stumbled to the front of the classroom, feigning clumsiness to imply feebleness. Larry followed behind him like an obedient dog.

In the confusion, one of the Americans panicked and attempted to push his way past the Russians. A rifle butt to the stomach sent him reeling to the floor, jolting him back to reality. He clutched his stomach, writhing and moaning.

While the guards were occupied with the Americans and searching cots and belongings, Dillon took the opportunity to question Larry. In a low voice, he said, "You talked a lot in your sleep last night."

"What'd I say?" Larry asked, rubbing his eyes.

"Something about your wife and how sorry you were for what happened."

Larry grunted.

"What did you mean?"

Larry felt Dillon's piercing glare, but didn't dare look him in the eye. "It didn't mean anything."

"Sounds like someone's guilty conscience is getting the best of them."

"My conscience is clear," Larry shot back.

"It better be, because someone alerted the Russians to the fact a large gathering of local townspeople was taking place at Holly's ranch. The timing of the attack was too good to think it was purely coincidental."

"If you think it was me, you're barking up the wrong tree."

"We'll see," Dillon muttered. As Larry was about to reply, Dillon clenched his teeth and said, "Be quiet. Don't say anything else."

The Russian soldiers parted and stood at attention when Petya Ruslan walked in. The atmosphere became tinged with an odd combination of reverence and hatred, and Dillon recognized the big

Russian as the same man from yesterday and the same one at Holly's ranch.

Dillon noted the man was dressed in civilian clothes, and at times seemed to be in command of the mission. He wore a sandy colored vest, which no doubt concealed his weapons and provided information about his last deployment. His muscular frame and scarred face indicated he had both faced hell and dished plenty of it out. He did not carry a firearm, yet the knife in the scabbard was one to cause alarm. The scar running down the side of his face clued Dillon to the fact he had been wounded in a knife fight. It also clued him to the fact he wasn't as deft at knife fighting as he wanted people to believe. Posturing was half the battle, and this dude was good at it from the way he dressed, his commanding gait of ownership, claiming whatever space he was in, and the suspicious eyes taking in his surroundings, not missing anything.

Dillon knew he'd better be on his game.

With the skill of a surgeon, the man whipped out a knife from under his vest.

Petya Ruslan clasped his hands behind his back and strolled over to the line where the men stood. He inspected each man as if they were a commodity needing to pass a test. He stopped in front of Larry, and eyed him up and down, not so much in an accepting way, rather contempt. He spoke in Russian, which elicited bouts of muffled laugher from the soldiers.

Larry could only helplessly stand there, impotently taking whatever insults had been said about him. He hung his head in shame.

Ruslan addressed the prisoners. "Stand at attention if you want to live."

One of the men in line cracked a half smile, smirking. Ruslan sprang on him with the force of a killer whale on a hapless seal. In one deft move he thrust his knife up and sliced the man's ear. It took the man's brain a long second to register what had just happened. Once his ear started burning like the devil as if someone had splashed gasoline on it then threw a match, he let out a gasp, instinctively putting his hand to his ear, cupping it.

Ruslan threw him up against the brick wall and shoved his massive forearm into the man's Adam's apple. "You want to smile again?" Ruslan pressed the knife just inside the man's right nostril.

The man stiffened and didn't even take a breath.

"No more trouble?"

Speaking like a ventriloquist, the man said, "No, Sir."

"Smart answer." Ruslan casually withdrew the bloody knife and wiped it on the man's shirt. Then he roughly grabbed him by his collar, now stained in blood dripping from his ear, and shoved him to the door leading to the hallway. Ruslan addressed a guard. "Take him to a medic and have that bloody mess sewed back together."

Dillon stood in line with the others, barely able to control his anger. The inability to strike back grated on the moral code that directed his life. He balled his fists, then released them. He had worked tirelessly to put criminals behind bars during his former stint as district attorney. He had won multiple cases against the dregs of society, so to do nothing while these bullies were throwing themselves around and laughing while they did it disturbed him immensely.

"My name is Petya Ruslan and I am your new master. I do not give orders twice. Cooperate and you will be treated well. Disobey and you will die at my amusement." Ruslan walked the line and observed each man as he waved his knife, at times drawing the cold metal down the side of a prisoner's face. He enjoyed instilling fear and seeing the men react.

Dillon used his peripheral vision to watch Ruslan. When emboldened, Dillon flicked his eyes to the knife. It was familiar, the shape, the handle, the length of the blade. During his time in the military, he recalled meeting a special unit operating in Afghanistan. The unit was from Italy and the men carried a local Italian-made knife called the Fulcrum, manufactured by Extrema Ratio. The unique overlapping rectangle handle design was unmistakable. It wouldn't surprise Dillon if the knife was taken from one of the dead men's bodies as a war trophy.

Finally, Ruslan stopped in front of Dillon. He took his sweet time, sizing up Dillon from head to toe. Dillon was shorter than Ruslan, yet stockier, with tree trunks for legs, strong arms, and an attitude oozing trouble. When he stepped directly in front of Dillon, Ruslan expected a flinch, an eye twitch, fast blinking eyes, rapid breathing, anything to indicate fear or nervousness.

There was nothing, and that infuriated Ruslan.

He used the tip of the knife to draw blood from Dillon's nose.

Still no response.

"You will be trouble."

"I assure you I will not be."

"Why?"

"I have my reasons," Dillon said, looking directly into Ruslan's cold eyes.

"You expect me to believe that?"

"I give you my word."

Ruslan paused, choosing what he would divulge about the fire set at the ranch house. "If your word relies on the wellbeing of your wife or daughter, *I* can assure you not to trouble yourself."

"What are you talking about?" Dillon's cool demeanor evaporated. His expression morphed from one of casual indifference to perplexed concern.

"Since the house was of no use to us, Colonel Burkov had it burned to the ground."

Larry, who was standing next to Dillon, asked, "The house burned?"

Ruslan jerked his head toward Larry. "That's right. Corporal Andrey Koshkin had the pleasure of torching it. Is this a problem?"

Dillon's hand twitched at his side.

Ruslan sensed he had hit a nerve. He nonchalantly turned his back to Dillon, letting the information sink in. Chandler reached over to Dillon and squeezed his arm, holding him back. Dillon's tense muscles relaxed. Knowing Chandler had his back provided some semblance of assurance.

Ruslan whipped around. "Are you not curious about the house?"

Dillon shrugged. "It can be rebuilt. Anything is replaceable."

"Anything?" Ruslan paused for effect then stepped to the side and glanced at Larry. "Even wives?"

"Why does my wife have anything to do with this?" Larry asked. "Was she in the house?"

"Ah, so there was someone in the house? No?"

Larry's eyes nervously bounced around. "I uh, I uh, don't know."

"If there was, they are dead now, so no need to worry about them anymore."

Dillon thought Larry was about to cry like a baby, and suspected Larry hadn't signed up for his wife to be hurt. While Ruslan was quite convincing about having the house burned, Dillon wasn't so sure about it. House fires resulted in black, billowing smoke, could be smelled from miles away, and Dillon had seen no indication a house had caught fire. Either the guy was straight up lying, or whoever had set the fire did a poor job or placed the accelerant in a way it wouldn't cause damage to the house. If it was the latter, then they had a friend among the Russians.

As expected, Larry started blubbering. Between the wailing and crying, his words were a jumbled mess of uncontained emotions.

Ruslan couldn't be bothered anymore with Larry. He came back to Dillon, who he considered a worthy opponent.

"You," Ruslan said, tapping his knife on Dillon's chest. "What was your profession?"

"I was an assistant District Attorney. I prosecute those who break the laws of the United States."

"Ah, a lawyer. Liars, all of them. They hide a liter of truth in an ocean of deception." Ruslan waved the knife around to emphasize his contempt.

Dillon remained silent. He'd been insulted much worse before.

"Let me tell you my profession. I do whatever is necessary to get the job done. I worked my way into Spetsnaz by delivering what was required. While in Africa I learned methods of torture even the UN investigators swore were perpetrated by indigenous people. Countrymen are most savage upon their own countrymen. Wouldn't you agree?"

Dillon said nothing.

The more Dillon thought about it, the more he was convinced Ruslan's knife had come from the Italian unit he had met. The thought of those brave men tortured by a sadist like Ruslan turned Dillon's stomach. Yeah, he planned to kill Ruslan first.

After Ruslan became bored with toying with the Americans and not being able to break through Dillon's stoic demeanor, he left, motioning for Andrey Koshkin to come with him.

The prisoners stood stoically, waiting for their next directions.

CHAPTER 23

"Dillon," Chandler said, speaking in hushed tones. "He's got your number and will be watching you. Be careful what you say, and don't be fooled by anything he says."

"I'm trying not to," Dillon said. "He told me things he should not have unless he planned to kill us at the end of all this. Worse than that, he is so perceptive that it makes me think someone in our group is a traitor."

"I've got my suspicions about that too," Chandler confirmed. "Dillon, you have to show confidence to the troops or they won't follow you when the time comes. Know that I have your back and we'll find a way to flush out whoever it is."

Approaching steps sounded in the hallway. "Shh, we'll talk later."

With the grace of a prima ballerina, Colonel Mikhael Burkov, dressed in a pressed uniform adorned with medals and military braid, entered the room. Petya Ruslan followed behind. Burkov's presence was as much for show as it was for power. The soldiers stood stiff at attention, unblinking eyes transfixed and focused beyond the classroom, beyond the beige walls and posters of unfinished classroom projects.

Ruslan shot an annoyed glance at Burkov, but knew his place and it wasn't wise to question Burkov in front of his men. Ruslan took a step back to let the Colonel pass.

After counting the men, Burkov left without saying a word. He exited the classroom, gave orders to one of the soldiers, then stepped back inside.

"Please pardon the confusion, and I do humbly apologize for any inconvenience we may have caused you."

One of the soldiers handed Burkov a clipboard. He took it and read the names and professions of each man. Burkov strolled over to the men and acknowledged them by a slight nod. "You may be wondering why we are here and what we plan to do with you. I would like to assure you we mean you no harm as long as you do as you are told. Any type of insubordination will not be tolerated and will lead to solitary confinement. I can also assure you once we have what we need, we will leave and you may go back to your farms and shops, wives or girlfriends. Are there any questions?"

There were no inquiries.

The door opened and a guard shoved Ryan into the room. He fell to the floor and rolled on his back.

Ryan had a cut above his left eye, which was swollen shut, a purplish bruise on the left side of his face, and a busted lip. Dillon immediately went to Ryan and helped him to his feet.

"As hosts in your great country," Burkov said, "I would like to extend an invitation to everyone here to be our guests at a bountiful American breakfast. We are civilized people, and know you must eat. The food will be hot, and you may eat all you want. I don't want anyone to go hungry." Burkov stepped toward the door. "Andrey, take several men and escort our guests to the cafeteria."

Andrey Koshkin saluted his commanding officer. "Yes, Sir."

After Burkov left, Andrey motioned the men to the door. In heavily accented English, he said, "Cafeteria, this way."

With two guards flanking the men, they walked single file toward the cafeteria. Two more guards brought up the rear, and Andrey followed several steps behind them.

The school hallway had lockers lined on one side, and brightly colored banners with the school's mascot, the Hornets, decorated the walls. Drawings of hornets, ranging from caricatures with friendly faces to those worthy of the dinosaur age were taped to lockers. School pride ran deep.

Dillon was curiously drawn to the childish drawings, and he couldn't take his eyes off them. Mesmerized, in fact.

Hold 'em Hornets, Halt 'em Hornets, Hang 'em Hornets, Hi Jack 'em Hornets, and various other clever uses of words starting with the letter H had been used for slogans. There were even two hornets high fiving each other. The imagination of teenagers never ceased to amaze Dillon. The teens had not yet been encumbered with the adult stresses of bills and mortgages, problem kids, problem spouses, bosses, taxes, and health issues, all which had the propensity to kill creativity. Their minds were free to create and solve, and to think outside the box.

Dillon kept staring at the hornet images.

Why?

Was there some sort of hidden meaning in the drawings? Some higher authority guiding him to a solution? A vague Bible verse popped into his mind, and Dillon searched for the words. He blocked out the extraneous noises of shuffling feet, coughs, whispers, Russians barking orders... He cleared his mind of chattering voices to concentrate on this moment.

Right here.

Right now.

Nothing else mattered. He searched for the truth in the moment, tapping deep into his subconscious. Somewhere the truth was here, right before him. His breathing slowed, a spiritual peace engulfed him, and the meaning came to him clearly as he recalled the precise words from *Deuteronomy 7:20. "Moreover, the LORD your God will send the hornet against them, until those who are left and hide themselves from you perish."*

That was it!

He was the hornet, and he planned to fight the Russians with whatever he had, using whatever tactics and weapons were at his disposal.

This was his home, and the Russians were invaders.

He was in it to win.

And he didn't plan to fight fair.

CHAPTER 24

"What do you mean you know why the Russians are here?" Holly asked.

"I mean just that."

"Come in. We all need to hear this. Nico, you too. Come sit at the table. I think we should all holster our weapons."

Nico held a chair for Dorothy, then sat opposite her. He was in full Border Patrol mode. While he had been in Austin, John and Tatiana Chandler spoke highly of Holly, Amanda, and Cassie, relayed by their son Chandler. Anyone with a military sniper background would be a good judge of character. Dorothy was the wildcard in the bunch. A hanger-on, like a groupie at a rock concert.

Dorothy sat down at the table and relayed what she knew. "A neighbor of mine saw me at my house and came over to check on me since she hadn't seen me in a couple of days. I explained what happened at the ranch and how the Russians raided the wedding party and took the men."

"What did your neighbor have to say?"

"She said several days ago a friend of theirs had asked her

husband and several others if they could help out at their ranch. They would pay in food, so her husband jumped at the chance. While they were repairing the fence the cows had knocked down, they needed more tools. Her husband volunteered to go to the barn to get the tools and that's when he saw a Russian military helicopter fly over the house. He was positive of it. The chopper flew to where the other men were working. He couldn't exactly see what happened, but heard a few gunshots. Like warning shots."

"What did he do?" Holly asked.

"He didn't know what to do, so he hid in the barn. It only took a few minutes for whoever it was to find the house. He said he heard foreign voices. He thought they were Russian, but he wasn't sure. He crawled to the top of a stack of hay then jumped behind it to hide."

"They didn't find him?" Holly asked.

"No," Dorothy said. "They searched the barn and fired some rounds into the hay, but it only scared a rat that ran across his arm."

"That's all good to know," Nico said, "but why are the Russians here?"

"This is where it gets interesting," Dorothy said. "My friend's husband is in the oil business. He did some type of roughneck work at that discovery well made last year."

"What discovery?" Nico asked. "Holly, have you heard anything about a discovery?"

"Not a thing. There could have been, but we didn't arrive here until after the grid went down. We've been too busy trying to survive. We haven't paid much attention to the rumor mill."

Nico let that sink it. "Dorothy, go on. Tell us the rest."

"Apparently, there was a lot of talk about how big the oil field was. I don't remember all the numbers and such, but someone said it was like finding Spindletop on steroids. The amount of oil in the ground would match what Saudi Arabia has."

"They have a lot of oil," Nico commented.

"And," Dorothy said, "I've seen trucks carrying oil field equipment."

"How's that possible?" Holly asked. Modern cars aren't working. That includes trucks."

"These weren't American trucks. They were Russian. The rumor mill has it the Russians are rounding up all the able-bodied men to work in the oil field."

"What? Why?" Holly stared at Dorothy in disbelief.

"I don't understand," Nico said. "It would be foolish to go house by house to round up men."

"They don't have to," Dorothy countered. "Somehow they are finding out about large gatherings, like town hall meetings...or Cassie's wedding. They come in, take who they want, and kill the rest. Like what they did here."

"But they didn't harm you or anyone else at this table." Nico was getting impatient because things weren't adding up. "Weren't only close friends invited to the wedding? Do you think it was someone at the wedding who is in cahoots with the Russians?"

"Like who?" Dorothy sat back in her chair and folded her arms across her chest. "One of us? Unlikely. We were all shot at, including Anna and myself. I certainly wouldn't put my life or my daughter's life in danger to help the enemy. It had to be one of the guys."

Nico was deep in thought, but the mention that the traitor could be one of the men in the close knit circle brought his head up. "Let's go over who was here. Dillon, Ryan, Chandler, an elderly neighbor who was killed, and who else?"

"Larry Monroe."

"It can't be him." Holly scowled and rubbed the back of her neck at the mention of her longtime neighbor. "I've known Larry for a long time. My parents always talked highly of him. Besides, his wife was killed. Why would they kill the wife of someone who was helping them?"

"She would've been collateral damage," Nico surmised. "Nothing more, nothing less. It happens in war."

"There's no way Larry would put his wife in danger. Absolutely no way." Holly demonstratively shook her head. "It certainly couldn't be one of us either."

Amanda and Cassie cast suspicious glances around the table wondering if anyone in the room could be the traitor. Kate didn't know what to think. She decided the best course of action was to keep silent and to watch for indications anyone was being deceitful.

Too wound up to remain seated, Holly scooted her chair back, then paced the length of the table. "It couldn't be one of us. A Russian soldier searched the house for us, but when he found us, he motioned for us to be quiet. He could have taken us all out with his AK."

"*What?*" Nico asked incredulously.

"We were hiding in a secret room. We knew someone was in the house searching for us. We could hear him going room to room, opening doors and so forth. When he found us, he looked directly at Anna, and that's when something in him changed. Why would that be, Dorothy?"

The room suddenly became silent.

Anna's gaze bounced around from one adult to the other. While she didn't understand the implications of what the grownups were talking about, she knew it wasn't good. Dillon and his friends had been taken in the raid. The man she trusted to help her and her mother was held prisoner by the Russians. Her mother was being ganged up on. Anna sniffled and dropped her chin.

"Dorothy? Why would that be?"

"I don't know. I've never seen him, never met him. I'm nobody. I'm barely scraping by raising chickens and selling eggs." Dorothy's gaze zeroed in on Holly. "You think it's me?"

Holly didn't answer.

Nico divided a glance between Holly and Dorothy.

"Well," Dorothy huffed. "If this is what you think of me then I'm leaving. I'll walk home if I have to." Dorothy pushed back so hard on the chair, it fell over. "Anna, let's leave."

Anna's eyes were rimmed in red. She hiccupped and sniffled, and began to say something when she burst into tears.

Dorothy addressed the group as if she was a teacher scolding her classroom. "Now look what you've done. You've upset my daughter. She's crying."

Holly dropped her shoulders, recognizing playing the blame game wasn't getting anybody any closer to the truth. "I'm sorry, Dorothy. I'm wrong to question you. I'm stressed and worried about Dillon and the others," she said. "For everyone here, including you. I'm truly sorry. I don't want you or Anna to go. You are welcome here."

"That's right," Cassie said. "Anna is like a little sister I've never had. Please stay."

"Can we?" Anna asked, searching her mother's eyes for affirmation.

Dorothy didn't answer immediately. "Okay, we will, but only for a few more days."

"One good thing has come of this," Nico said. "We know we have at least one Russian on our side. The question is why?"

CHAPTER 25

Corporal Andrey Koshkin listened with feigned interest as Colonel Burkov shouted orders.

Once the prisoners had eaten their fill of the hearty breakfast–just like Burkov had promised–they were allowed a bathroom break then escorted onto the football field.

The rest of the soldiers ate the same fare the Americans were offered: scrambled eggs, bacon, sausage, toast, jam, pancakes, syrup, fruit, and unlimited coffee. Unlike the simple Russian breakfast food of black tea, rye bread, and sausage which the other soldiers demanded, Andrey grew to enjoy the American style breakfast. It was more pleasing to the palate, not bland and heavy like the Russian food.

Andrey was in mid-bite when Burkov bellowed, "Corporal Koshkin! Come here."

Andrey immediately placed the fork on the plate, dabbed his mouth with a paper napkin, then a swift pivot and a few steps later he approached his commanding officer, saluting him.

"Go get the horse. Saddle him and bring him to the football field.

I want to ride him."

"Yes, Sir," Andrey replied automatically. "Right away."

Andrey had been chosen to work with Cowboy once Burkov learned he had been raised on a farm with working horses. While Andrey viewed riding horses as a favorite pastime of the rich, he nevertheless recognized Cowboy's verve. He was a magnificent animal, sturdy and smart, and Andrey had seen the horse react to Dillon's orders. Andrey's rudimentary English allowed him to converse in simple sentences with complete words. The contractions the Americans used were quite confusing, especially spoken with the southern drawl, which sounded more like singing than words. A one syllable word became two. Phrases unique to the Texan culture made even less sense.

He learned fast though.

Andrey listened and mentally repeated English words he heard or those he thought were words or phrases. One particularly strange string of sounds Dillon used when riding Cowboy perplexed Andrey. The words were spoken in front of Cowboy's name, and for the life of Andrey, he could not understand them. The best he could come up with was *whydem*. He used an English to Russian translator app he had on his mobile phone, yet regardless of how he typed the word, there was no translation. It was quite frustrating.

Coming to the corral where Cowboy was penned, Andrey spoke to the horse in low tones, and approached him using careful movements. Jerky or fast movements tended to spook horses, a fact he had learned at an early age, and he still bore the scar above his left eye. Hooves tended to do that to the skin of a young boy. He was lucky not to have lost an eye.

Andrey saddled Cowboy and led him to the football field where the Americans were standing on the fifty-yard line. The prisoners were spaced randomly, milling around and talking, waiting to hear the reason for their imprisonment.

"Silence!"

The bullhorn sounded loud and clear.

The Americans took notice.

Dillon glanced at the stadium's press box. A guard armed with an automatic weapon was stationed there where he had a 360 view of the high school and surrounding woods.

Built during the 1960s on the outskirts of the town of Hemphill, the high school served not only Hemphill, but other rural communities as well. Only one two-lane road had access to the high school, and even the entrance to the school was guarded.

However, as with other prisons, and regardless of how well it was locked down, there were always deficiencies, and Dillon was determined to sniff those out.

From the moment he had been captured, Dillon observed the guards, their habits, and whether or not they were friendly or talkative. He memorized their weapons and their ease at handling them. Though he did not understand Russian, it was fairly simple to gauge who was in charge and who had the most clout.

Mingling with the others on the football field, he noted the distance from the football stadium to the woods. An escape during daylight was out of the question, although nightfall or when the guards changed might be doable.

The land had been carved out from a once pristine and a nearly impenetrable tangled thicket of virgin forest and underbrush, some of which remained. One side of the land sloped to a stream, which meandered for a while until it fed into a bigger stream. Animal trails snaked through the woods, patted down by countless trips of deer and other mammals. While an animal trail would be a logical path to follow, it would also be the easiest for his pursuers, so he decided natural spaces in the woods where he could run through would be a better escape route. Perhaps a fallen tree would provide a natural path, one his pursuers would overlook.

Andrey entered the stadium and led Cowboy onto the field dotted with weeds and low growing dandelions. The horse stopped to nibble at the edible flower but Andrey tugged him away.

"Ah, such a magnificent animal," Burkov said. He strutted over to Cowboy and inspected him, running his hands over Cowboy's mane, and down his shoulders.

Cowboy held his head high and blew a hot breath out of his nostrils, snorting his uneasiness. Out of the corner of his eye, he watched Burkov's movements and listened to the sounds the man made.

Cowboy had been around enough people to recognize who was good and who wasn't, and Burkov fitted into the latter category. He wanted nothing to do with this man.

When Cowboy spotted Dillon in the crowd of prisoners, his eyes got big and he whinnied softly, taking a step toward him.

Burkov jerked him back and Cowboy's head spun around. He stamped his feet and tossed his head, blowing hard through his nostrils. Burkov struggled to get the increasingly agitated horse under control, and he thought about how he'd appear to his men if he couldn't control this horse. Burkov had come prepared though.

He took out his whip, flicked his arm back, and cracked the whip in the air, testing it. Like a ring master, he made several figure eights in the air, and with all his power he cracked the stinging leather on Cowboy. The horse jumped and screamed. Burkov held tight to the reins, hitting him repeatedly with the whip while yelling angry profanities.

The shear brutality inflicted on Cowboy stunned the prisoners and the Russians. Brutalizing the enemy was one thing, but an animal? What kind of sick, twisted mind could enjoy that?

Dillon made a move but Chandler held him back. "Don't, Dillon," he hissed. "No matter what he does, don't intervene. We have to think about Holly and Cassie. Think about Amanda. We can't help them unless we live."

Dillon's muscles relaxed and agreed with Chandler's sage advice. When the time came, Burkov would get his comeuppance, and if Dillon had anything to do with it, well, it couldn't come soon enough.

After several agonizing minutes, Burkov gained control of Cowboy, and while he may have broken the horse's will to resist, he hadn't broken his spirit. Cowboy must have sensed there was a time to fight, and this wasn't it.

With Cowboy under control, Burkov tested the saddle, making sure it had been put on properly and was tight enough. He somewhat trusted his subordinates, yet he had learned saboteurs were quite clever and could engineer a hit on his life by making it look like an accident. A loose saddle could result in a fall from a horse. And if the rider hit the ground awkwardly, death or paralysis could follow. Burkov wasn't about to become a statistic.

Andrey mentally bit his lip. "Excellent work, Sir. He is ready to ride."

"Have you ridden him yet?"

"No, Sir. The pleasure is all yours." Andrey knew better than to ride the horse, especially since Burkov had mentioned it first.

Upstaging a high ranking officer never had good consequences. Andrey knew his place.

Burkov mounted Cowboy and sat tall in the saddle.

Cowboy snorted once and tossed his head. He didn't like having Burkov in the saddle any more than Dillon did.

"This is just like John Wayne in the movies," Burkov said, pleased he had shown Cowboy who was boss. He addressed the prisoners. "I shall now show you how to properly ride a horse." Burkov kicked Cowboy, prodding him to move.

Nothing happened.

Burkov lurched in the saddle and kicked Cowboy again, this time harder.

Cowboy lowered his head, waving it from side to side. He flattened his ears and his tail switched in a show of aggression.

"Go!" Burkov shouted. He jammed his heels into Cowboy's side.

Cowboy stood firm.

Burkov kicked him again, harder, more violently. "Run!" he shouted. The heat in Burkov's face rose to an elevated level, his heart beat fast, sweat broke out on his forehead. "What the hell is wrong with this animal?"

Cowboy pawed at the ground.

Burkov dismounted Cowboy and stood to his side, glaring at the animal. "Andrey, what did you do to him?"

"Nothing, Sir. I saddled him as you instructed and brought him to you."

Burkov paced the length of Cowboy, his footsteps heavy on the ground. He couldn't let a mere beast embarrass him in front of his men and the prisoners. Any indication of weakness or the possibility he was losing control could have dire consequences. He knew all about going for the jugular and dispatching a weakling who got in his way. Putting a hit on one of his adversaries required finesse and planning, and it gave him great satisfaction knowing one more obstacle was out of the picture. But Burkov never had an animal upstage him. This was new territory and it confused and scared him.

In a fit of anger, Burkov drew his pistol and sighted it at Cowboy's head. A collective low gasp came from both the prisoners and the Russian guards.

Nobody moved. Nobody said a word. Nobody breathed.

Andrey's mind raced for solutions to mitigate the tense situation, and unless he intervened, the outcome could be disastrous. He took a chance. "Colonel, may I have a word with you in private?"

Burkov shoved the pistol against Cowboy's head.

"Colonel?" Andrey said urgently.

Burkov whipped around. "What!"

"I need to speak with you in private."

"Now?"

"Yes, Sir."

"Very well. This better be good." Burkov holstered his pistol and went with Andrey. They walked a few steps away where they talked in private.

Dillon stared at Chandler. "That bastard was about to kill Cowboy."

Chandler nodded. "I know."

"Why didn't you tell him the magic phrase?"

"I thought about it, but I couldn't bring myself to tell him. Cowboy would be better off dead than with that psychopath."

Burkov strolled over to the prisoners and acted as if nothing had happened. His face was tranquil, his posture normal, his gait relaxed.

The madman had surfaced, and that was disturbing and enlightening at the same time.

CHAPTER 26

The soldiers glanced around nervously and spoke in low tones, while the American prisoners listened intently, trying to discern the subtle underlying meanings of the foreign words. While the Americans didn't understand the Russian language, they did understand the concern and worry the soldiers were showing. It was obvious Burkov had hidden the undisciplined side of himself away from his subordinates, away from his superiors, because anyone who would kill an animal for not obeying would certainly unleash his anger on unsuspecting humans.

When Colonel Burkov addressed the Americans, there was no indication he had been in the throes of a meltdown five minutes earlier. The way his demeanor changed on a dime worried Dillon.

"I suppose it is time for me to address the reason you are here. It is quite simple. America is rich in natural resources, and while Russia is equally rich, certain unforeseen factors have required us to seek additional resources. Those reasons do not need to concern you. Therefore, I will not address them."

Burkov took a breath.

"The Russian people need what you and I are standing on. Not the dirt or the grass, but the riches under the dirt, in the formations where decomposition and pressurization of decaying plant and animal life turned into oil and gas.

"We are shorthanded due to circumstances beyond my control. American men can work as well as Russian men. We need you to work on the rigs. While we cannot remunerate your time, we will treat you with compassion and make sure you are fed and clothed. Do you have any questions?"

Burkov observed the men's reactions, and while they tried to contain their displeasure, he knew otherwise.

"Good. You will be escorted back to your quarters to await further instruction. Training will start tomorrow, and you will be educated on safety and proper procedures. I sincerely hope you are satisfied we are not savages. Once we are finished, you may go back to your lives. I ask for your cooperation in all this."

Burkov dipped his chin and left.

* * *

A short time later, the guards escorted the Americans back to the classroom which was now their holding cell. Dillon, Chandler, and Ryan were huddled near a wall discussing what they had learned.

"That's it?" Ryan asked in bewilderment. "They need oil? Why didn't the Russians just increase their oil imports instead of detonating an EMP? Don't they realize how many people have died because of it?"

"I'm not an expert on world oil," Dillon said, "but I do remember reading a report about how Russian oil fields were being depleted at an alarming rate. Apparently, the money from their exports pays for their military."

"This is all starting to make sense now," Chandler said. "When I came back from my deployment, I had a job waiting for me where the discovery well was made. Talk was the oil field was huge, and I mean huge. Like the biggest in the world type of huge. All the landowners around here were going to be rich because of the oil and gas pooling laws in Texas. That includes Holly's and Amanda's land."

"I think I understand now," Dillon said. "When the EMP struck, we all were just trying to survive. Nobody was concerned about royalty checks or the oil rig sitting idly in the pasture. The Russians were waiting until the maximum number of Americans died due to natural causes, starvation, lack of medical care…whatever. They came in with their helicopters, fuel trucks, generators, and…" Dillon was deep in thought. "And that explains all the oil field equipment stacked near the school."

"But why do they need us?" Ryan asked. "Why didn't they just get more Russians to do the work?"

"I don't know," Dillon said. "I guess they are short on able-bodied men. Who knows what's happening on the world stage? Maybe there's a war somewhere. What all this tells me is the Russians aren't as well equipped as they want us to believe. There's a crack in their veneer and all we need to do is to find a way to get in."

CHAPTER 27

At Holly's house, Nico led the discussion about how they were going to rescue Dillon, Chandler, and Ryan. Voices were tense with emotion.

Reload sat by Kate's side, taking in the voice intonations and the underlying meanings. He sensed Nico had taken charge and was giving directions.

Anna sat on the floor next to Reload and placed her head on the big dog's back. At first Reload didn't know how to react to the child, so he waited for Kate's guidance. Through the tone of her voice and body language, it was clear to Reload he should tolerate the extra attention.

Holly had been outside getting a fire going in the grill so she could boil water for coffee. She had kept the coffee for a special occasion, and had planned to serve it at Cassie and Ryan's wedding, but this gathering would do just as well. Besides, they needed some semblance of normalcy in this crazy world.

Communications had been down for months and the only news came from people who had escaped the big cities, telling horror stories of what was happening.

Gangs ran rampant and controlled entire neighborhoods, routinely plundering homes rumored to still contain supplies of food and water. Hospitals had been looted of food and medicine, while veterinary offices had been stripped of cat and dog food for surviving pets.

Gossip indicated pets remaining in the cities disappeared at night. Even more disturbing were the people who raised dogs to be sold and butchered as food.

People did what they needed to survive, and Holly was thankful she had gotten out when she did. She shuddered at what might have happened to her if Dillon hadn't been there to help her when the plane clipped the Harris County Courthouse. Dillon had saved her, now it was time she returned the favor.

"Coffee's ready," she said, walking into the dining room. She poured coffee for Nico, Dorothy, and Amanda. Cassie waved her off, instead opting for a glass of cool well water which she flavored with a pinch of Tang, courtesy of the goody bag Chandler's mom had packed. Months earlier Dillon had rigged up a pulley system for the indoor well which kept the water at a constant seventy-two degrees.

After petting Reload for a while, Anna went to the living room where she perused the bookshelves for something to read. She found listening to grown-up talk quite boring. She wished Dillon was here because he always made time to talk to her and show her how things worked. He had told her a lot of stories, and since the TV was useless, Anna relished the time Dillon spent with her. There were times she wished she had a dad like Dillon.

"I'm afraid this is the last of the coffee," Holly said. She poured the last drop in Nico's cup.

"I've come up with a plan," Nico said.

All eyes were trained on Nico, and even Anna listened in from the adjoining room.

"We'll do this in layers," Nico began, "so that each person does what they are best at doing. Nobody needs to take stupid chances, so let's go around the table and assess what skills each one of us has to offer."

"My dad taught me how to shoot a rifle," Cassie said eagerly, "and also how to use a pistol to protect myself."

Dorothy piped in. "I don't have the training you have. I don't know how to shoot."

Right as Kate was about to speak, Nico stopped her. He already knew she was a crack shot. The bravery she demonstrated at the Alamo spoke volumes. The discussion was about to take a turn for the worse and he needed to nip it in the bud. "Dorothy, you can be the lookout. Can you do that?"

"Yes."

"Great. Okay, listen up. This is what we are going to do to rescue Dillon."

At the mention of Dillon's name, Anna closed the book she had been reading. She moved away from the bookshelves and tiptoed to the foyer next to the dining room, just out of sight of the grownups. While Nico laid out his plan, Anna recalled a conversation she had with Dillon when he showed her how to shoot. They were in the pasture, where Dillon practiced shooting.

"Why is it so long?" Anna asked, referring to the lightweight pistol.

"This is a Walther P22 with a silencer on it that makes it look longer. When you shoot, it will be quiet like in the spy movies." Dillon showed her the ten-round stainless steel magazine then inserted it into the gun's handle. He pulled the slide back then released it.

"Why did you pull back the top of the gun and let it go?" Anna asked.

"The top of the gun is the slide. I pulled it back so it will take a cartridge–a bullet–from the magazine, and put it in the barrel for firing. You only have to do it one time after the magazine is inserted. Do you understand?"

Anna nodded.

"After you fire, the slide snaps back and automatically pushes another cartridge into the barrel so you can shoot faster." Dillon didn't bring up the issue of recoil since this pistol's recoil was minimal, even for a child.

"Can I try?"

"Of course." Dillon put ear protection on Anna then placed the gun in her hands. He positioned her for an accurate shot at the target.

Anna held her arms straight like Dillon told her to. She locked her right elbow, left hand supporting her right one.

"Keep your eyes open, and hold the pistol tight. Keep your trigger finger off the trigger until you're ready to shoot."

Anna aimed the pistol at the target and peered through the sights. She pulled the trigger and a bullseye appeared on the five yard target.

"Keep going until the slide locks back. That means there are no more bullets in the magazine."

Anna fired all the rounds until the slide locked back. "Why did it do that?" she asked.

"It's out of bullets."

Anna accepted the explanation without further questions.

"Good girl!" He patted her on the back.

Anna gave the pistol back to Dillon and he made it safe. He retrieved the target and showed her. "This is very good. All bullseyes. You're a regular Annie Oakley, I do believe. Do you want to show your mom?"

"I can't wait to show her."

The memory was fresh in her mind, and as the conversation continued at the dining room table, Anna recalled the other story Dillon had told her about Denmark during WWII. The funny names of Copenhagen and Gestapo didn't make much sense to her, but Dillon told her about a spy who used a .22 pistol with a silencer to rescue people.

Good guy, .22, silencer, and escape were the only important details that mattered to her. She'd show the adults she could do what big girls did. Her heart beat faster and her little palms dampened at the thought of what she had planned.

She went upstairs and retrieved her pink Hello Kitty backpack. With cat-like movements, Anna crept down the stairs to the room where the guns were hidden under the hardwood floor. She stopped and listened to the adults talking. Good, they were still busy.

Taking a chair, she scooted it to a shelf where the Phillip's screwdriver was located. Kneeling, she pulled back the rug and spotted the board she had seen Dillon remove. She worked the deck screw until it popped out of the board. She removed the board, then another one, until she found the hidden stash.

She was confused by all the boxes of ammunition, long barreled guns and some that looked like military weapons she had seen on TV. Tentatively, she pushed the rifles to the side. There, she spotted what she was after.

Her heart pounded.

It was the spy gun Dillon had let her shoot. It was in a holster and only the tip of the silencer peeked out. A thick rubber band was wrapped around five shiny silver magazines. She picked them up and tested their weight. They were heavy so they must be loaded.

Anna unzipped her Hello Kitty backpack and adjusted the gun and magazines until they settled on the bottom. She fluffed her jacket to conceal them.

As she was about to replace the floorboards, she remembered hearing about the cyclone fence around the school. She'd need something for that too. She spotted the knife Dillon had used to demonstrate how to cut wire. Using both hands, she picked up the sheathed knife with the steel nub sheath that fit through the hole in the knife blade. When both were fitted together properly, it made heavy duty scissors. She placed the sheathed knife in the pink backpack and zipped it up.

Anna worked quickly to replace the floorboards. She put the Phillips screwdriver back in place and returned the chair back to its original spot, just in time too.

"Does everybody understand what to do?" Nico asked. He made eye contact with each woman to make sure everybody was on the same page.

"We do," Holly replied.

"Okay then. Gear up and put on the darkest clothes you have." Nico stood. "I'll get the truck."

"What about me?" Anna asked. "Am I dressed okay?" She had on a pair of blue jeans and a green top.

"You're staying here," Nico said.

"What? No!" Anna exclaimed. "I'm too scared to stay here. I'll be all by myself. The boogie man might get me. And there's no light or TV and—"

"There's no other choice," Nico said. "It's too dangerous for you to come with us. Reload will stay with you. Right, Kate?"

"Sure. That's fine," she said. "Reload is good company. And he won't let anybody in the house."

Anna lowered her head, and the fake tears came easily. "Suppose you don't come back. Then what do I do?" Through red-rimmed eyes she begged her mother for support. "Let me come with you.

Please. I'll be quiet and I won't be any trouble. I promise." She sniffled and waited for a response.

"Nico, Anna's a brave little girl," Dorothy said. "She won't be any trouble. I assure you."

Nico scratched the side of his head. "Well," he thought a moment. "I guess she can come with us, although it's against my better judgment. I suppose it would be scary for her to stay here all alone. But make sure she stays quiet and out of the way."

"Thank you," Dorothy said. "She won't be any trouble. I promise."

"It'll be dusk soon. Meet out front before then. I'll bring the truck around."

CHAPTER 28

A mile south of the school, Nico cut the lights to the truck and went off road. The truck bounced along the uneven ground, the shocks squeaked, and Nico prayed the woods would absorb the sound. He spotted a thicket suitable for hiding the truck. Cutting the wheel, he backed the truck in to make it easier for a hasty getaway if needed. He cut the engine and pocketed the keys.

The sun's rays touched the tops of the pine trees, casting a warm glow feathering skyward. A breeze came by, brushing the oaks, and weathered leaves floated to the ground.

"Holly," Nico said, "do you have the spare key just in case something goes wrong?"

"I do."

Nico glanced over his shoulder at the women sitting in the back seat. "I need everyone to stay quiet and to watch where you walk. We don't need anyone spraining an ankle. I want everyone to walk single file behind me. Holly, you'll bring up the rear. Dorothy, keep an eye out for anything unusual. Anna, you stay quiet. Understood?"

Anna nodded. She pursed her lips together, put her fingers to her lips and made a motion with her thumb and index finger like she was zipping her lips closed.

"Let's get out of the truck and take a few minutes to go over the plan. We need to be in place by the time it gets dark."

Nico exited the truck and carefully pushed the door into place. The click echoed louder than he would have liked. "Shhh," he whispered. He listened for footsteps where none should be or the sounds of guns being readied for firing, or any foreign sounds among nature's whisperings.

"Anna," Nico said, "you stay next to the truck and don't move."

Satisfied they were alone, he gathered the group. He spotted a bare patch of ground, took a stick, and drew the perimeter of the school compound in the dirt. While Nico had never seen the school, Holly had found an old high school yearbook and showed it to him so he could understand the layout. He drew the layout, including the football field.

"I'm guessing the Russians will have one guard stationed at the football stadium concession stand. Here," he said tapping the ground, "at the top of the stands. The guard will have a good view of the area around the football field, but won't be able to see the other side of the school. That's where we will be. Now, I'm also guessing they will have constructed guard towers on this side of the school. It won't be as high as the one in the football field. We'll have to watch out for them.

"Remember, darkness is our friend. Don't be afraid of the dark. But we need to work fast while it's dusk when the light plays tricks on people's eyes, and before night vision glasses are useful. Also, the woods are thick, and the trees can stop most high-powered bullets."

"If we get separated, how will we get back to the truck?" Holly asked.

Nico unzipped his backpack and took out several light sticks. "On the way there, I'll drop a few light sticks on the ground with the skinny end pointed in the right direction where the truck is parked. I'll place them so they can't easily be seen unless you're looking for them."

Once the issue of getting lost had been addressed, Nico took a few minutes to go over strategy and what to do in case an epic fail occurred or if someone was captured or injured. "I know what I've said may be disturbing, but we have to consider the big picture. Is everyone on board?"

He scanned the group to make sure they understood what was expected of them. "Good. Let's go. I'll lead the way. Dorothy, you keep Anna close to you." Nico glanced to where he had told Anna to stay. A worried expression spread across his face.

Anna was nowhere in sight.

Nico palmed his head and let his hand stay there. He mumbled a string of obscenities that would have shocked a hardened sailor.

He ended it with a pronounced, "Crap!"

* * *

Anna had plans other than to wait around for the grownups to decide what to do. Time was 'a wasting, as her mother always said, so she shouldered her Hello Kitty backpack, slid away from the truck, skidded around to the other side where she couldn't be seen, and dashed into the woods.

She had been in the woods near Holly's house several times, but she had always been with someone. This evening while she walked toward the school, the trees seemed especially large and foreboding and the breeze whistling through the leaves was more worrying. Her imagination ran wild with images of the boogie man and wild animals lurking behind the trees in front of her, waiting to snatch her.

Further she walked away from the safety of the group, closer to the school. Once when something scurried nearby, she let out a surprised yelp. She cupped her hand over her mouth to muffle a scream.

Go away! she told the imaginary demons.

Gathering her courage, she found a trail leading to the school. Finally, the buildings appeared. Crouching down, she ran to where the bushes came to within a few yards of the cyclone fence. She noticed a strange type of wire looping against the fence. She figured it was barbed wire, but there were no barbs. How dumb could those soldiers be?

The sun dipped beneath the horizon and within seconds, the land became quieter.

Darker.

Scarier.

UNDEFEATED WORLD

Crouched next to the bushes, Anna made herself as little as possible, listening to muffled voices of the Russians interspersed with laughter. She flinched at the sound of a gunshot.

Her eyes roamed over the compound for Dillon, and she listened for American voices. A group of men was sitting on the ground next to the main entrance of the high school. Squinting, she spied Dillon. Next to him were Ryan and Chandler. She took off her backpack and lowered it, thinking the pink color might be noticeable. Hunched over, she ran along the edge of the woods, taking cover where she could until she found a spot close to the cyclone fence.

The guards in the tower scanned the compound, watching the prisoners for any type of movement indicating an attempted escape. A new guard approached the tower and yelled something in Russian to his comrade stationed above him. He slung his rifle over his back and proceeded to climb the ladder.

Anna took advantage of the guards being distracted while they changed shifts.

Belly crawling on the ground, dragging her backpack, she inched to the fence. While she had brought along the special knife to cut the fence, as luck would have it, the fence had not been properly secured.

As she was about to squeeze her tiny body through the opening, she realized her backpack was too big. She removed the knife from her backpack and took it out of the sheath. She hooked the forward end of the blade over the metal nub to create a pair of wire cutting scissors, just like Dillon had done.

The first clip of the fence was quite easy, but she had to use all her strength on the remaining ones. Sitting back, she estimated she had made a hole big enough for an adult to slip through if they pushed the wires to the side. A tiny girl like Anna could slip through without a problem.

She had not been detected.

So far, so good.

She wiggled through the opening and pushed her hand against the shiny ribbon wire to shove it aside. A stab of searing pain gripped her and she instinctively jerked her hand back. She had sliced the fleshy part of her thumb. A thin line of oozing blood trickled down her hand and dripped to the ground. Anna bit her trembling lip, determined not to cry.

Thinking she was low enough, she wiggled through, but a wire caught on the back part of her shirt. She tugged, trying to get free. She twisted back and forth, pushed up and down. The wire sprung loose, slapping her back. She fell to the ground and landed flat on her belly with a pitiful cry. Anna remained motionless for a few moments until she calmed down. Pushing up on her hands and knees, her back stung like the dickens. The more she moved the worse it stung. She reached around under her shirt and her fingers came in contact with something warm and wet.

Her fingers were covered in blood. Her hand was bleeding and now so was her back. She sniffled and wanted to cry.

Anna thought about what she should do.

She searched her backpack and found a few Band-Aids in a side pocket. She wiped her bloody hand on her jeans, tore the Band-Aids open with her teeth, then placed them over the cut.

Even with her hand bandaged, it still throbbed, and she had no idea what to do about her back.

Stifling a cry, she grabbed her backpack and glanced at the guards. They were in the tower smoking cigarettes and laughing, unaware of Anna.

She slipped through the opening and dashed to the nearest shadow. Dillon and the others had not yet noticed her. If only she could get their attention. She picked up a rock and threw it, only for it to land feet away. She threw another one, but wasn't strong enough to hit anybody.

With her backpack secured, she took a chance and darted to the group. Like a baseball player sliding into home plate, Anna slid feet first into Dillon, startling him. He whipped around.

"Anna! What are you doing here?" Dillon scanned the area, checking if the guards saw what had happened. They were still busy smoking and talking in the guard tower. Dillon put his hands under her arms and whisked her to the middle of the group. "Make some cover." The other men positioned their bodies to hide Anna. Dillon noticed her bleeding hand, and her shirt stained with blood. "You're hurt. What happened? Why are you here? How'd you get in here?" He rapidly fired off the questions before Anna had time to answer. Then he scolded her. "You shouldn't have come here."

"Don't be mad at me," Anna said. "I'm here to rescue you."

"What? You? How? Where's your mom? We need to get you to

a doctor. You're hurt."

"I'm not hurt that bad," Anna lied. Her back was throbbing. "I remembered what you taught me. Check my backpack. It has everything you need."

Dillon tore open the backpack to find a Walther P22 with a silencer. He pocketed the extra magazines and stuffed the knife in his waistband. Dillon patted Anna on the head. "Don't ever do this again. Do you understand?"

Anna didn't answer.

"Do you?"

She nodded.

"Good," he said gruffly. "Thank you, though."

Anna gave him the thumbs up sign.

"Did you come here alone?"

"No. Holly and Nico, and my mom are—"

"Who's Nico?"

"He's Kate Chandler's boyfriend."

"Kate must be Chandler's sister?"

Anna nodded. "Holly, Nico, Kate, my mom, and Amanda are in the woods not far from here. They were going to rescue you, but I beat them to it."

"Stay down, and stay behind me. That's an order." Dillon addressed Chandler, Ryan, and Larry, who were sitting next to him. "Chandler, you're best rifle shot, so I'll get you a rifle. Ryan, give Anna some first aid on her hand. Larry, you help Ryan."

A guard walking along the perimeter of the school noticed the commotion in the circle of men. "What's going on here?" He used his gun butt to push the Americans out of the way as he plowed toward the center of the group.

When the guard saw Anna, he said, "What the—"

CHAPTER 29

Dillon slid behind the guard and cupped his left hand tightly over the man's mouth and nose, forcing his head back and exposing his vulnerable neck. With one deft movement, Dillon sliced the man's throat, severing the vocal cords and the carotid artery. The guard gurgled and struggled feebly before slumping to the ground where the Americans held him down. He bled out in seconds and lost consciousness. Death soon followed.

Ryan had put his hands over Anna's eyes so she couldn't witness the gruesome death.

Chandler took the guard's AK-74 and crouched in a huddled position. Now armed, he scouted their escape routes, noting the four guard towers, two of which had a good view of the compound. The rear of the school appeared to be the best option due to the short distance needed to run for cover in the woods. Still, the odds of outrunning two machine guns weren't good. Chandler didn't want to go there.

"Dillon," Chandler said, "I can take out a machine gunner once the silence is broken. I won't have time to take out both guard towers before they get shots off."

"What do you suggest?" Dillon asked.

"I think our best route to escape is the back wall. Use your silenced .22 to take out the second gunner. You'll be able to get close enough for a good shot."

Dillon nodded his understanding. "Good plan. Wait for my signal to proceed. If I don't give the signal, you don't move. We can't afford to fail."

The guards in the tower were preoccupied and had not yet clicked on the floodlights, and had forgone their hourly rounds. Most of the Russians were inside the school enjoying the benefits of electricity supplied by portable Russian generators not affected by the EMP, whiling away their time playing chess and card games.

Low clouds darkened the moon, plunging the East Texas woods into darkness. Crickets chirped, and a light breeze cooled down the compound.

Dillon figured it was now or never.

He headed toward a guard tower and placed one foot on the wooden ladder, swearing under his breath when the board creaked. He decided to trade silence for speed so he could move high enough to be covered by the platform's shadow in case the neighboring guard glanced in his direction.

Dillon glanced up and listened. This was not the movies, so there was no trap door to overcome. This was life or death, and one wrong move could result in catastrophe. The towers had been hastily constructed with lumber being their primary component. Dillon reckoned the Russians had probably hijacked any contractor unfortunate enough to be on the premises when they raided the builder's supply store.

All was still and quiet. Dillon took a deep breath, exhaling it, then another one, focusing on what he needed to do. He filtered out external and internal distractions.

Focus. Breathe. Repeat.

The top of Dillon's head breached the plane of the tower floor and he stretched to get a good view. A Russian soldier sat in a chair facing away from him. He had earbuds in and was listening to some type of American rap music, his foot tapping to the beat while he moved his head in time with the music.

Dillon lifted a foot to the next ladder rung, his body stiffening at the unmistakable feeling of a cold rifle barrel jabbing him hard in the back. He froze, and a brief thought crossed his mind he could whip around and shove the rifle away before whoever it was got a shot off. But if a shot was fired, all hell would break out, and Americans could get killed, including Anna. Before Dillon took any action, the guard spoke.

A heavily accented Russian voice said, "Be quiet and do exactly as I say."

Dillon nodded. The rifle barrel in his back was quite persuasive.

"Are you Dillon Stockdale?"

"I am."

"You were about to walk into a trap. The ground over there is a minefield." The man shoved the rifle barrel harder into Dillon's back, forcing him to step off the ladder.

"Who are you?" Dillon turned around, and recognized the man as the Russian who set fire to Holly's house.

"My name is Andrey Koshkin." He lowered his AK-74.

"You son of a bitch. You're the one who torched the house."

"No. I only made it look that way."

"Liar," Dillon said, testing him. He suspected the house had not burned, yet wanted to confirm it. "I saw the smoke."

"Smoke from bushes only. House fires cause black smoke. The smoke was not black."

Dillon mulled that over, knowing Andrey was being truthful since grass fires resulted in gray smoke. "Did you see any women in the house?"

"I did. I found them in a hidden room. The little girl who was with them just gave you a backpack."

"Why are you helping us?"

"Colonel Burkov is a killer and a madman. I want no part of this. If I help you, will you help me?"

"Are you defecting?" Dillon asked.

"Yes."

"Then I'll do whatever I can to help you. If you double cross us, I swear I'll—"

"I assure you I will not."

Dillon accepted Andrey's answer.

"Put on my coat."

"Why?"

"Just do it. From a distance you'll look like one of us."

Dillon shrugged on Andrey's coat.

"Come with me." Andrey motioned for Dillon to follow him. They moved over to where the prisoners were.

Chandler saw Dillon and the Russian soldier walking toward them. Dillon showed no sign of distress, yet Chandler wasn't one to be fooled. If this was a trick, he'd be ready. He kept the safety off his AK-74, positioning the rifle so he could fire it.

"Everything is okay," Dillon said when he reached the group. "Meet Andrey Koshkin. He'll be helping us."

"Can he be trusted?" Chandler asked, dubious about the man's motives.

"He's already helped Holly and the others."

"How?"

"I'll explain later."

"Dillon, you take the AK from your friend and pretend to be the following guard for a service mission I am leading," Andrey said. "Make sure everyone knows to follow my footsteps exactly once we get to the other side of the fence."

Dillon and Chandler passed the instructions to the other Americans.

The group walked single file as directed. Ryan carried Anna on his back. He'd sacrifice his life before he let the little girl be harmed by an exploding mine.

Dillon brought up the rear, with Chandler in front of him as they walked toward the gate. The grass appeared normal except for a slight difference in color of a few blades of grass sticking up as straight as a metal yardstick. Chandler recalled what a sergeant taught him in camouflage school: *There are no straight lines in nature*. He understood what those odd colored blades of grass were: hidden triggers for the land mines.

Two-thirds of the way across the minefield, one of the guards stationed in a tower called out angrily to them. Dillon's eyes flicked to Andrey for a cue.

Andrey swiveled around, brought up his AK, sighted the guard, and fired. He missed. Dillon tossed his AK to Chandler, knowing the trained sniper had better skills than he did. Chandler sprang into action and leveled the rifle at the guard. In the moment it took the guard to understand what was happening, Chandler fired. The single shot struck the guard in the face. He was dead before he hit the floor of the tower.

The floodlights flickered on.

The prisoners' escape had been compromised.

Russian shouts rang out.

"Hurry," Andrey ordered, without bothering to keep his voice low. "We have to hurry!"

The single file broke up as prisoners panicked, rushing to the woods. More shots were fired and Dillon ducked, but the muzzle flashes coming from the woods confused him. Ah, he understood now. His friends were in the woods.

Suddenly a loud explosion rocked the ground. Dust and debris flew into the air like missiles, and Dillon was thrown to the ground. Stunned by the blast, it took him a few seconds to get his wits about himself. A wet and warm liquid dripped down the side of his face. He wiped it away with his fingers and was shocked to find his hand covered in blood. Dillon palpated his scalp and face checking for injuries. Finding none, he made sure he had all his limbs, so the blood must be someone else's. Feet away, a bloody corpse was face down in the dirt, arms and legs blown off. Dillon scanned the other survivors and accounted for Chandler and Ryan.

God help them all. They were going to need it.

A stampede of blurred forms rushed the compound.

Dillon fumbled with his .22, handling it like he was drunk.

"Don't shoot!" a man yelled coming up to Dillon. "I'm Nico Bell. I'm with Holly and the others."

"Are they okay?" Dillon fought to clearly speak, fighting the muzziness in his head.

"Yes. I told them to stay in the woods in case anything went wrong."

Andrey Koshkin appeared and Nico spoke to him in Russian. While Dillon didn't understand the conversation, it was apparent they were fervently discussing the situation.

Shots were fired.

"We need to go now!" Nico ordered.

"I'll cover you," Andrey said. "Go. And may God by with you."

"And with you," Dillon said.

Andrey crouched and readied his weapon. "Be careful. There is a spy among your people. I do not know who it is. It was not by accident you were captured at the wedding. Colonel Burkov makes it his practice to recruit spies in every territory."

The ragged survivors dashed out of the compound and into the woods where Holly and the others were waiting. Some of the American prisoners decided it was safer to scatter in different directions than to stay together, and Dillon didn't fight them on their decision. He wished them luck.

"A snapped twig at the wrong time could get us killed," he said to the group, taking the lead. "If we are separated, head to Rally Point A. If you don't know where that is, follow Chandler or me. It appears we have some help, so hold your fire until we are fired upon or until we give an order."

Chandler spoke urgently, instructing the survivors what to do. He helped to lead the way, and using the glow sticks as a guide, pocketing them as he ran, they made it back to where the truck had been hidden.

Chandler, Larry, and Ryan–who still had Anna on his back–followed Dillon to where the women were hiding.

The convoy of survivors moved cautiously through the woods as sporadic gunfire from the other side of the school picked up in intensity. Strings of thuds were followed by the occasional long twang of a ricochet heading off to parts unknown.

Chandler raised his hand in the universal gesture to stop. Shadowy figures moved in the woods, dashing behind trees to take cover. One person peered out from a large pine, and Chandler focused his senses on the person. Obviously a woman by her small stature and the way she moved, and there was something familiar about her. He recognized her. "Kate? Is that you?"

"It's me," Kate said, stepping away from the tree.

Chandler gave his sister a brief hug. There was no time for an emotional reunion, so hugs and tears of happiness would have to wait for later. Kate stepped over to Nico and hugged him.

"You know him?" Chandler asked.

"He's my fiancée."

"Say what?" Chandler gave his apparent future brother-in-law a critical glance.

"I'll explain later. He can handle himself and can probably teach you guys a thing or two."

Chandler gestured a peace sign to Nico.

"Listen, everybody," Kate said. "We have a truck hitched to a hay wagon. It's nearby and we need to get to it before it comes within range of the Russian's rifles."

"Andrey," Dillon said, "stay next to me until I have a chance to explain you to the group." Since Andrey had made no attempt to clarify the location of Rally Point A, Dillon felt he could trust him, yet the spy issue was still in the forefront of his mind.

As they approached the truck with the hay wagon, Dillon stopped, bent at the waist, and put his hands on his thighs. He gasped for air, fighting the urge to heave. It had been a long time since he had pushed his body to the brink of exhaustion. As the group gathered, he mentally checked each one off his list.

Who was the spy? Who among this group would turn traitor and put the lives of fellow Americans in danger? They had escaped, they were alive, but they would never be truly safe until the spy was exposed and punished.

There was only one punishment for spying.

Death.

Whoever it was would pay one way or the other, and Dillon planned to make sure they did. He had taken an oath to uphold the constitution of the United States, and by God, he was going to do that.

CHAPTER 30

The group clambered aboard the hay wagon and squeezed in together, legs hanging off the flatbed trailer.

"Kate," Dillon said, "this is our plan. You and Nico take Andrey Koshkin to Rally Point A. He is on our side and can give you an idea of what we'll be facing. Find one of the VFW guys and have him recruit every rifleman he knows. Tell them to bring their own weapons and ammo. Chandler and I will ride with you for a couple of miles, then get off and try to delay the Russians for a while."

Kate nodded. "Got it. To let you know, Andrey was the soldier who saved Holly's house and our lives. We'll take good care of him."

"I already know, but thanks for verifying."

"I hope the truck can handle the weight of all these people," Nico said. He suspiciously eyed the truck then hopped in the driver's seat. Kate rode shotgun.

"Don't worry," Dillon assured him. "The truck can carry a lot of hay. The only thing to remember is that you'll need extra braking distance with all that extra weight."

Nico handed Chandler the AR-15A2 rifle he had been holding. "I understand you can get some use out of this." Nico then passed him a bandolier of 20-round magazines. "These are loaded with 77 grainers."

"Thanks. It's my favorite sniping ammo," Chandler said. He placed the bandolier over his head and across his chest. "One more thing, Nico. Take good care of my sis."

Kate rolled her eyes. "I know how to take care of myself just fine."

"I'll take care of her," Nico said. "You can bet on it."

* * *

Minutes later, Nico had pulled the truck onto the highway, driving only as fast as he thought was safe without losing anyone out of the flatbed. Maneuvering the truck was about as easy as running through waist high water. Once they were about two miles from the compound, Dillon rapped on the truck to get Nico's attention. He motioned for Nico to pull over.

"Time for us to cause a diversion," Dillon said. "Come on Chandler, let's go." Both men hopped off the trailer and disappeared into the woods.

Nobody spoke as Nico drove along the country road. Sporadic gunfire echoed in the distance, and Nico said a silent prayer to keep Dillon and Chandler safe. Minutes passed, and Nico slowed the truck, worried about the pair of headlights coming in his direction. "Kate, let me handle this. If anything goes wrong start shooting."

Kate nodded. "I wonder who it could be?"

"No telling." Nico rested his hand on his handgun, preparing to draw it if necessary. He squinted as the old car ambled closer. "Who around here drives a POS like that?"

"*That* POS is an egg yolk yellow 1973 Ford Gran Torino," Kate said, "and I'm guessing it's stocked with a case of warm beer. Pull up to it, but let's be cautious, just in case I'm wrong."

The old Ford pulled alongside the truck, and a satisfied grin spread across Kate's face.

The driver of the Ford rolled down the window. "I thought the party was at Holly Hudson's house. We decided to follow the lights and the gunshots to find out where the action is in this one horse town." Uncle Billy tossed a grin at Nico then took a long pull on a warm beer.

"I thought that was you, Uncle Billy," Kate said. "Luke too?"

"Yup, I'm here," Luke said, leaning out the window. "I didn't want Uncle Billy to have all the fun!"

"Are y'all here to party or to fight?"

"Both!"

"You can help us by picking up Dillon and Chandler." Kate waited for Nico's approval.

"Who am I to say no?"

"They're back that way." Kate hitched her thumb in the direction where the two ran into the woods. "On second thought, I'm coming with you. I don't want them to overshoot and run into the Russians. Nico, you know the way to the rally point."

Before Nico had time to protest, Kate had swung open the door of the truck and dashed to the Gran Torino.

"Be careful, Kate," Nico said, worry lines etching his face. "I need you to stay safe."

Uncle Billy opened the driver's door, got out, and stepped over to the trunk. He popped the trunk and took out three fully automatic M-4 carbines with magazine bags. "Don't worry. We'll be careful. These are the real deal." Uncle Billy turned one of the carbines over and tapped the automatic option on the selector.

Nico nodded his approval.

* * *

Crouched in the woods, Dillon and Chandler weighed their options on how to slow down the Russians.

"What's the plan?" Dillon said. "I don't have a lot of ammo."

"My AR with this type of ammo," Chandler held up a bullet, "is good out to six hundred yards, even without a scope. I shot your AK-74, and it's dead on to about three hundred yards." Chandler shifted positions. "I'll go to the top of the hill so I can control the road and the field beyond. I'm guessing they'll take cover and send a group to flank me. They'll probably have night vision and body armor, so at distance, shoot single shots at their head or pelvis."

"Good thinking," Dillon replied. "A pelvis hit means they'll lose their mobility, but can still pull a trigger. Be sure to take cover."

"Right. If they get too close you can use the full auto position. Replenish your ammo with theirs. Stay low, and if they are silhouetted by the moon, shoot. Got it?"

"Yeah," Dillon said. "We can make it happen. Remember, we have a reason to live. I've got Holly and Cassie, who's going to be a mother. You've got Amanda and the rest of your family. Focus on the task and we'll get there. Let's not forget Anna showed incredible bravery. Remember what she did for us." Dillon was a bit sharp, but he had to be sure Chandler's head was in the game. "Good luck."

"Good luck to you too," Chandler said.

* * *

Chandler stationed himself at the top of the hill, using scattered boulders for cover. In the distance about twenty men followed a Russian armored vehicle. A man holding what appeared to be giant binoculars was standing in the open hatch of the vehicle, exposing his head and torso. Those giant binoculars were in fact Thermal Night Vision, which could track movements of warm bodies, including Chandler's and Dillon's.

Chandler rolled over on his stomach and set his mechanical rear sight on five hundred yards, waiting for the slow moving vehicle to enter his selected kill zone. He identified the Russian standing in the vehicle as his target. Chandler pressed his cheek against the smooth stock and took up the slack in the trigger. He swept off the safety, took up the slack, and pulled the trigger. The instant the bullet jerked the man's head, the thermal binoculars flew out of his hand and landed on the top of the vehicle. Chandler used Kentucky elevation to put one in the device, shattering it into useless glass and metal.

Now they were on even terms.

Taking aim, Chandler first selected officers and machine gunners, snap shooting the remainder.

Dillon watched the master in action, and waited for his own turn at bat. Five men broke the horizon of the hill, silhouetted by the moonlight. Dillon cursed the AK sights which were nearly useless at night. He regretted forgetting to ask Chandler for tips on sighting at night. Regardless, he angled the sights to get the maximum amount of moonlight. When ready, he pretended he was on the range shooting steel, where each steel disk represented a head shot.

Three men went down. Two were still at large. Dillon listened for any careless movement the men might make to give away their position.

Twenty yards to his right, the sound of something large slipping on gravel got his attention. Dillon switched to full auto and fired, emptying the magazine. He inserted a full magazine and racked the bolt carrier.

"Weapon down!" The order was laced in a heavy Russian accent.

Dillon froze. There was no time for indecision.

He thought quickly and made a motion to throw his weapon down. In one deft movement, he launched himself to the ground, twisted his body around and emptied several rounds into the soldier.

The Russian soldier collapsed to the ground, and in one last desperate attempt he swung his own AK in Dillon's direction, only to be met by a final life-ending bullet to the head.

Dillon gathered the soldier's ammo to replenish his dwindling supply, and as he was gathering the ammo, the hair on his arms prickled. Footsteps approached. Dillon pivoted around ready to send a blast of bullets.

Chandler appeared on the horizon, and Dillon let out the breath he had been holding.

"Thank God it was only you," Dillon said.

"I should have alerted you."

"No worries."

"Let's gather the spoils and get outta here," Chandler said.

"The load is too heavy and will slow us down. Let's hide what we can't carry then leave."

Once Dillon and Chandler had gathered the ammo and guns, they picked a hollow log to hide their bounty in, then headed to the road where a car idled toward them. Chandler recognized the poor driving.

"Did someone call for a yellow cab?" Uncle Billy asked in his best smartass dialect. Kate sat shotgun while Luke was in the back seat.

"I can't say I did," Dillon said, scratching his head. He didn't recognize the driver, but from the way Chandler was acting, the newcomer was on the up and up. "I'll take the ride nonetheless."

Luke threw the door open. "I'm Luke. Hop in." He went around to the back of the car and popped the trunk lid with the set of extra keys his uncle had procured for him.

Chandler introduced his sister, his uncle, and his brother to Dillon.

"Nice to meet y'all," Dillon said.

"Come see our newfound treasure." Luke gestured for Dillon and Chandler to come over. Inside were two rifles, two pistols, two combat vests, and four grenades. A bar-b-que MRE rounded out the bounty.

"Uncle Billy?" Chandler yelled. "Where'd you get this?"

"Well, once upon a time there was a slight detour—"

"We need the condensed version."

Uncle Billy huffed. "The long and short of it was while driving here I got a doozy of a headache so I stopped at a gas station that was open to buy pain reliever. But the owner wasn't very hospitable because he decided to relieve me of my life, which I can tell you I didn't take kindly to, so as of now he's somewhere near the pearly gates, or the other ones down under, maybe the ones near Australia, 'cause parts of that country are about as close as you can get to Hades, although parts of West Texas comes in a close second. Davy Crocket had it right when he said, you may all go to Hell and I shall go to Texas." Uncle Billy was met with blank looks. "Oh, never mind. Since I couldn't let good ammo, guns, and gear go to waste, I did the proper thing and now they're in the back of my car. That's it in a nutshell. Besides, don't mess with Texas, and don't mess with Uncle Billy."

"Thank you for that extraordinarily awesome rendition of your trip, Uncle Billy," Chandler said. "Let's head back to the hollow log and top off this trunk load."

"Smart aleck," Uncle Billy said with a hint of mischief in his voice.

"Uncle Billy, I pity the person who does mess with you."

CHAPTER 31

Upon their arrival at Rally Point A, the group sought out familiar faces. Hugs and thanks for finding one another safe followed.

Ryan, with Larry by his side who was holding Anna, asked if anyone had medical supplies. "We have an injured girl who needs medical assistance."

"I'm a veterinarian," a man said. "Can I help?"

Ryan approached the man. "I was in med school before the grid went down, and I can handle it. Do you have any medical supplies?"

"I've got a nylon bag with various first aid items, some blankets, and a tarp."

"That'll do. Thank you."

Ryan shook out the blanket and put it on the ground. Larry gently placed Anna on the blanket.

Dorothy came running up, emotionally overwhelmed at finding her daughter. An expression of horror spread across her face when she saw her. She knelt next to Anna and touched her forehead. "Baby, what happened?" Before Anna had time to answer, Dorothy threw an angry glance at Dillon. "What have you done to her? You promised you'd keep her safe."

Dillon opened his mouth to explain, but Ryan answered, "It's not as bad as it looks. All she needs is a few stitches and a good antiseptic." He dug around in the nylon bag searching for the items he needed. "She'll be fine, I promise."

"Your daughter is a hero, Dorothy," Dillon said. "You should be proud of her."

"Is that true?" Dorothy gazed upon Anna with a mixture of motherly love and confusion.

Anna nodded. "I helped break them out, Mommy. I heard them talk about a spy and I couldn't let anything happen."

Dorothy gasped at the revelation. "A spy? Here? Who?"

"We don't know who it is," Dillon said.

"Oh." Dorothy glanced at the ground then put an index finger to her face, rubbing her cheek. "I, uh, I don't know anything about it." She flicked her eyes to Dillon. "I'm just glad my daughter is okay."

While Ryan stitched up Anna, Dillon stepped away and motioned for Chandler to join him and Holly. "Gather the people we can trust and ask them to meet me at the pecan tree, over there." Dillon jerked his head in the direction of the tree. "Specifically, Cassie, Amanda, Nico, Luke, and Uncle Billy. Once Ryan is finished with Anna, we'll talk with him."

"Dillon," Holly said, "I need to talk to you."

"What about?"

"I had to tell Larry his wife died at the house when the Russians ambushed us."

"How'd he take it?"

"Not good. He couldn't believe it at first, and after the initial shock wore off, he started crying and swore he'd kill as many Russians as he could to get back at them for what they did." Holly stepped closer to Dillon and leaned into him. "There's been a lot of rumors about who the spy is. By now, Larry is ready to kill anyone who looks guilty."

Dillon rubbed the stubble on his chin. "We can't afford to have a hair trigger temper on an operation requiring stealth. I need you to stay with Larry and to keep an eye on him. Can you do that?"

"Of course."

"When the Russians attack, he'll be able to channel his anger and take out as many as he can."

"Okay. Also, you need to hear Nico and Kate's story before assigning tasks." Holly stopped talking as people approached her and Dillon. Addressing Nico, she said, "Can you give Dillon a brief rundown on what happened at the Alamo?"

"Sure," Nico said. He gave a short recap of their Alamo experience, tactics, shootout, and Kate's bravery, along with the world of drug dealers.

Chandler leaned into Dillon and whispered in his ear. Dillon nodded in agreement.

"Gather 'round, everybody, and listen up." Dillon said. "We are going for a two-pronged attack. Mission A will be to defend this area, while Mission B will be to attack the Russian base at the school. If your mission goes badly, take the wounded and survivors to Rally Point B until the rest of us can meet up with you. Cassie and Ryan will proceed with the children and any non-participants to Rally Point B. Use tarps and brush to camouflage your group so the Russian drones do not discover your location. Uncle Billy will supply you with an M-4 or an AK-74. I need to address everyone else now, so good luck, and God speed to you all."

As the meeting broke up, Dillon took Holly by the elbow and guided her to a spot out of earshot of the others.

"What's going on?" she asked.

"I hate to say it, but I'm convinced Dorothy is the traitor. I'm guessing she'll slip away to warn the Russians at the school when we start to leave. Don't do anything to stop her, because we are going to use her to our advantage."

Holly's eyes flicked around, making sure nobody was listening. "I've had my suspicions about her for a while now."

"Alright, we're on the same page regarding that." Dillon searched for the right words regarding what he needed to say. "If anything happens to me—"

"Shhh," Holly put her fingers to Dillon's lips, quieting him. "Don't say anything else. I'm not prepared to say goodbye to you. Keep the faith that everything will be okay."

"You're right. Holly, time's short. I need to address the rest of the group."

"I understand."

Dillon stepped over to a picnic table which he could use as a podium for him to address the gathering crowd. He estimated there were fifty people, ranging in age from a teen to eighty plus. He straightened his back and took a deep breath, his eyes roaming over the crowd, all waiting for guidance from him. He felt honored he had been trusted to lead these people, yet at the same time he felt the weight of responsibility and regret on his shoulders. Some of the people would lose their lives.

"We have little time to accomplish a big task. If every person here was a trained warrior, we could meet the Russians on equal terms. But we have to be realistic. My best fighting days are in the past, a status some of you older veterans share with me." He noted the heads nodding in agreement. "Some of you are great shots, but have never faced men in battle. Some of you may have little experience with weapons. Regardless, everyone here can help us to secure a victory.

"Our Russian ally, Andrey Koshkin is to my left," Dillon said. "Andrey, raise your hand so everyone knows who you are."

Andrey took a step forward, stood for a moment, then stepped back.

"Andrey tells us we are facing fifty trained Russian soldiers. Twenty of them are Spetsnaz, the equivalent of our Special Forces. The Russian leaders are ruthless and will give no quarter to civilians who raise arms against them. I've also learned there are two hundred additional soldiers they can call upon from their ship at Beaumont's harbor, as well as special purpose attack helicopters. Instead of Russian machine guns and grenades we face today, we could be facing missiles and mini-guns launched by some of the most experienced combat pilots in the world. We need to get it right the first time.

"The scenario is bleak, but know we will never get a better chance than now to defend our homeland from invasion. We are healthy, we are not starving, and we have persevered and adapted to this new world thrust upon us. We are survivors."

"Yeah!" a shout came from the audience. "We are survivors! Let's go kick those red commies out of our country!"

Dillon let his speech sink in while the crowd geared themselves up for the battle. He whispered to Holly, "Are the tarps up yet?"

She gave the thumbs up.

"Can I have everyone's attention now?" Dillon shouted. After a few moments the crowd quieted so he could be heard. "Folks, I need half of you to stand entirely under those tarps to your right. Once there, stay under them completely and do not look out from under the tarps regardless of what you hear. Any mistakes will cost lives. Please move quietly and wait for me to tell you to come out."

A large man in a muscle shirt bullied his way through the crowd. He bellowed, "Who are you to give us orders? I don't like being pushed around by a lawyer, because the only good lawyer is a dead lawyer."

Nico came out of nowhere and laid him out with a savage haymaker punch so powerful he followed the guy to the ground. Kate came running over with rope, and with Nico's help, they hogtied the man. A red bandana knotted tightly around his mouth kept him quiet.

Nico said, "Calm down now so I can hear the crickets chirp. If you don't I'll put a bullet in your head to keep you from giving us away."

The man glared at Nico.

A strange buzzing noise filled the air. "Now!" Dillon barked. "Under the tarps."

The buzzing emanating from overhead came closer. Not as loud and threatening as a helicopter, but loud enough it was noticeable.

The drone swooped in and hovered near the treetops, swiveling to get a 360 degree view. It disappeared as quickly as it had appeared, the buzzing fading away with it.

"Well done everybody," Dillon said. "The Russian drone has revealed our location, but not our strength. It would have only seen half of you. Now is the time to implement the plan. If anyone does not want to participate, say something now." The group went quiet as both young and old nervously glanced around, waiting. Dillon scanned the group, finding no takers.

"Since everybody is on board, we will divide into two groups. The Mission A group will stay to defend this area, while the Mission B group will use the truck and trailer to attack the school first thing in the morning. Nico Bell and Kate Chandler will command Mission A. They have experience defending against large forces. Chris Chandler and myself will lead Mission B. We will have fewer people, so we'll have to move fast with the selection process." Dillon motioned for Chandler to stand. "It's your turn to take the podium."

"Hi, I'm Chris Chandler. I'm a trained U.S. Marine sniper. I need everyone who can shoot five shots into one inch at a hundred yards with the rifle they have with them to raise his hand." One man and one woman raised their hands. "You two, come over here. You'll be on team B." Chandler addressed the crowd. "How about anyone who can put five shots into one and a half inches at one hundred?" Nobody raised their hands. "How about five shots into two inches at one hundred?" The group raised their hands in unison. "Excellent."

Chandler hand-picked the next sixteen shooters based on the guns they had, a mix of high powered bolt guns with a number of 7.62 NATO battle rifles. Chandler needed powerful cartridges to go against the AK-74s and the Russian heavy machine guns.

"Luke," he said, "you're with me on Team B."

"Got it, big brother."

Chandler raised his voice to be heard over the low din of the crowd. "Everyone else is on Team A. Non-participants will go with Cassie, Ryan, and Anna. Good luck, everyone!"

While Chandler was shaking hands and reassuring the group, Holly came up to Dillon. "You were right about Dorothy. She slipped away while Chandler made his selections."

"Don't worry," Dillon said. "I've suspected her for a while, and she's playing right into my hands."

CHAPTER 32

Team B headed down the road, using the truck hauling the hay trailer as transportation. Hay bales were used to supply cover for the riders. With only twenty-one members, Team B was a good deal leaner than Team A.

Taking advantage of the travel time, Chandler moved from team member to team member, giving each person their assignment so they would be able to take their position the moment they stopped near the school.

Dillon, who was driving the truck, decided to make an unplanned stop.

"Why are we going down this road?" Luke asked.

"Your brother mentioned explosives earlier, which got me to thinking. Oil exploration requires seismic charges and perforators for the perforator gun. I spoke to one of the team members who just happened to be a volunteer fireman. He told me where the nearest explosives distributor was located. We're making a quick shopping trip."

"Are you sure about that?"

"He had no reason to lie."

"What are you going to do with the explosives?"

"You'll see."

At the end of the dirt road, Dillon stopped the truck. Ahead were two buildings, dark and deserted. One of the buildings, known as a magazine, housed the explosives. It was a sturdy structure made of reinforced concrete with thick steel doors. Steel hoods secured the locks.

Dillon swore. He'd have to find the keys.

He exited the truck, went to the office building, and pried open the door. It smelled like it hadn't been occupied in a long time. Clicking on his flashlight, he made a cursory search and determined it was indeed empty. A chair had been knocked over and papers were scattered on the floor. Papers rustled, startling Dillon for a moment, and he crouched until he realized a rat had scurried across the papers.

A desk sat in the middle of the room. A row of lockers was on the back wall.

He opened the lockers and found two backpacks and one satchel. He emptied those on the floor. Next, he opened the top desk drawer, pushing around pens and note pads, an old candy bar that had been chewed on, a stapler, and pencils. He shut the drawer and searched the other one. Way in the back, he found a key ring.

Bingo.

Holding the backpacks and satchel, he raced out of the building and went next door to the building housing the explosives. The third key on the key ring did the trick and the lock popped open.

The room was lined with wood secured by nails painted over with non-sparking putty. Various explosives were neatly arranged in boxes. The sausage shaped yellow packages of extra gelatin dynamite were exactly what Dillon needed. One summer when he was in law school, he had worked on a seismic crew and had become familiar with explosives. Classic dynamite would be leaking nitroglycerine due to aging, while gelatin dynamite was sealed and much safer to transport.

He needed detonators and connecting cords, which he found. He planned to use Detcord for connection, and boosters to assure the gelatin would have full detonation. Since military detonators were in stock, he grabbed an old blasting machine to complete the shopping trip. Dillon took care to transport each item separately in the backpacks and satchel.

He hoofed it back to the truck.

"Chandler, you drive while I make the charges."

Dillon crimped the detonator caps on the Detcord and threaded them into the capwells of the boosters. Each booster was surrounded by three gelatin tubes and a charge which he wrapped together with excess Detcord. The unit could be detonated using the blasting machine, a Russian grenade, or a shot from a powerful rifle.

"We're here," Chandler said. He stopped the truck about a mile from the school. Team B unloaded quietly.

"The darkness favors the Russians with their night vision equipment," Dillon whispered. "We are going to wait until they take off the equipment at dawn before we sneak up to the outer fence for the breach. If we don't have an opportunity to hook each charge to the blasting machine, Chandler and one of our better shooters will shoot the boosters to detonate. Any questions?" After a beat he said, "Good. We'll rest for a little while until it's time to leave."

* * *

Nearing daybreak, the group walked carefully through the woods, mindful of a possible ambush. When they came up to the school, three volunteers crept up to the fence where they placed the explosives on all sides except the side with the minefield.

Dillon held his position with Andrey on the minefield side. He had expected some sort of surprise, knowing Dorothy had arrived first, and thus the Spetsnaz troops would be ready at the school.

A large dull green tarp covered some type of equipment on the athletic field, but there was no movement under it. Dillon wondered what kind of surprise awaited them. He clenched his jaw in frustration.

Andrey stared hard at the minefield. "They've changed it." He squinted into the first light of dawn, searching for those straight lines which were a first class ticket to the graveyard.

Movement at the nearest guard tower caught Dillon's attention. The guards were taking off their night vision equipment. "It's time," he mouthed.

Three rapid reports of gunfire broke the silence of the night.

Explosions rocked the compound.

Chandler's snipers had timed the detonation perfectly.

On three sides of the compound, the fences were shredded. Posts had been snapped in half as easily as a child breaking a pencil. Razor wire bent into grotesque shapes.

Shouts and random gunfire peppered the adjoining dark woods.

Aimed gunfire from the woods dropped a number of Russian guards.

Inside the compound, the Spetsnaz soldiers made a decision to spring overwhelming fire on the attacking force. As a group, they rushed outside then scattered in twos, firing their AKs and machineguns as they went while their body armor took the impact of incoming fire. They fired a continuous onslaught of lead and steel. Chunks of wood splintered from the mature trees taking the hits, while others were chopped down.

Orders where shouted in Russian.

Someone screamed.

Three of Dillon's volunteers schooled in explosive placement anxiously waited in the soft earth of a two foot deep depression, camouflaging themselves with dead leaves and pine needles. A large tree trunk offered some protection.

The Spetsnaz soldiers cautiously advanced into the woods, unknowingly coming to within throwing distance of the volunteers.

Using the crunching leaves as cover, a volunteer pulled the pin on a grenade, and the others followed his lead.

The rustling of leaves was the only indication something wasn't right.

A lead soldier turned to fire, and as he did, several grenades rolled behind him. In the millisecond it took his mind to comprehend the severity of the situation, the grenades detonated before he or his nearest comrades had another thought or were able to utter a warning. Blood and bits of flesh rained down on the hidden volunteers, yet they held their position.

The American snipers pounded the remaining Spetsnaz soldiers without mercy. In the space of a few seconds, the soldiers had all been shot dead.

* * *

Dillon and Andrey made it to the back gate by taking advantage of the loud gunfire reports and confusion from the battle. Andrey studied the landmine pattern, using the light by the gate. "This has to be wired, but I don't see it." His attention went to the rear guard towers then back to the gate, searching. "I still can't find anything. I don't want to take a chance."

"We'll go around," Dillon said. "You keep an eye out for soldiers."

While Andrey kept watch, Dillon went to work on the fence, snapping the wires with the wire-cutting bayonet.

When he cut the last one, Andrey said, "Let me go first."

"I can't let you do that."

"I can see better in low light than you can."

Dillon reluctantly agreed, lamenting the fact he hadn't had eye surgery to correct his vision before the grid went down. Andrey's eyes were at least twenty years younger than his. He would definitely have better sight at night than Dillon would.

Andrey's sharp eyes strained to differentiate the grass from fine lines leading to a mine. He scanned the area, noting the straight lines where none should be. "They've mined inside the fence too."

"Then we'll crawl," Dillon offered. "Make sure your equipment is cinched down tight. We don't want a loose strap sending us into the next county." Dillon slung his AK on his back and secured the sling. A quick grab of his AK was now impossible, so he was prepared to use his pistol if necessary.

Dillon and Andrey belly crawled through the hole in the fence then out into the newly laid minefield. As they loosened their equipment, an AK being racked broke the silence.

Dillon froze.

CHAPTER 33

"Nice of you to drop in." Petya Ruslan emerged from behind a wall. He carried a shortened AK, leveling it directly at Dillon and Andrey. "It appears there are traitors on both sides."

Colonel Burkov roughly pushed Dorothy out from behind the wall. He held a knife to her throat, pressing it against her pulsating jugular.

Her face was contorted with deep worry lines and an expression of bewilderment. Her hands feebly tried to pull Burkov's forearm away. "But I cooperated. Please, no."

"Shut up," Burkov snapped, pressing the knife harder into Dorothy's throat. "Put your weapons down if you don't want to see this woman's blood spurting everywhere. You too, Andrey. You'll be dealt with later."

Dillon didn't move. Neither did Andrey.

"I'll slice her throat from ear to ear." Burkov said.

"Please, Dillon," Dorothy begged. "I have a daughter who needs me. Do as he says."

Dillon reluctantly placed his weapons on the ground. This

wasn't going as he had planned.

Andrey glanced at Dillon. "Why would you save the life of this woman who is a traitor?"

"The question you should be asking, Andrey," Ruslan said, "is what will happen to you?" He strutted over to Andrey and faced him. "Russia doesn't like traitors."

Dillon needed to act fast to create some type of diversion. "Dorothy, what will your daughter think of what you are doing?"

"Leave my daughter out of this." Her words were short and curt. "The Russians were only going to get the oil then they would leave us alone. Nobody would have gotten hurt if you had cooperated."

"They must have threatened you. Or Anna."

Dorothy dropped her gaze to the ground.

Dillon realized he had hit a nerve. "It was Anna, wasn't it? They threatened her, not you." Dillon addressed Colonel Burkov. "What kind of man threatens a child?"

"I'm here to win at all costs," Burkov replied. "I take no prisoners, a fact you'll find out in a moment."

Burkov jerked Dorothy and shoved her toward a large tarp draped over a bulky object. Burkov put the knife in his belt and pulled his pistol. "Roll the tarp off. Dillon needs to see his surprise."

Dorothy backed up to a steel beam with a ratcheted spool of wire rope attached to it. She reeled in the rope, which pulled off the tarp to expose a Russian attack helicopter.

"What?" Burkov feigned surprise. "Are you not surprised at this magnificent creation of our military force?"

Dillon wasn't about to be goaded into a fight he couldn't win. He'd bide his time and wait for an opportune moment, or a careless oversight.

"Well then, let me tell you about it. This," Burkov said, sweeping his hand toward the chopper, "is an Mi-24 attack helicopter with rockets and machine guns. It has the thickest armor available, and will easily wipe out the men you call a resistance. I call them undisciplined and untrained heathens who have no place in the new world I plan to create."

"What are you talking about?" Dorothy asked.

"My dear, you are such a simple woman, and one who has a simple child."

"You bastard," Dorothy spat. "You threatened to kill my child if

I didn't cooperate. You said all you needed was the oil and then you'd leave."

Burkov scoffed. "The complexities of our operation are beyond your comprehension. I almost feel sorry for you. Almost. I have no need for simpletons." He brightened. "On the other hand, I do have a use for you."

Dorothy rushed at Burkov, and when she raised her hand to slap him, he roughly grabbed her by the wrist, forcing her to the ground. He twisted his boot into her back to make her lay still. Dorothy looked at Dillon, and mouthed, "I'm sorry."

When Dillon made a move to help her, Ruslan jabbed a hard rifle butt to his kidneys, buckling Dillon to his knees.

Two gunshots sounded, followed by two tower guards falling to their deaths. Their bodies hit the ground with a thud and puff of dust. Chandler's expert sniping skills were picking off the enemy one by one. It was too bad he didn't have a clear shot of Burkov and Ruslan.

Burkov sensed the situation he previously had under control was becoming unstable. He motioned for two of his guards to accompany him to the helicopter. He jerked Dorothy up from the ground and forced her into the chopper.

Sensing it was now or never, Andrey rushed Ruslan and threw his body into the big Russian, knocking him off balance. Ruslan pounded his smaller compatriot, balling his fists into Andrey's back. During the scuffle Andrey became entangled with Ruslan's AK shorty.

Andrey had his boots dug into the dirt, and with a burst of adrenaline spurring him on, he bent at the waist and looped his arms around Ruslan's legs, lifting him up. With Ruslan off balance, Andrey leaned forward and stumbled to the grassy part of the compound.

In the split second when Ruslan understood what Andrey was doing, and the unmeasurable amount of time it took for his body to register his comprehension, his eyes showed a brief flicker of understanding the horror of the inevitable. He didn't even have time for his muscles to tense.

The explosion ripped apart his consciousness.

There was no pain for Ruslan or bright lights or angels waiting to escort him to the afterlife. The man who had no conscience, who killed without remorse, who did not value life, was met with something worse than death.

A black void of unspeakable horrors reached to him, surrounding him into a chillingly cold pit of damnation where he sunk further, deeper, to be trapped for eternity.

Ruslan's back took the force of the landmine explosion which ripped apart his spinal cord, severed major arteries, and split his head like a watermelon. All that was left of him was his face contorted in terror, his torso intact, his head hanging by loose skin on his neck.

Dillon had been thrown back and hit the ground hard next to a guard who wasn't as lucky. He was obviously dead, impaled by a piece of wood the explosion had propelled through the air at bone-breaking speed.

Stunned by the blast, Dillon shook his head, trying to stave off the ringing in his ears. He wasn't sure if he was alive or dead. He opened his eyes to a fiery world bending and creaking, and the buildings shimmered as if heatwaves had engulfed them.

The concussion he had sustained played havoc on his ability to think, and he was experiencing a disconnect between his brain and his body. His eyesight was blurred while his arms and legs wouldn't move the way he wanted them to. Dillon forced himself to stay conscious and it took him a few seconds to regain his composure. The whumping of helicopter blades brought him back to reality. Burkov was piloting the chopper, which was still on the ground. Dillon clearly saw Dorothy through the open doors. She was on the floor, pleading with him with her eyes to help her. Even after all she had done, and though her traitorous actions had cost lives, Dillon could only think if she died, Anna would be motherless.

An idea came to him as the chopper lifted off the ground.

A moment of hesitation gripped him because he was sure if he followed through, he'd go straight to Hell. Still, he couldn't let Burkov get away.

Dillon pulled a grenade off a dead soldier, stood up, and hurled it through the helicopter door where it landed next to Dorothy. He fell to the ground and covered his head with his hands, waiting for the fiery explosion and resulting shrapnel.

He tensed.

He waited.

Nothing happened.

Then he realized what he had forgotten to do. His concussed

brain didn't register he needed to pull the pin before he threw the grenade. At that moment, the fight went out of him.

All the planning, the heroic effort by him and others, the loss of life, was all for nothing. His muscles relaxed and he went limp. The Russians were going to win after all. The Americans had lost and he couldn't deal with it.

He was so incredibly tired.

Dillon's body was spent and he hurt in places he didn't know was possible. He closed his eyes, rested his head on the ground, and waited for blissful unconsciousness to take him away from the pain, the fight, the disappointments. His world faded to black.

* * *

Chandler and Luke arrived just in time to see the helicopter fade away over the treetops. They sprinted over to Dillon, standing over him. Rivulets of blood streaked his face and neck, and had soaked into his shirt. Bits of dirt and grass were embedded in his skin. His bloodied face was expressionless and he was as still as a corpse.

"Do you think he's alive?" Luke asked, wondering what exactly had happened to the crumpled man.

"It's not good," Chandler said, shaking his head. "I'm not sure what happened here, but he put up one heck of a fight. The place is littered with body parts and dead Russians."

"I guess we can bury him out at the ranch. It's the least we can do for him. If you need to check the compound, I'll stay with him to make sure nobody touches him."

Dillon popped open his eyes and sat up.

Chandler and Luke jumped.

"I'm not dead yet, so don't go burying me."

"Good God Almighty!" Luke exclaimed. "I nearly peed in my pants. We thought you were a goner."

"Well I'm not. I heard everything you said. I was only resting."

"Your rest is over," Chandler said. "Stop feeling sorry for yourself and let's see if anybody else is alive." Chandler hooked an arm under Dillon and helped him up. "Are you okay to walk?"

"Give me a moment." Stars appeared in his vision and Dillon wobbled on unsteady legs. Chandler held him so he wouldn't fall over.

"I think you need to sit down," Chandler said.

"I'm good. Just give me a moment." Dillon scanned the compound. "Where's Andrey?"

"He's over there," Chandler said, jerking his thumb in the direction where Andrey was.

With Chandler's help, Dillon hobbled over to Andrey and assessed his injuries. Kneeling, Dillon put his index and middle finger to Andrey's neck. "He has a pulse." Dillon inspected Andrey's head, noting the bleeding. He opened his uniform and checked for wounds. "He has a number of shrapnel wounds which aren't life threatening. It's the head wound he needs to be treated for."

Chandler dug around in his backpack. "I've got pressure bandages. It should stop the bleeding and hopefully he'll stabilize until we can get him medical care." He handed those to Dillon.

Dillon applied the pressure bandages to Andrey's most severe wounds. "In the meantime, until we can get him help, we need to stay on course."

"Can I do anything?" Luke asked.

"Yes. Get the truck and bring it over here. Leave the trailer though."

"On it."

"Chandler, see if you can find any rocket propelled grenades or handheld missiles. I have a sinking feeling that Team A is in real trouble."

"Why's that?"

"Burkov is piloting the helicopter, and I'm guessing that's where he's headed."

While Chandler and Dillon searched the compound for additional firepower, Luke hoofed it to the truck. Unhitching the trailer, he sped back to the compound.

CHAPTER 34

Rally Point A had one structure, an adobe style house over one hundred years old marked by a historical landmark sign detailing its history. The property had been willed to the city for use as a park, but improvement funds were not forthcoming. The result was a partially constructed park that had never opened.

Nico appreciated the bullet resistant structure, yet decided not to use it. "We can't use it."

"Why not? It would be a good place to defend." Kate recognized the value of the thick walls.

"The problem is we are facing an army this time. They will have military weapons that can blow the house apart. At the very least, the house is a bullet magnet and there's not any cover near it if we need an escape route."

"Regardless, we'll need to make sure it stays empty, while making it appear occupied so it will draw fire. That way, we'll be able to locate where the Russians are."

"You're a smart woman, Kate."

"You're a smart man, Nico."

"I hope you still need me."

Kate grinned. "Always."

* * *

Nico and Kate asked the men and women of Rally Point A to gather around them. Before sending the team members out, Nico gave a few tips.

"Choose cover as opposed to concealment. Hiding behind a bush is concealment. If you brush against a bush causing it to move, you'll draw fire. The bush will not stop fire. That's bad. Don't choose bad. Choose good. A rock formation or a dirt berm is cover, and will stop incoming fire. It's important to remember that cover can be penetrated with enough rounds shot into the same spot. I once shot through a three-eighths inch steel disk with a single magazine from an M-16. So, don't let them see you, and don't feel you have to stay in the same spot if you are seen." Nico let the information sink in. "Alright, then. Wait for my shot to start the action. Good luck, and God bless."

While Nico gave the speech, Kate left to go to the adobe house. She placed a Coleman lantern on a table, and made a broken broomstick to look like two rifle barrels sticking out of the windows.

The team scattered to the spots they had picked earlier. Several took cover in a shallow stream, taking advantage of the sand and gravel composition of the bank. Large trees provided additional cover to hide behind. Others found a rock outcropping to use as cover. A few unwise members chose to climb trees, not factoring in the difficulty of moving if the situation required it. Still others picked uneven ground to ensure a vehicle would not choose their location as a path and run over them.

The tarps used earlier to hide from the drone were cut into sniper blankets and adorned with plants and leaves from the surrounding area. The snipers were positioned hundreds of yards out from the center of the adobe house, making it difficult for the Russians to spot them.

All was quiet.

The morning sun brushed the tops of the trees, casting a golden glow over the land, burning off the night's dew. A crow cawed in the early morning hour, and an owl soared over the land, searching for a daytime place to roost.

Team A scouts spotted two armored personnel carriers stopped in the road half a mile out. Soldiers exited each vehicle, spreading out in a large line. They walked behind the carriers.

The carriers reached the outer perimeter of Rally Point A, as per the description from Dorothy. From a distance, Rally Point A looked like a picnic area with a structure for community use, and of no military value. The Russian commander ordered the vehicles to drive closer to determine if the area was abandoned.

The commander opened the hatch to get behind the machinegun. He peppered the area randomly, failing to find any of the Americans who were supposed to have been there. Several Russian soldiers crept closer to get better intel. They came back and reported no sightings. The commander radioed Colonel Burkov for instructions. He told them to stay in place and wait for him, explaining he'd be arriving by helicopter.

* * *

A mile away, Uncle Billy observed the scene through a pair of binoculars from the safety of his Gran Tornio. While he could not see the details, he caught sight of the Commander and an idea came to him.

"Holly, do you think you could throw one of these grenades?"

She hefted the weight, holding the grenade in her hand. "I could throw it, but it's so heavy I might miss the target."

"Can you drive better than you can throw?" Uncle Billy tossed a grenade back and forth between his hands.

"You bet I can. What exactly do you have in mind?"

"Get behind the wheel and you'll find out."

CHAPTER 35

The failure of the Russian expansion to go as planned had become personal for Colonel Burkov.

His well-thought out plans were being unraveled by a group of backwoods East Texas hillbillies who brewed their own liquor. Earlier, he had found a moonshine operation, tested the liquor, and spat it out, disgusted by the foul flavor, akin to what horse piss must taste like.

He'd show them who was boss.

Burkov piloted the Mi-24 helicopter to Rally Point A, hovering high above, giving him an excellent view of the area.

The Americans were well hidden, he'd give them credit for that, no doubt skills learned from Indians who passed it down from generation to generation. He'd read about them in textbooks. Savages who could disappear into the desert or woods like ghosts, leaving no footprints or other traces they had been there. These East Texans were no different than the savages.

And like the Indians who had inferior weapons, these Texans would be annihilated in the same fashion.

Hovering the helicopter, Burkov used thermal vision to hunt his prey. A shotgun pattern of hot spots indicating where the people were hidden dotted the landscape. He could use the helicopter to take them all out, yet he wanted to get up and personal when he personally executed the leaders. Dillon Stockdale would be first on the list.

"Squad commanders, I will draw their fire so you can see them and eliminate them," Burkov radioed.

He decreased the altitude to fifty feet. "Dorothy, you sit behind me."

Dorothy didn't move.

"Do as I say, or I'll toss you out and everyone will see you fall to your death."

Reluctantly, Dorothy moved behind the pilot seat. Through the open door, she peered out onto the land, and for the first time, she feared for her life. Burkov had threatened her that if she didn't cooperate, he'd kill Anna. As a mother, she felt she had no other choice but to cooperate with the Russians, even if it meant being a traitor.

Burkov turned the helicopter slowly three hundred and sixty degrees to make sure all the Americans got a good look at him and at Dorothy. He took pleasure in letting the Americans know who the traitor was among them.

She hung her head in shame.

The Russians manning the armored carriers let loose a deadly volley of fire, peppering the land, shredding trees and anyone unlucky enough to be struck.

Larry Monroe had been one of the unlucky ones, and Dorothy witnessed him jerking under the force of the bullets shattering his body. She hadn't signed up for any of this, and felt helpless by the threats the Russian Colonel levied against her daughter.

Damn him.

* * *

Random fire hit the attack helicopter, which took evasive action, flying fast out of reach of the bullets.

Nico cursed at the break in discipline when the Texans fired. He was not yet ready to spring the trap.

The Texans fired when there was a lull from the Russians' side, and the cat and mouse game continued for several minutes. The helicopter sustained minor damage by the small arms fire.

Burkov piloted the helicopter to an altitude which would be sufficient for launching the rockets. He nosed the chopper in the direction of the adobe house and fired a rocket. The house exploded into a massive debris cloud of rock and timbers, and when the dust settled, only a shell was left.

An evil smirk spread across Burkov's face, and he took pleasure in punishing Hemphill and its people for their arrogance. By the time he was finished, there'd be nothing left except the spoils of war. Oil, and lots of it.

* * *

Uncle Billy and Holly were sitting in the Gran Torino, hidden under the canopy of a massive oak. He was briefing Holly on his plan to take out the chopper while he counted grenades. "See that hill over there?" he said.

Holly nodded.

"Wait until the helicopter gets close to the other side, then hit the gas to get it up to sixty. I'll be in the backseat throwing grenades. With any luck, I'll toss one inside the chopper."

Holly couldn't believe what she was hearing. She put her hand to her forehead and kneaded the space between her eyebrows. "This isn't the *Dukes of Hazzard*, and I'm no Daisy Duke."

"Maybe not, but those boys sure did put on a show. If I'm gonna meet my maker, I want to do it in style."

"*I'm* not ready to meet *my* maker yet," Holly said in all seriousness.

"Then keep your head down."

"The odds of tossing a grenade into a fast moving helicopter while we are pushing sixty miles per hour aren't good. I don't even want to think about it."

"Then don't. Let me do the thinking."

"I don't want to think about that either."

* * *

221

Chandler and Luke made it to the edge of the property where they found a shady spot to hide their wounded friends, Dillon and Andrey. They took the downtime to commence with their own plan.

Chandler studied the landscape, searching for one of his nearby snipers, knowing anyone out this far would have to be a great shot. His eyes roamed over the land for anything out of place. Perhaps a tree where none should be, an uplift in the otherwise flat land, or unnatural colors in the forest would be a dead giveaway. While he scanned the area, his eyes kept focusing on a patch of grass leaning the opposite way the wind blew. He admired the sniper's ability to camouflage himself to near invisibility.

The grass moved and the report of a high powered rifle startled a flock of birds in a tree, and the flap of wings momentarily vexed Chandler.

Luke spotted the victim. "One of the armored carrier gunners went down, courtesy of our sniper."

"Whoever it is, I want him on my team," Chandler said. "Stay here, Luke."

Chandler picked his way carefully toward the sniper, while showing his hands were empty. He didn't want the guy to think he was a threat. Much to his surprise, the guy wasn't a guy, but the girl who raised her hand at his first accuracy question.

"I'm Maggie."

"I'm Chandler."

"I know who you are. Your brother Luke is over there," she said. "Now that my position has been compromised, I think we need to get outta here."

They ducked at the sound of automatic fire in the background.

"Time to go," Chandler said. "I need your help."

"What do you need?"

"I need you to position yourself behind those rocks," he said, pointing in a southerly direction. "It will give you a clear line of sight when the chopper makes a pass. Take out the door gunners then duck if you take on fire. While you're doing that, Luke and I will be in a truck. He'll be driving while I'll be in the bed of the truck firing Russian RPGs at their own chopper. If I'm seen before I'm in position, assume the outcome won't be good. I'll probably be a goner, Luke too."

"Who am I to refuse a couple of heroes?" Maggie said. "Give

me five minutes to get in position. Good luck and Godspeed."

Back at the truck, Luke took the driver's seat while Chandler was seated in the bed. He took the safety cap off the rocket propelled grenade, already in the launcher. He kept the other three RPGs in their carrier, which he placed on his back. He put a tarp over the launcher to conceal it the best he could. From a distance, it might look like a bale of hay.

"You ready?" Luke yelled.

"As much as I'll ever be little brother. Let's roll!"

Luke hit the gas, the tires spun, leaving a trail of grass and gravel. He made it to the highway and floored it.

Chandler crouched low and held on to the launcher, waiting for the helicopter to make an appearance. Flying low and fast, the chopper rose above the treetops and came straight toward the diminutive looking truck.

CHAPTER 36

Seated behind Burkov, Dorothy gauged her options, none of which were any good. The noise of the whirling blades drowned out the chatter in her mind, and her thoughts focused on her life and what she needed to do. As a single mother, she had struggled to raise Anna and provide a stable home. She worked two jobs, raised chickens, and when she had downtime she cleaned other people's houses with Anna in tow. Dorothy regretted leaving Anna home alone so much, but had noticed her daughter possessed a mature quality other children her age did not. Dorothy now realized that quality would help Anna face her future.

She herself had been branded as a traitor, and once Burkov had paraded her around in the helicopter for everyone to see, the whole town knew it. She and Anna would be outcasts. She would probably go to jail for a long time if convicted of treason, thereby leaving Anna motherless. There was one person who would take Anna in though, and that thought gave her the courage she needed.

Dorothy thought about the events leading up to her current predicament, and she wondered if it was part of a bigger plan, one in which she would be a major player. Like a row of dominoes standing rigidly and seemingly indestructible, the entire line could be toppled by a tap or a wiggle, and Dorothy considered herself the defining domino.

Her life had had several defining moments, one of which was Anna's birth. She was a heroic little girl who all by herself braved the night to find her mother the antibiotics she needed; the brave little girl who tried to defy Burkov; the brave little girl who tried to rescue Dillon.

Nothing would destroy Anna's will and spirit, and it was now up to Dorothy to be the domino which could topple the rest.

She had the power now and she knew what she had to do.

In the folds of her shirt, she removed the grenade Dillon had lobbed into the helicopter. At the time when Dorothy surreptitiously hid the grenade, her actions had gone unnoticed.

Holding the grenade in her hand, she wondered how many seconds she had between when she pulled the ring and when it would explode. Flashes of scenes from war movies came to her, and she figured she had around five seconds.

A calming and spiritual influence washed over her and guided her next action. She grasped the grenade and looped her index finger through the pull ring.

"Colonel Burkov," Dorothy said. "Look what I found."

Burkov wasn't used to being told what to do by an inferior, but something in her voice indicated steadfast resolution, and he didn't like the sound of that. He held the helicopter steady then took a furtive peek over his left shoulder at her. His eyes dropped to the grenade she held. He neither blinked nor breathed for fear of startling her into accidentally pulling the ring. An explosion in a confined area would cause the most destruction and would be absolutely deadly, and he stood no chance of surviving it.

There was no noise, no commander to impress, no war to win, no politics to play. There was nothing anymore in the world, but him and her. He needed to distract her.

"Dorothy, don't do this," he said, his voice low and steady. "What would Anna think of her mother?"

"How dare you bring my daughter into this, you bastard."

"Please, just think a moment. I can get you anything you need. Anything at all. I have connections in high places. You want a home.

It's yours. You want money. I can get that for you. Anna can go to the best schools in Russia, and—"

"Shut up! You tricked me once and you're not going to do it again."

"Dorothy, you're a brave woman, and the kind Russia needs." Burkov kept lathering on the accolades while his right hand moved toward his hip where he kept his sidearm. "I can get you a good job, if that's what you want. You can teach English and I can get you the training you need."

He unsnapped the holster.

She hadn't noticed.

"You want me to teach English to people who would wage war against the United States? Then you don't know me very well."

In one deft motion, Burkov withdrew the pistol, aimed it at her, and—

The helicopter took a direct hit from a rocket propelled grenade, shaking it violently.

Dorothy stumbled and the grenade flew out of her hand and lodged next to Burkov.

The pistol fell away from him.

The chopper dropped dangerously close to the ground before Burkov regained control.

Out of the corner of the eye, he saw Dorothy lunge for the grenade. He reached for it at the same time she did.

With one hand, he tried to keep the chopper steady while struggling with Dorothy with the other.

She was stronger than he anticipated.

Before he could utter another word, she pulled the safety ring.

Burkov opened his mouth and screamed, "Noooo—"

A wave of panic gripped Burkov so tight he couldn't breathe. He had a brief thought about the life he wouldn't live and how all his cunning and posturing to become a general would be cut short by this woman. This inferior woman, and he cursed her with all the fervor he possessed. His life and all the pomp and circumstance which was his birthright came to him, and his goal of becoming general was within his grasp, so close he could taste the success.

A second ticked by, then another.

In one last desperate attempt, Burkov decided to jump. If anyone could survive the fall he could, and broken bones would be a small price to pay for his life. He fumbled to unbuckle himself, losing a precious second in the attempt. He bent over and took a step toward where the sky shined blue and the green trees swayed.

He grasped the edge of the door.

Escape was a second away.

Dorothy closed her eyes and whispered, "Anna, for you. Be brave for your mother. I love you."

The grenade detonated the spare rockets, and the resulting fiery explosion ripped apart the helicopter and blew with such a tremendous force that the shockwave ripped off the tops of nearby trees.

Wire, metal, fuel, and indistinguishable pieces of the flaming helicopter rained down on the East Texas land. The cockpit landed with a heavy thud, gouging a furrow in the dirt.

Blades sliced through trees.

Pine needles sizzled from burning debris.

No distinguishable body parts were left.

* * *

Chandler, Luke, Holly, and Uncle Billy gasped at the explosion and a brief mixture of jubilation and horror followed at the realization that not only was Burkov dead, but so was Dorothy.

Their undulating emotions were cut short when another attack helicopter appeared over the treetops.

Chandler barked an order. "Man the guns and give them everything you've got!" Just as Chandler was about to let loose, he recognized the differences between the two helicopters. "Wait! Don't fire. It's one of ours!"

The attack helicopter bore United States markings.

Chandler had never seen a more beautiful sight. Whoops of elation, high fiving, back slaps, and general euphoria abounded among the ragtag patriots as the chopper laid down firepower on the Russians, who were quickly overpowered.

Minutes later, the American attack helicopter came in for a landing just short of the Mi-24 main wreckage.

A man stepped out of the chopper, and it was clear he was in command. He had on the uniform of a high ranking officer, his back was washboard straight, hair cropped short, and he carried an air of undeniable determination.

"I'm Colonel Samuel James, U.S. Army." He took a sweep of the area. "Who's in charge here?"

Chandler walked up to the Colonel and extended a hand to shake. "I'm Chris Chandler. Dillon Stockdale is the man you want, but he's out of commission for now." Chandler waited for additional questions, but when there were none, he asked one of his own. "We've had no intel for months now. Can you tell us what's been happening?"

"The Russians launched a coordinated EMP attack on the continental United States. There have been reports of massive casualties from the breakdown of infrastructure and resulting disease and starvation. That's the bad news. The good news is that there have been pockets of people like yourselves who used guerilla style tactics to inflict as much damage on the Russians as possible. The United States of America thanks you, Sir."

"You're welcome. It was our duty," Chandler said. "What about our borders? Are they secure?"

"Yes. That was one of our main priorities, and the reason we couldn't get here before. We knew the Russians were in East Texas and gearing up to claim Texas as one of their sovereign territories. They wanted the oil in East Texas, and they were going to do whatever they needed to secure the commodity. Earlier today, we sank two of their ships in the Gulf of Mexico, and shot down several of their fighter jets."

"We were able to do that?"

"Affirmative," Colonel James said. "Several of our bases were EMP proofed, including our fighter jets and attack helicopters stationed there. I flew in from the Gulf of Mexico when we intercepted Colonel Burkov requesting reinforcements. We pinpointed his location and decided you could use the help."

"It came just at the right time. Thank you. Can you tell me anything about the grid coming back on?" Chandler asked.

"We have teams working on it as we speak," Colonel James explained. "Some of the major cities now have a few hours of electricity every day. I can't tell you when your area will be resupplied, but with any luck you may get intermittent service. It should be enough to watch TV or to use the oven. I can tell you the Americans living in the country had it much better than those in the cities. We are working to restore law and order in the cities. Just know the government is still functioning. The President wants to rebuild America into a pre-eminent world power again."

"That sounds good," Chandler said. "We are very grateful. Feel free to check on us from time to time." Chandler shook the Colonel's hand when the pilot restarted the Blackhawk's rotors.

"It's been a pleasure. I hope to meet Dillon Stockdale on my next visit."

"Before you go, I have a couple of requests. Do you have a doctor on board? Dillon needs medical attention."

"I'm afraid not. I can give you a surgical hospital kit. Would that help?"

"Absolutely."

"What else do you need?"

"Ammo. We are precariously low."

"We can do that too. I'll have my gunner deliver what you need. For now, I must go."

As Colonel James left, Chandler saluted him. The colonel stepped into the Blackhawk and said something to the gunner, who immediately instructed several soldiers to deliver the ammo and the medical kit.

* * *

Three days later Dillon was resting in a makeshift hospital in Hemphill. He had been treated by Ryan, who used his medical school training to tend to his future father-in-law and the other wounded patients.

Andrey was sitting in a wheelchair, and although heavily bandaged, he was alive and would recover thanks to the antibiotics provided in the surgical kit. Due to his bravery and the fact he saved many American lives, he had been assured he would be given quarters and be placed on the fast track to become an American citizen.

"I'm glad you made it, Andrey," Dillon said.

"Me too."

"What are your plans?"

"I'm not really sure. I have a distant cousin in Austin, so I think I'll go there."

"Chandler's folks are in Austin, and I'm sure they can help you. Did you know his mother descends from a Russian sniper?"

"That is quite interesting. I think I would like to meet her."

"I'll try to arrange it."

The door squeaked open and Holly came in. She carried a tote bag with clean clothes, some toiletries, and homemade goodies.

"Dillon, how are you doing?" Holly asked, setting the tote bag on the nightstand.

"Not too bad," he said. "Ryan tells me I can go home in a couple of days. I'll be good as new."

"I've missed you." Holly leaned over and kissed Dillon on the forehead. "I'm ready for you to come home."

"I am too." He reached for her hand and held it in his.

"I'll just leave you two alone," Andrey said. "I'll be in the waiting area."

"There is no waiting area," Dillon said.

"I know. I'll pretend."

After Andrey left, Holly said, "Anna is waiting outside the room. Have you considered what we spoke about earlier?"

"I have."

"What are you going to tell Anna about how her mother died?"

"I've already decided to tell her that her mother died a hero."

"How can you be certain of that?"

"The explosion that took down the Russian chopper came from within. It had to have been Dorothy. I think she must have kept the grenade I threw–the one I forgot to pull the pin on. I had a concussion and wasn't thinking clearly at the time."

"But what she did could amount to suicide."

"Or a very heroic act that saved a lot of lives. We will never know for sure, but that's what I choose to believe."

"Alright. What about the other issue we discussed?"

Dillon didn't answer the question. "Bring Anna in and we'll both tell her."

Holly went to the door and opened it. "You can come on in."

"Anna!" Dillon exclaimed. "Come here."

The wisp of a girl ran into the room and stood next to Dillon's bed. He sat up, leaned against the headboard, and propped a pillow behind his back.

"Are you okay?" she asked hesitantly.

231

"I'm okay. The docs say I'll be home in a few days." Dillon patted the bed, motioning for Anna to sit down. "There's something I want to tell you."

Anna's eyes became hopeful.

"I know you've had a lot of questions about your mom."

Anna nodded.

"Your mom died a hero, Anna. You should be very proud of her. We all are."

Anna's gaze fell to the floor. "I heard some people say bad things about her."

"Listen to me, Anna. Grownups aren't perfect, and when you grow up you'll understand that. We all make mistakes, including your mother, but that didn't make her a bad person. She did what she had to do to protect you. We heard from one of the Russian soldiers who told us Colonel Burkov threatened your mom that if she didn't cooperate, he'd hurt you."

Anna's eyes got big. "Is that true?"

"I'm afraid it is. He can't hurt you anymore, because your mom made sure of that. She sacrificed her life so you'd be safe."

"I wish she was still here. I'm really sad."

"I know."

"Did it hurt when she died?" Anna's face was flushed and her eyes red and teary.

Dillon reached under his pillow to get a Kleenex then wiped away a tear on her cheek. "No Anna, your mom didn't feel any pain. The moment someone dies, it's very peaceful, and there's no pain, only the love of our Heavenly Father."

"How do you know?"

"Anna, I've never told anyone this. I was visited by an angel once. It happened when I drowned in the swamp, before Holly saved me. When the moment came, when I died, it was the most peaceful feeling in the whole world." Dillon cleared his throat and swallowed a lump that had formed. "It's hard to explain because it's not an Earthly feeling. It was warm and peaceful. I had no worries, and I was blissfully happy. Do you understand?"

"I don't know."

"Well, let me help you. Have you ever held a warm puppy in your hands?"

"I have."

"Were you gentle with the puppy?"

"I was."

"And were you happy?"

Anna nodded.

"It's a little like that. Heaven is like holding a warm puppy. Right now, I know your mom is happy, not because she isn't with you, but because she's in Heaven. That was her eternal reward when she sacrificed herself so all of us would be safe. She died a hero, and that's something only the bravest of people can do. So don't listen to anyone who says anything different. Promise me that."

"I promise," Anna said, sniffling. "What's going to happen to me? I don't have anywhere to live."

"Holly and I have been discussing something else."

"What?"

Holly came forward and took a seat next to Anna. "Sweetie," Holly said, "Dillon and I want you to be our daughter. We want to adopt you. But we want to know what you think about that first."

Anna's gaze flicked from Holly to Dillon then back to Holly.

"But you're not even married," Anna said.

Dillon and Holly broke out laughing.

"We will be soon," Dillon assured her.

"Okay." Anna scratched her chin. "Does that mean Cassie will be my big sister?"

"She will be. I've already talked to her and she's excited for you to be her little sister. She's an only child, but won't be if you become our daughter. So…what do you say, Anna?"

"Umm, I think it's okay." Anna perked up. "Can I get a dog?"

"That would be a great idea, especially since Buster is missing," Dillon said. "Perhaps we can get you a puppy."

Anna nodded. "I'd be really gentle with the puppy, and I think my mom would approve of me living with you and Holly. So you'll be my new parents?"

"We'll be your parents forever."

Anna's eyes brightened at Dillon's comment. "What do I call you?"

"You can call us whatever you want to."

"Sweetie," Holly said, "I'll never replace your mom and I don't want to. When Dillon and I adopt you, you'll be my daughter, and I'll be honored to be your second mom." She took Anna's hands in hers. "For now, call me Holly. You can call Dillon by his first name or Dad. It's your choice."

"Okay. I'll decide later. Is that alright?"

"It sure is."

Holly rose and stretched. "I think it's time we go home. Dillon has had enough excitement for the day." She placed her hand on Anna's shoulder, directing her to the door, and glanced back at Dillon. "I'll be back in a couple of days to take you home. For now, we'll leave you to rest."

"I'll see you then."

As the door closed, Anna peeked back inside. She stood at the door, hesitated, then blurted, "Bye, Dad."

"Bye, Anna. See you soon."

After the door shut, Dillon was left in the quiet room. His thoughts took him to everything that had transpired over the last few years, and how he thought he'd never find happiness again after the death of his wife. Fate intervened when he found Holly, and through the miracle of the Lord, Cassie and Ryan's lives were spared when the plane crashed. They came together, and now were expecting their own child. Dillon leaned back and rested his head on the pillow, clasping his hands behind his head, realizing he had found happiness. He was going to be a grandfather. He had a family again, a second generation was to be born, and life went on.

He was a lucky man, and he knew that now.

He closed his eyes and said, "Thank you, Lord. Thank you for all your blessings."

CHAPTER 37

One Week Later

"Good boy," the elderly rancher said, patting Buster on the head. "You're fitting in good here, and you're going to make a fine ranch dog. Stay here while me and the missus head into town."

The man and his wife hobbled down the front porch steps of their ranch house, stepped on the walkway of sandstone slabs, then to the truck where he held the door open for her. He glanced at Buster and said, "We'll be back later."

"Hun," the wife said, "do you think he'll run away while we're gone?"

"Nah, where's he gonna go? There aren't that many people left, and I suppose whoever owned him dumped him because they couldn't feed him. It is what it is."

"We should have put him in the house with Skippy. He's so well behaved and friendly."

"It's too soon to leave him in the house."

"But, Hun, suppose something happens while we're—"

"Now don't fret about that. He'll be just fine. It's nice this evening."

UNDEFEATED WORLD

The rancher backed the truck out of the yard, and proceeded down the gravelly path to the farm-to-market road.

"He'll make a good ranch dog. Sure was terrible what happened to old Gus." The rancher briefly thought about his favorite dog and his unfortunate demise. He shook his head. "The old dogs aren't any match for a pack of coyotes."

"Life can be cruel on a ranch."

"Sometimes it is." The rancher glanced at his wife and patted her arm. "He'll be okay. I know he's already your favorite. Don't worry, we won't be gone that long. I doubt the store has much of anything. When we come back, I'll let him into the house. How's that?"

"That would be wonderful. And thank you for humoring me by driving me into town," she said. "I wanted to do something normal, especially after all that has happened."

"I know. I'm glad to take you shopping. Sorry we got off so late."

"Think we'll be home by the time it gets dark?"

"I'm sure we will. I heard on the ham radio a fog bank is rolling in from the Gulf, so we'll need to be careful about getting stuck in bad driving conditions. I'm sure nothing will happen while we're gone. The dog will probably be right where we left him."

* * *

Buster sat on the front porch and watched the truck disappear beyond the tree line. The crunching of tires on gravel became less and less until only the sounds of the country remained. His ears flopped down on his head, his eyes drooped, and tinges of desperation and loneliness came to him. As a dog accustomed to the presence of his pack, being alone was unnerving, and he cautiously checked his surroundings.

The unfenced yard had slabs of sandstone paving a path from the house to where the truck had been parked. Two pecan trees shaded the otherwise sunny yard where grass grew unhindered. A barn sat back from the house surrounded by thick woods.

Buster's eyes flicked to the woods and the dark spaces hidden among the trees.

In the short time he had been with the older couple, they had shown him kindness by feeding him until his belly was full, and by talking to him in soothing tones when he shivered. They put an old blanket on the porch for him to sleep on.

This wasn't home, though, and he preferred the energy of Holly's home she shared with Dillon, Cassie, and Ryan.

Where were they? Why hadn't they come to get him? He missed their voices and the unique ways they interacted when they greeted each other.

He couldn't understand the reason he became lost, only that the loud explosions had startled him and hurt his ears. He recalled shivering at the pressure of the helicopter's whumping blades high overhead, lashing wind and noise, resulting in panic and blood and terror which had become too much.

It had been fight or flight, and Buster had chosen flight, a choice unbecoming to a dog of his stature. He ran and ran until his muscles cramped and his thirst drove him to rest. He ran over anthills and clambered under barbed wire fencing, yelping when a rusted barb nicked his skin. He dodged fallen logs and a patch of cactus. Stinging stickers dug deep into his tender pads, and he briefly stopped to lick his bleeding paws.

A noise had startled him and he jerked up, tucked his tail, and ran because he had to, until the noise in his mind of panicked voices and mechanical screechings were no more.

He had become impossibly lost in the tangle of trees and brush, pastures and cows, and galloping horses. He darted past darkened houses void of laughter or the wafting scents of human habitation. Food cooking, soap, clothes hung out to dry, cars with tanks filled with gasoline, boots, or worn carpet trapping a plethora of scents indicating life was alive and well.

With the rancher and his wife gone, Buster was alone again.

He lowered his body to the porch slats. He sniffed the dried mud the rancher tracked in earlier when he returned from his work in the pasture.

He sniffed the sweet traces of talcum powder the woman had left as she brushed past him. Her cotton dress, freshly washed and dried by the sun's rays, lingered in the air.

Buster huffed a warm breath and rested his head on his paws.

The wind rustled the leaves of the oak trees, blowing them around. The pine trees loomed tall and stately. An animal scurried in the brush and Buster pricked his ears, listening, waiting. He lifted his snout, his nostrils twitching, testing the wind for an answer.

A cloud floated in the sky, casting an island of a shadow on the land, darkening it.

More clouds rolled over the land.

A red cardinal flitted across the sea of green trees and tall grass then landed in a tree. It sat perched on a limb, preening its feathers. Occasionally it stopped to sing a tune, twittering a pleasant melody, the song of the land. Another one answered and the cardinal flew away, leaving Buster listening to the wind whistling through the trees.

A thick fog bank floated in from the warm Gulf water, draping the land in a misty monotone, clinging to the air and obscuring visibility. Buster lifted his snout and tested the moist, salty air hinting of sea creatures and the ocean. Fine particles of water collected on Buster's dark coat, and he felt the chill of the air. He padded to his blanket and pillowed into it.

How long had the man and his wife been gone?

Time meant nothing to Buster, and without anything to do or to keep him occupied, he became drowsy. His eyelids became heavy until he could no longer fight the urge to sleep. He drifted back to his home, back to where Cassie waited for him, and he felt the comforting strokes of her warm, soft hand across his back. He dreamed of chasing a ball thrown in the house, and the hearty laughter echoing when he clumsily slid across the floor.

His dreams floated to the home where Dillon and Holly were a couple, where Cassie and Ryan would become parents. He dreamed of—

Buster woke with a start and sat up on his haunches. Perhaps it was intuition, or his superior senses, but whatever it was, it was dark and his eyes had already acclimated to the low light. The moon hung in the sky like a lamppost, a hazy light casting a yellow pall across the land.

A coyote yipped far in the distance and Buster cocked his head in the direction so he could understand the meanings of the yips and howls. Others joined in.

The padding of four legged creatures darting in the woods, snapping leaves and twigs garnered his attention. He stood tall and growled low in his throat, sensing the presence of a similar species.

Unable to see through the fog, Buster relied on his olfactory and acute hearing senses.

He lifted his nose high in the air as a breeze drifted by, capturing the scents of the animals clinging to droplets in the fog. His nostrils twitched to understand the peculiar odor dominating his senses. He had smelled the scent before, a wild and untamed odor, and as his mind whirled to identify the animal, Buster realized his precarious situation. He was being stalked by coyotes.

He moved with caution and backed up toward the front door. He clawed at it fruitlessly to get in.

A blur of snarling teeth and bristling fur burst out from the cover of the misty fog and darted into the yard. Like soldiers trained to subdue their opponent with precise maneuvering, the coyotes scattered to flank each end of the porch, cornering Buster. The large male leading the pack was front and center. Yellow eyes rimmed in black locked on Buster for the kill. The coyote lowered his head and cautiously put one paw in front of the other, inching closer to the porch.

The dog inside the house barked.

The coyote flanking Buster to his right also crept closer while the other one blocked an escape to Buster's left.

Buster bared his teeth and growled.

Without warning, the large male barged forward, and as he scrambled up the steps, he lost his footing on the slick wood, wet with fog. The coyote thrashed and tumbled down the steps, legs flailing in the air. He yelped when he landed on the hard sandstone rocks leading to the driveway.

In the sudden confusion, startling the other two coyotes, Buster took a running start and leapt over the coyote to his right. The Olympic worthy jump propelled him high above the coyote and when he landed, he did so with a solid thud.

Buster dug his large paws into the wet grass to gain traction, bolted out of the yard, dashed to the woods, and with wild abandon ran blindly through the fog.

Branches slapped his face. Twigs snapped under the weight of his legs. Dirt and leaves flew in all directions.

Buster sensed the coyotes were running with an exclusive fervor to kill, while he ran with equal vehemence to live.

He sprinted across a pasture where cows stood watching the life and death chase. A thousand pound bull snorted and emerged from the center of the herd, alarmed at the sight of the dog and coyotes. The massive bull lowered its head and stampeded across the land, its thundering hooves pounding hard on the grassy plain.

The coyotes scattered at the sight of the charging bull. A single kick could be deadly.

A rabbit dashed from the clump of high grass where it had taken cover.

One of the coyotes saw the splash of brown and white darting across the pasture, and suddenly its attention was on the lesser prey. The coyote took off in hot pursuit. A moment later, there was a flurry of fur and growling, then a high pitched squeal silenced by the jaws of the coyote. Taking the limp, lifeless body of the rabbit, the coyote hurried away with its prize.

The others joined their pack member to find a suitable spot to share their spoils of the chase.

Buster ran further away from the coyotes and from the man and woman who had rescued him, until their memory meant nothing. He ran through the woods with the ease of a lighter dog, fast and powerful, until his legs became wobbly. He slowed to a trot, and finally to walking.

He came upon a fallen tree, its bark soft and branches pliable, ferns and mushrooms sprouting from the wood. He padded to the other side where the dirt was soft. He scratched at the dirt then huffed his wet nose in it. It smelled of the damp woods and earth, of the animals that had crawled the length of the once magnificent tree. Exhausted, Buster curled into a little ball and fell into a fitful sleep.

* * *

Hunger gnawed at the massive animal roaming the woods. Standing thirty-six inches at the shoulder and weighing close to four hundred pounds, it was a formidable beast.

It was hungry and it was on the prowl.

Its face and neck were scarred from fighting, its massive body muscular and covered in stiff, dark colored hairs. It had long side whiskers, a straight tail, short legs, and a larger head in proportion to its body. The animal had four tusks which grew continuously, two on top, two on bottom, and the constant gnashing of the tusks resulted in scissor sharpness, excellent for slashing and stabbing prey.

It had small eyes and poor eyesight, yet huge ears resulting in superior hearing, and a long snout for a keen sense of smell.

It was a wild boar that had descended from domestic hogs which escaped or were released when Texas settlers fled the bloody fight for Texas independence.

As the years passed and as one century turned to another, the domestic hog mated with European boars. The cross breed adapted to the new environment and established traits needed to survive in the wild. Bristly hair replaced the fine whispery hair of the domestic variety, and males grew long tusks needed to fight for breeding rights and to claim territory.

This evening the solitary male walked the paths it had taken before, rooting for grubs and searching for acorns. It had checked the normal places for food, but with the exploding hog population, others of its species had already depleted the food sources.

It needed animal protein, and lots of it.

Sticking its snout into the dirt, it pushed aside leaves and twigs, and recognized a familiar scent. A dog had passed by just minutes before, and had left an unmistakable odor of fear.

The wild boar knew about fear and pain, and the limping from a bullet lodged in its thigh had become more pronounced. It was no longer the revered bush beast it once had been, dominating the other male hogs and forcing them to flee for their lives. Sensing the wild boar's weakened state, one of its former contenders had forced the boar to less sustainable territory containing poor food sources.

When the wild boar recognized the dog's scent, it followed the trail. Tame dogs were no match for the massive beast, and it had made a meal of pets many times before. Easy prey, exactly what it needed tonight.

With its snout to the ground, the boar followed the scent trail.

Gradually, the scent became more pronounced until the boar spotted the dog, yards ahead, sleeping, unaware of the impending danger. Its feet and nostrils twitched in the low light. The dog was big, yet it could be easily subdued. A seventy-pound dog was no match for this particular boar.

Stealth was not in the boar's repertoire of skills, so it did what it did best; it used its massive girth to plow ahead. Thundering hooves gouged the soft earth, leaving hoof prints an inch deep. It trampled grass and rotted logs, and when it approached the dog, the boar readied his impressive set of razor sharp tusks.

The kill was moments away.

Lost in the tangled woods, Buster had fallen asleep exhausted next to a sapling, but even while sleeping, his nostrils twitched and his mind worked to identify the odors of the woodland. Granted, he had never smelled anything remotely similar to a wild boar, but the instinct of his wolf forebears, some of whose DNA lingered in Buster, recognized the danger, waking him and spurring him into action.

It was the boar's pungent odor of wallowing in a foul soup of urine, rotted vegetation, and putrefying dead animals from the day before which alerted Buster to its presence.

Buster opened his eyes to the horror of the wild boar lowering his head for the upward killing thrust of the tusks and the ripping of flesh.

In the millisecond it took Buster's brain to process the boar with those menacing three-inch tusks, Buster thrashed and wiggled his legs, dug his paws into the dirt, tucked his tail, and tore out of there.

If Buster had been a cat, he would have used up all his nine lives.

The boar's tusks missed its target, and instead dug into a small sapling. With a mouthful of bark, the boar jerked his head, jarring loose its tusks. Hunger drove the boar to a maddening level of aggression.

It took off running after Buster. The enraged boar ran across the land, foaming at the mouth, long strings of drool dripping from its jaws.

Although massive and injured, the boar was unfazed by its girth or the bullet wound to its leg. Full of adrenaline, it barreled through the brush, hot on Buster's trail.

Gradually the boar tired and lagged further and further behind, until it lost sight of the dog and no longer heard the animal crashing through the woods. Undaunted, the boar put its snout to the ground and began tracking Buster, winding around trees and bramble, fallen logs, and ant mounds.

The space between Buster's scented prints became less and less, until the boar recognized the dog was now walking. The boar traipsed through the woods, carefully choosing where it would step.

It lifted its snout and got a whiff of a strong scent of the panting dog, which the boar now recognized as fatigued. Experience had taught the boar once its prey was fatigued, mistakes followed.

The dog was now his to kill.

Taking advantage of being downwind, the boar came within yards of Buster, then the pounding of its hooves alerted Buster to its presence.

The dog once more bolted out of harm's way, yet this time the boar was intent on chasing and capturing the dog.

It would run until it died if that was the case.

Buster's long legs galloped like a racing greyhound, the boar's legs like a trampling bull, unfazed by any obstacle it encountered.

Further they ran until Buster recognized a familiar sign among the grayed trees and hidden animal dens, stock ponds, and pastures of cows.

Scrambling under a barbed wire fence where a natural depression in the land had formed, Buster's newfound determination propelled him to top speed and untamed cunning.

The finish line was within sight.

* * *

The survivors sat in a circle around the campfire near the front of Holly's house. The dancing light cast shadows of flame on their faces. Embers glowed and the fire crackled.

Reload sat by Kate's side, Nipper by Amanda. The group was thankful for a rancher returning Cowboy who was pastured nearby. Dillon surmised Cowboy had escaped during the fighting at the compound, wandering around for a while until a friendly face found him.

The only one missing was Buster, and the group felt his absence.

Conversation had died down in the evening hour. Without light to prolong the day, bedtime came early.

Dillon stoked the fire with a long stick. His gaze went to the people he had put his life on the line for. Holly had her arm around Anna, while Cassie sat next to her soon-to-be husband Ryan. Chandler and Amanda, and Nico and Kate were together as well. Uncle Billy and Luke rounded out the group.

Uncle Billy rose from his chair. "I'll be back in a moment."

"What's he up to?" Chandler asked Kate.

"No telling with Uncle Billy," she replied. "Luke, do you know?"

"Not a clue," Luke said, scratching his head.

"Before we turn in for the night, I'd like to take a moment to thank each of you," Dillon said. "Although you were not in uniform, you conducted yourselves with utmost bravery. We stood together and we fought together. Be proud of that. We reclaimed our land because of patriots like yourselves. People who put country above themselves, who risked their lives to fight the invading enemy. This is our home. Our land. It's where Cassie and Ryan will raise their child–my grandchild. It's where Amanda and Chandler will make a home for their children. It's where Nico and Kate will establish their own homestead."

Cassie cleared her throat and stood. "Dad, can I say something?"

"Sure."

"It's been some kind of ride, hasn't it?" Cassie acknowledged her friends with a nod of her head. "There's not a finer group of people anywhere. We've helped each other, loved each other, fought at times, but we stayed together. I'd like to remember a brave man I met in Louisiana who's been on my mind a lot lately. He told me he lived his life by the three Fs. Here's to you Garrett wherever you are, and to faith, family, and firearms."

"And to a fine bourbon." Uncle Billy hobbled back to the circle. "Holly, I hope you don't mind." He held up a bottle of bourbon. "I found this squirreled away in a top kitchen cabinet."

"Not at all." Holly grinned. "I had forgotten about it. It was my dad's favorite he used for special occasions."

"I think this counts as a special occasion. I even found some old Dixie cups. Who wants a shot?"

The group answered a collective, "I do," except for Cassie and Anna.

As Uncle Billy handed out the Dixie cups, a crackling, humming sound interrupted the silence. Uncle Billy tried to place where the sound was coming from. "Do y'all hear that?"

"I heard something," Cassie said. "I think it's coming from the woods."

Uncle Billy dismissed Cassie's observation. "No, not that. I hear that too. It's different, like uh, a uh..." Uncle Billy snapped his fingers, "like an electrical current. That's it! Listen. Shhh."

"I still think I hear something running through the woods."

A lamp flickered in the house.

Cassie rose excitedly. "Did you see that! A light came on!"

Uncle Billy glanced at the house. "I don't see anything. It was probably the ghost of the Double H Ranch. You know about that, don't you?"

"Uncle Billy, stop kidding. I swear I saw a light. Look. There it is again."

Hope rose. A few seconds passed and a humming noise zipped along an electrical line going to the house.

The faintest of flickering lights clicked on.

Instantaneously, the mood became joyous.

Somebody clapped. Another whooped.

Uncle Billy removed his cap and slapped his leg. "It is coming back on! Halleluiah! Why, dog bite my buttons! Let's go in and see if the TV works. Then we'll—"

At that moment, all seventy pounds of Buster came crashing into the camp. He barreled over a chair and a kerosene lamp, zeroed in on Dillon, and leapt into his lap as if he was a small, fluffy dog. Dillon wrapped his arms around the large dog, trying to control his flailing arms and legs before he too toppled over. Buster pawed and tried to climb higher on Dillon.

Nico sat stunned.

Kate had her mouth open.

Cassie expressed a sound of disbelief.

Ryan put a hand across Cassie.

Uncle Billy protected the prized bourbon bottle by holding it close to his chest.

Luke jumped.

But it was Holly who got off the shot.

Stunned by the unexpected events and from emotions changing from surprise to elation to disbelief, the blast of the gunshot reset the group, shocking them back to reality.

Mere feet from the camp, a boar lay dead on its side, bleeding out the last of its blood pressure.

To say the friends sitting around the campfire were dumbfounded would have been an understatement, and it took them a while to realize what had happened.

Dillon was the first to speak. "Holly? How'd you—"

"When a dog like Buster runs for his life, there's a reason. I knew something was after him. While everyone was gaping at Buster, I kept my eyes on the woods."

"What did you shoot it with?"

Holly holstered her pistol and patted it. "My trusty Smith and Wesson .44 Magnum.

"I thought you always carried a Glock."

"I normally do, but I wanted to carry something different." Holly paused for effect. "I was bored." She gauged the group's reaction then broke out laughing at her own joke. Giggling, she clutched her stomach. "Bored. Boared. Get it?"

A chorus of groans followed her lame joke.

After the groaning and eye rolling ceased, Dillon asked, "What should we do with it? Eat it?"

"I vote yes," Uncle Billy said. "I can make sausage."

Dillon placed the heavily panting Buster on the ground. The dog stood there shivering, pressing his body against Dillon. At the sight of the boar, he put his paws on Dillon, jumped, and tried to climb up him. Dillon took Buster by the paws and gently placed them on the ground. "It's dead, Buster. Go on. Go check it out for yourself."

Buster wouldn't budge, so Dillon took him by the collar and led him to the dead boar. Buster held back, stretching his body away from the animal while Dillon held him steady. The dog refused the coaxing, so Dillon straddled Buster, put his hands under his ribcage, and hoisted the dog next to the boar.

Buster diverted his gaze away from the boar, refusing to look at it. Dillon wouldn't let Buster run away. Curiosity got the best of Buster, and he took a glance at the beast, stretching his neck as much as possible to get a better sniff of the boar. Instinct and his keen sense of smell alerted the dog the beast was dead and could cause no more harm.

Dillon released his hold on Buster. The dog tentatively took a step toward the boar and sniffed it, running his nose along the dead animal.

Buster untucked his tail and waited for Dillon's approval. "Good dog," Dillon said. "You slayed it." It wasn't true, but Buster didn't know that. He only knew he was back with his family where he should be. He wiggled from side to side, slapping his tail against his haunches.

Dillon led Buster to Holly. "Will you take him in, please, and check him over for injuries? I think it would be a good time to take the other dogs in too."

"Sure."

"Chandler, get the truck and let's haul that thing where we can field dress it. I don't want to do it so close to the house."

"I'll get a lantern," Chandler said.

"I'll come with y'all," Ryan said. "Cassie, I think you should head on into the house. There's been enough excitement for the day."

"Okay," Cassie replied, following the others inside. "I'll try the TV to see if it works. I'd like to watch the news." Uncle Billy and Luke followed her inside.

The night had become darker, and a cool breeze brushed the land. Kate shivered. It was quiet now that everyone was gone.

Rising from the chair, she stretched and yawned. "Nico, we should go on in too. I'm tired, and I need a good night's sleep."

Kate reached for Nico's hand and tugged him to join her, but he hesitated.

"Let's sit here for a while longer. It's peaceful. Just you and me...like on Padre Island."

Kate laughed. "Don't tell me I'll have to save your life again."

"Nothing like that." For a while he studied her face, and the way her mouth curved when she smiled. Nothing was said, and the seriousness of the situation suddenly struck Nico. He shifted in his chair, scratched his chin, cleared his throat, then again. His eyes darted around.

"What's going on?" Kate asked. "I've never seen you so nervous."

"There's something I want to ask you."

"What?"

"This isn't easy for me. Give me a minute."

Seconds ticked by and Kate waited, then a moment of clarity came to her. Her eyes twinkled. "Yes."

"Huh?" Nico said. He scratched the side of his head and shifted his weight then came back to her.

"The answer is yes."

"You don't even know what the question is."

"Yes, I do. The answer is still yes."

"You'll marry me?"

"I've already said yes several times. How many more do you want me to say?"

"How did you know what I was going to ask?" Nico was quite puzzled.

"Remember when you were talking to my mom at the dinner table the night before we left?"

"Yes."

"That's how I knew."

"But we were speaking in Russian."

"I understand Russian."

"What? You never told me that." He was somewhere between irritation and relief.

"You never asked."

"Oh. So all this time you knew what we talked about?"

Kate nodded.

"I can't believe it. I thought you only knew a few words and phrases."

"After Ben died, I filled up my time with night classes. One of them was Russian. The language came easily to me because I grew up listening to the words being spoken although I never paid any attention to the meanings."

"Makes sense."

"There was one thing you said that I didn't understand."

"What was that?" Nico asked.

"My mom said something about praying we would have a long and happy life. Then she said something about fruit. What was she talking about?"

Nico rose from his chair, and reached for Kate's hand. She stood. He brought her close and wrapped his arms around her. He leaned in and ran his thumb across her lips, inviting her to—

Luke came running up.

"What the—" Nico's expression of loving tenderness morphed into one of sheer exasperation. "What the hell is the matter with you, Luke? Can't you see I'm busy?"

Kate leaned back from Nico and put her hand to her mouth to stifle a laugh about the bad timing her brother was known for.

"What I'd do? Bad timing again?" Luke put his hands in the air in an apologetic gesture.

"What do you want?" Nico growled.

"Uncle Billy sent me out here to tell you the TV works. Reports are coming in from all over the place about what's been going on. It's incredible! He said you'd want to see it too."

"Oh, he did, did he?" Kate glanced at the house. "Luke, do me a favor."

"What?"

"Tell Uncle Billy if he interrupts me again, I'm going to hotwire his Gran Torino just like how he taught me and steal it. Then tell him I'm going to strip it down and sell it for parts. Let's see how fast he shuts those curtains he's trying to hide behind." Kate waved at the window where Uncle Billy was hiding. A shadowy figure disappeared behind the ruffling curtains.

"Okay," Luke said. "I have no idea what's going on, but I can't guarantee he won't come out and have a talk with you."

After Luke left, Kate said, "I think we'll be telling our kids about this someday."

Nico cracked a wry smile and lifted his eyebrows twice in quick succession. He leaned into Kate, whispering in her ear, "Still want to know what fruitful means?"

"I think I know but tell me anyway."

"It means we won't be getting any sleep tonight."

"That's what I thought. We have a big trip tomorrow, and we still need to pack for it," she reminded him.

"We do, but first things first." Nico flicked his eyes in the direction of an upstairs bedroom.

Kate wrinkled her nose. "No way."

"Where then?"

Kate glanced at the Gran Torino, back to the house, then to the car. "I have an idea."

"What?"

"I'm going to steal it anyway."

"That's a V-8 engine, Kate. Do you know what to do with it?"

"I know exactly what to do with a big engine. Wanna find out?"

"You don't need to ask me twice."

Kate took Nico's hand and led him to the car. He slid into the passenger seat, trying out the seats in the old car.

"Check the glove compartment for 8-tracks."

Nico opened the glove compartment to find it stuffed with dinosaur sized tapes. "I can't believe people used to listen to these." He picked up an 8-track tape, inspected it, and shrugged.

"According to Uncle Billy, an 8-track player was the hottest thing there was back in the 70s."

"I don't understand."

"All the cool dudes had 8-track players in their cars."

"Let me guess. Uncle Billy used to be a cool dude."

"Hey, he still is. Buckle up, and I'll get this baby started."

While Kate worked her magic under the steering column, fiddling with wires, Nico perused the selection of tapes. He found one he recognized.

The car's engine roared to life, and Kate tossed Nico a mischievous smile. "Ready?"

"Just a moment. Let me pop this in." He got the 8-track to work and turned up the volume. After a few moments, he drummed his thumbs to the beat of an old Peter Frampton song. Nico leaned to Kate and whispered the lyrics, "Baby, I love your way."

Kate grinned. "I love your way too. Hold on." She put the car in gear, gassed it, tires spinning and throwing dust and gravel in the air. She sped off down the dirt road, leaving a trail of dust. When she got out to the blacktop, she floored the pedal. The windows were down, her hair blowing in the wind. Music blared.

Nico had an arm propped on the window ledge, and his thoughts went to what was ahead for them in this new and undefeated world.

Tomorrow would be a new day, with a new set of challenges, but the survivors were together. They had survived by using their wits, by being prepared, and by never, ever giving up in the face of unrelenting adversity.

They were winners, and they would live their lives not by how society dictated they should, but by how they were meant to live. Marriages would take place, children would be born, schools would reopen, store shelves restocked, some would go back to work, some wouldn't. Yet it wouldn't quite be the same, because nothing ever stayed the same.

Time didn't stop for anyone or anything, yet they would all live a long and fulfilling life because...

They believed in faith.

They believed in family.

They believed in firearms.
Forever.

THE END

BEHIND THE SCENES

A Note From the Author

Hi readers, this is Chris. Well, we finally reached the end of the series with all the major characters surviving. Halleluiah! I wasn't sure who was going to live or die, and had thought about what would happen if one of the good ones were killed. In real life, good people do die, but since this is a fictional world, I like the good guys to win and to come out ahead, and for the bad guys to get their comeuppance. Even in fiction, sometimes the plot and characters have a life of their own and don't always behave themselves and end up doing something entirely different than what was planned.

For this series, everyone behaved. Well, most everybody. Uncle Billy didn't because he never conformed to society's standards. He didn't care about how much money was in the bank, or how he dressed, but he sure was a stand-up kind of guy.

The more I wrote about Uncle Billy, the more I liked him. He reminds me of Uncle Buck of the *High Chaparral* series. If you've ever seen the show, you might see some similarities between the characters.

Thanks for staying with the EMP Survivor series! I hope everyone has enjoyed the ride. I know I have. The characters became like friends, and I'm sad to see them ride off into the sunset like Kate and Nico did. But weren't they great characters? I've received some mail about having a spinoff series with Kate and Nico, so if you're interested in what happens next after the grid boots back up, write me and let me know.

The world they knew before would not exist anymore. It would be replaced by a new world with a different set of challenges other than surviving the initial fallout from the EMP.

Also, check out the anthology titled, *The Will to Survive*, containing short stories by several post-apocalyptic authors, including myself. My story had been rattling around in my head for years so I've finally decided to make it a novel or perhaps a short series. A glimpse of it is in the anthology. I got the idea one day while driving to work early in the morning along Interstate 10. As I was driving east, clouds appeared over the massive freeway exchange of I-10 and the 610 Loop. The radio was on, cars bumper to bumper, red taillights of cars in front of me were distracting, but all I could concentrate on were those clouds. An idea came to me at that moment about what would happen if those clouds were biological warfare instead of rain clouds.

So, a morning commute inspired the story.

I plan to release the first book in mid-2018, so if you want to be notified of the release, please send me an email at Chris.Pike123@aol.com.

I'm also thinking about a short series with Nico and Kate after they leave the Double H Ranch. I hope to release at least of one those in the series in 2018.

Available books in the EMP Survivor Series:
Unexpected world – Book 1
Uncertain world – Book 2
Unknown World – Book 3
Unwanted World – Book 4
Undefeated World Book – 5

Book 3, Unknown World, is a standalone book and continues the EMP survivor series as Amanda and Chandler face new struggles in their quest to survive. Just go to Amazon, and type in keywords: Chris Pike EMP Survivor Series. Or type in the book title. Book 4 is the story of Kate Chandler and Nico Bell. The series will be wrapped up in Book 5 – Undefeated World scheduled for early 2018.

BEFORE YOU GO...

One last thing. Thank you, thank you, thank you for downloading this book. Without the support of readers like yourself, Indie publishing would not be possible.

CHRIS PIKE

I've received a lot of emails from my readers, and for those who have written me, you know I always answer your emails, and I don't spam either.

An easy way to show your support of an Indie author is to write an honest review on Amazon. It does several things: It helps other readers make a decision to download the book. It also allows the author to understand what the readers want. For example, my readers asked for no F-bombs or adult situations. I listened and followed through with the requests. I've learned good writing and editing is extremely appreciated and I will always strive for that.

So please consider writing a review. It will be forever grateful. A few words or one sentence is all it takes.

* * *

I've had a lot of help along the way from some special people, first and foremost my husband, Alan. He was the brains behind the expert firearm and knife content in the book, and was my consultant on shootouts and how men would react in certain situations. Being a woman, I know how the ladies think and react, but not always the men.

When writing I use inspiration from my life, expand upon my experiences, and fictionalize them. The Gran Torino in the series was based on the car I had in college. I loved that car, and if there was one thing I could do over in my life, I'd keep that car. It was a light yellow, two-door V-8 engine, although it did not have an 8-track tape deck in it!

Writing a book is not a solitary undertaking, and many people have helped me. Special thanks go to those who have inspired, cheered, edited, proofed, provided cover art, formatted, legal advice, narrated, or were sounding boards: daughters Michelle and Courtney, son-in-law Cody, editor Felicia, narrator Kevin, proofer Mick, cover artist Hristo, friends Anne, Mikki, and Mary, formatter Kody, helicopter consultants Ken and Robert, wild boar consultants Francis, Steve, Jim, Mike, and Cliff. A very special thanks goes to you ladies and gents.

For my readers who have written me and have connected with me on Facebook, y'all are the best! You've encouraged me and have allowed me a glimpse into your lives. I am truly honored. Thank you. For anyone else who would like to connect with me, email me at Chris.Pike123@aol.com.

I'm on Facebook at Author Chris Pike.

So until next time, remember to read, enjoy, learn, and save some more food.

And regarding the ongoing theme in the EMP Survivor Series, remember the three Fs: Faith, Family, and Firearms.

Forever!

All the best,

Chris

"It's time to say goodbye, but I think goodbyes are sad and I'd much rather say hello. Hello to a new adventure."

—Ernie Harwell

ABOUT THE AUTHOR

Chris Pike grew up in the woodlands of Central Texas and along the Texas Gulf Coast, fishing, hunting, hiking, camping, and dodging hurricanes and tropical storms. Chris has learned that the power of Mother Nature is daunting from sizzling temperatures or icy conditions; from drought to category five hurricanes. Living without electricity for two weeks in the sweltering August heat after Hurricane Ike proved to be challenging. It paid to be prepared.

Currently living in Houston, Texas, Chris is married, has two grown daughters, one dog, and three overweight, demanding cats.

Chris is an avid supporter of the Second Amendment, and has held a Texas concealed carry permit since 1998, with the Glock being the current gun of choice. Chris is a graduate of the University of Texas and has a BBA in Marketing. By day Chris works as a database manager for a large international company, while by night an Indie author.

Got a question or a comment? Email Chris at Chris.Pike123@aol.com. Your email will be answered promptly and your address will never be shared with anyone.

Made in the USA
Las Vegas, NV
11 January 2023

65429115R00144